THE TIGER'S CUB

Book Two of The Tiger Series

by Debi Emmons

Northern Bard Publications

Gray, ME 04039

Northern Bard Publications

53 Cambell Shore Road
Gray, ME 04039

ISBN-13: 978-0692400012 (Northern Bard Publications)

ISBN-10: 069240001X

Dedicated to

The friends and family
who kept asking for a sequel to
Night of the Tiger

Well folks, here it is!

With many thanks to

Model Derek Yates for portraying Chase Benton

Photographer Jse Yu for the beautiful photo of Derek
in a New Orleans-like alley

Model Belle Louve for portraying Aloriah Starbird

RedRope Photography for permission
to use Belle's photo

And a special mention to

Photographer Jodie Burkett and Belle Louve
for the cover on the First Print Edition of this book,
since they didn't get properly thanked
by the author on that project

Preface

The original print edition of this book just came out in October 2013, but there were some minor issues that I, the author, wanted to correct that I didn't really notice until it was too late to correct it with the first publisher.

Nothing major. Just the stuff that appeared on that last page. You know, the stuff that I *meant* to include, but for some reason missed that it wasn't there when I gave approval of the final file that was being sent to the printer.

Of course, there's also the fact that I changed publishers, and they opted to go a little larger for the third book in the series…

And they want to do the kind of covers I wanted for the books when I first started writing *Night of the Tiger*…

And they're talking doing a boxed set, and audio books, and other such things that would be interesting to see…

And, since the staff at Northern Bard are old friends, they also take my recommendations as to other authors we might want to publish…

So, with no further ado, I present to you the Northern Bard Publications printing of *The Tiger's Cub*.

Prologue: October 28, 2011

Teresanna Benton dropped her two costumed daughters at the library for an after school gathering with a Halloween theme, then turned her car around to head toward the high school. She had received a very cryptic text from her son, Chase, stating only that there had been "bully problems" after school, and although he was "fine", the school principal needed to speak to her. There had been "bully problems" since second grade, when Chase began to be one of the better students and had made other students, many of whom were struggling with their school work, quite jealous. When the taunts and jibes began to turn into swirlies and trash cannings, Kyle began bringing his son to the dojo in Milo for self-defense classes.

Unfortunately, although the bullying had eased somewhat by the time he finished middle school, Chase was looking more and more like his handsome father each year, and when he entered high school that September, the high school girls were quick to take notice. Dancing green eyes with a slight oriental tilt peered out of a strongly boned face beneath a frequently unkempt looking mop of wavy dark hair. A tall, still somewhat gangly frame and a quick smile made him popular with the ladies, but the upperclassmen weren't very appreciative of the competition, and the bullying had begun to escalate again. Biting her lip as she parked her car, Teresanna could only hope that Chase was truly "fine" and not bleeding like he had been the last time she went to collect him when he had texted her about "bully problems".

Entering the almost empty hallways, she immediately became aware of the distant sound of shouting voices, which grew ever louder as she made her way to the principal's office.

Worried that one of those voices could well belong to her son, she hurried along as fast as she could without actually running, only vaguely aware of the eyes of the few teen boys still in the halls watching her as she passed. It wasn't until she entered the main office and saw Chase sitting with the secretary, holding an ice pack to the right side of his face, that she allowed herself a relaxing breath and started noticing all the tiny details of the world around her again, starting with the worried look in the green eyes that turned her way.

"Ah, Mrs. Benton!" the secretary greeted cheerfully, "I'll tell Mr. Murray you're here."

Before the secretary could get out of her chair, however, the door to the principal's office popped open, spilling the argument that had been going on into the main office mid-sentence.

"....and I'll sue you for not protecting the

children we entrust to you to educate!" one man was shouting as he made his exit, followed by two other men, one of whom looked angry while the other looked abjectly uncomfortable. Teresanna identified the shouting man as Henry Reynolds, who had moved to the area from Massachusetts five years prior. The second angry man was the principal, Mr. Murray, and the uncomfortable man was John Bean, who had grown up in Greenville, but whose son seemed to worship Henry Reynolds's son, Brock, even when following Brock got him into major trouble.

"Mr. Reynolds, suing me will NOT make me allow your son to return to school until he has served the school board mandated suspension for starting a fight on school grounds, and you may want to tell your lawyer that I have the whole thing on the school security tapes this time!" Mr. Murray, despite the obvious anger on his face, was using the no-nonsense tone that all the students knew too well. "You DO remember being head of the committee that collected the funds for the security cameras, don't you?"

Mr. Reynolds started to sputter, trying to think of a comeback, but that was when Mr. Bean nudged him and drew everyone's attention to Teresanna. Mr. Murray beamed, seeing no anger in her visage.

"Mrs. Benton, so sorry to keep you waiting."

"No problem," she assured the principal, "I can see that you had other things to deal with."

The displeasure in her eyes as she looked at the two men whose sons had obviously been involved in this latest attack on her offspring made the men shuffle, suddenly remembering exactly who she was married to. Although John Bean had grown up with Kyle and Henry Reynolds had only encountered him when trying to force the townspeople to develop the area into a semblance of the Massachusetts he'd left, both knew that Kyle was not a man who would just lie down and let them blame his son for starting something their children were responsible for.

Mr. Murray saw the change in the demeanor of both men and tried not to smile. The small woman had, without a single word, reminded them of who their sons had targeted, and effectively negated the threat of the school being sued. He continued on as if he hadn't noticed a thing.

"I was just suspending two out of the six boys who made your son miss his bus. The other four are waiting for their parents to come and get them, at which time their parents will also be informed that they are being suspended for bullying, and since it's not their first offense, they won't be coming back." He ignored the surprise on the faces of both men that indicated they hadn't realized who their sons had been associating with. "Now then, if you gentlemen would please follow Miss Ross to the nurse's station, your boys should be ready to go home."

Turning his back on the two men as a signal for them to leave, he indicated his office to Teresanna and Chase, who obediently went inside with him. As the office door closed behind them, he sighed and allowed the rest of his remaining anger to dissipate. By the time the two Bentons had seated themselves, and Mr. Murray had made his way around his desk to take his own seat, a wry smile was affixed to his face and his eyes were twinkling.

"Could you fill me in about what happened this afternoon?" Teresanna asked, and Mr. Murray gave her a brilliant smile.

"Courtesy of the committee that insisted we needed security cameras, I can show you what happened. Unfortunately, you'll need your son to explain some of what it is you're seeing, as they didn't pay for microphones to be able to have sound with our visual, and a lot of it appears to be just a verbal disagreement."

Teresanna watched the security tape in silence as the after school ritual of the students milling around to get onto the buses that would take them to their homes unfolded. Chase passed through the crowd with a couple of friends, but when they got onto a bus and he continued alone toward his bus, he was suddenly surrounded by a large group of boys, most of whom were wearing school football jerseys. Brock Reynolds, the star quarterback, seemed to be the one in charge of the group, as he shoved Chase while his mouth was running a mile a minute. The buses started pulling away, and there were fewer and fewer students around, leaving Chase and the majority of the football team alone in front of the school.

"Brock and his cronies stopped me because he said he'd heard some ugly rumors about Cassie Plourde and me." Chase said softly in explanation. "He accused me of all kinds of nasty things that might have incited the others to think that I should be severely beaten, if not lynched, for soiling a good girl's reputation."

But as Brock continued to talk, the other boys in the football jerseys started to look uncomfortable, then slip away from the group in twos and threes, until the only ones left wearing jerseys were Brock and Jason Bean. The other four boys were bullies from Chase's grade school years who hadn't matured enough to stop the bullying, especially when they thought their victim was outnumbered. Chase continued his soft commentary with a wry observation.

"Obviously Brock didn't rehearse his little speech, because he shifted from trying to defend his girlfriend's honor to admitting that she'd told him during an argument that she thought I was cute, and wanted to break up with him so we could date. When they realized that they had been recruited to teach me a lesson when I hadn't done anything wrong, they decided that discretion was the better part of valor."

Teresanna's jaw dropped open and she almost came out of her seat when two of the boys grabbed Chase's arms in response to something Brock said, and held him still while Brock delivered a left hook to the right side of his face. Chase seemed to slump in response to the hit, but then erupted into action so fast that it was hard for the human eye to catch everything that happened. Lifting his feet off the ground, he put his entire weight on the two boys holding him so that they were pulled off balance, then he dropped his feet back down with enough force to allow him to lunge upward, breaking their grasp on his arms. As soon as his hands were free, he retaliated for Brock's strike with an uppercut that knocked Brock onto his back where he laid still, apparently knocked unconscious.

Seeing his fearless leader down, Jason leapt into action, taking a swing that Chase easily avoided before delivering a defensive strike of his own. When Jason joined Brock on the ground, also seemingly knocked unconscious, the other four boys seemed to realize that the odds weren't as stacked in their favor as they may have hoped, so they turned to run. Unfortunately for them, the security officer and several of the teachers had caught on to what was happening, so the four boys were swiftly stopped and taken into the school while Chase finally allowed himself to react to the left hook by wiping blood off his lip with the back of his hand.

Mr. Murray turned off the tape, and turned to see Teresanna's dark eyes fixed firmly on her son, who seemed to squirm before he slowly lowered the ice pack to show off the swollen right side of his mouth and cheek. Trying hard to look stern, she pulled his face around so she could get a better look, and then smiled.

"No stitches this time, at least."

Chase's hand automatically went toward his left shoulder, where his last encounter with the foursome who had stayed with Brock and Jason had left a permanent scar from a knife one of the boys had pulled on him, but the relief in his expression told both his mother and the principal that he had been expecting some form of punishment for giving two boys concussions. With a kind smile, Mr. Murray sent the boy out to wait in the outer office while he finished his discussion with Teresanna. As the door closed, Mr. Murray leaned against his desk and took a careful assessment of Teresanna's demeanor, which was very relaxed as she did her own assessment of the principal.

"He's not in any trouble for this is he?" she asked softly, and Mr. Murray gave a soft snort.

"Not on your life! In my opinion, he did exactly what he had to do to get out of that situation."

Teresanna smiled.

"Seeing the bruise on his face, I suspect his father will agree with you, and probably encourage him to take all the boys down next time."

Mr. Murray laughed as he opened the door to escort her out, finding the mother of one of the other bullies had arrived while they talked. The woman was staring at Chase with the appreciative look in her eyes that Teresanna had become used to seeing directed at her husband. With a sigh, she admitted to herself that her handsome son was going to break as many hearts as her husband had, and she only hoped that this battle over a girl wasn't going to become a common occurrence.

Chase remained silent until they got into the car and were on the way back to the library to pick up the girls. While staring out the window at the passing buildings, he sighed and expressed the very thought his mother had before they left the school.

"I remember Dad telling me about how this happened to him, and the way I scoffed at the thought that girls would ever find me cute." His next words had his mother fighting not to laugh even as her heart ached for him. "I'm not ready to be a heartbreaker."

Chase fell silent again, and there was nothing but the sound of the radio for several minutes before his sense of humor returned with a bang.

"Maybe I should just start wearing a bag on my head."

Teresanna finally allowed the laugh out, feeling much better about the day. The first few times that Chase had been targeted, he had come home in tears, and been depressed for months. He was showing a large amount of maturity by being able to just allow the day's violence to slip away and calmly joke about the apparent cause, which he, unfortunately, had no control of.

His mood changed again, however, when they entered the library, and everyone seemed to be staring at the bruise on his face. Although he was smiling and joking about how he had managed to get such a bruise, never coming near the truth, Teresanna saw the troubled look in his eyes, and she saw again the hurt child he had been.

On the ride home, Chase told 12-year-old Lynn and 10-year-old Angela the truth. Both girls loudly proclaimed him a slow poke for not managing to take out all six boys, making him laugh as they compared him to Jackie Chan.

"Yeah, but slower." Lynn insisted.

Chase got very sober again as they arrived home, and he saw his father adding more fake tombstones to their Halloween Cemetery display.

He always got a little nervous about telling his father about another incident, for some reason always worried that he would be blamed for starting the fight, even though Kyle had always listened to the facts before passing judgment. He let the girls jump out first and run over for hugs, both looking like miniature versions of Teresanna, before he took a deep breath and got out himself. Kyle looked past his wife and toward the car, still smiling about whatever Angela had just said, but his face changed dramatically when he spotted his eldest. In long, furious strides, he was at Chase's side in an instant, taking a very close look at the bruise.

"Who did this?" he rumbled, his tightly controlled anger obvious in his deep voice. His palpable anger made Chase take a deep breath before he answered.

"Brock Reynolds, and five others."

Kyle took a closer assessment of his son's condition, but when he didn't see any other obvious damage, his temper started to cool a little.

"So what happened?"

Chase gave a very short assessment of what Teresanna had witnessed on the video, not mentioning that the whole football team had been in on it at first. She saw the same flash of anger in Kyle's eyes that she had felt when Chase told of the two boys holding his arms while Brock got in the first punch, and when Chase mentioned, with regret in his tone, that both Brock and Jason had concussions, she saw pride replace the anger, but as the girls had done, Kyle tried to lighten the mood.

"You getting slow in your old age? You

should have been able to do six concussions!"

Smiling at his father, Chase shook his head.

"The little wimps ran off in four different directions!"

Kyle gave his son a playful punch to the arm before he called the girls to see if they wanted to help him put up more decorations. Chase collected his backpack and went up to his room, still hearing Brock's accusations in his head. He would never share the quarterback's words with his parents, but the words still stung a part of him that was seeking the acceptance of his peers.

"Freshman boys and senior girls don't date!" Brock had repeated that one more than once. It seemed to be some sort of rule as far as Brock was concerned, and it didn't seem to matter that Chase had no interest in a cheerleader who was obviously someone else's girl. It was when Chase had pointed out that he had no control over his looks, or how Cassie reacted to them, that Brock had told the other boys to hold him.

"Let me help you with those looks!" Brock had growled just before his fist connected with Chase's jaw. "No one will find you good looking when I'm done with you!"

Laying back on his bed and staring at the ceiling, Chase thought about how many times he'd been abused by the boys like Brock, all for things beyond his control. His looks, his brain, his father's money, all were things that he should be abused for if he tried to be humble and not be like Brock, who was all "in your face" about the fact that his father had money and he had a natural talent for football.

He thought about the girls he had as friends and the shallow ones like Cassie Plourde who were out to get the cutest and richest guys just to say they could.

But if he started acting like them to make them stop beating on him, didn't that make him as bad as them? Wasn't there another way to make them stop?

As he thought about the security camera, he started thinking about some of the moves he could have made. It was too bad he couldn't show some of the really tough moves to the other students so they would realize he was actually dangerous and stop picking on him. That was when a text came in from one of his friends, who was trying to talk him into doing something for the school's Talent Show, and Chase had what his mother often referred to as "a eureka moment".

"I should do a martial arts demo." He murmured, then went to find his father.

Kyle helped him all weekend, and when Chase went back to school on Monday, he had a new confidence that things would work out well for him in high school. Except for the bruise on his face, he was a new man, and was joking with his friends on the way into the building when Cassie Plourde stopped him.

"I'm sorry Brock did that," she said quickly as soon as their friends had moved on, "I was just trying to make him jealous because he's been talking about other women in front of me."

Chase couldn't speak for several minutes. He had been surrounded, yelled at and punched because she wanted to make her boyfriend jealous? Before he could stop himself, he gave her a devilish smile and leaned slightly forward, seeing a spark of interest on her face as she looked into his sparkling eyes.

"Cassie, it's great if you really find me cute, because I'd love to see you drop your quarterback boyfriend for this measly little freshman." Then he let the fury rise up and became very menacing, trying not to care when the fear of him showed in Cassie's eyes. "But if you ever use me like that again, you better watch out."

He turned and strode away from her, not looking back, and met back up with his friends a little way down the hall. Wade, his best friend since kindergarten, was giving him a comical look of shock.

"Who are you and what have you done with Chase?" he asked, and Chase sighed.

"I just want the nonsense to stop." he admitted, and since Wade had suggested the Talent Show, he continued, "Just wait until you see what I'm doing as my talent."

Two weeks later

Chase and Kyle stood side by side in the hallway, doing an exercise in calm breathing to center them while waiting for Chase's turn to perform. They had been practicing every evening, and had the routine down to split second timing. Chase was feeling more confident every day that he was going to win this round, and was very hopeful that he might be able to make it through high school without any more stitches.

When Chase was called to perform, he explained about the basics of Tae Kwon Do and the other martial arts that he had been introduced to. He and Kyle did an almost dance-like series of moves to warm and loosen their muscles, then Kyle put on a set of padded gloves, and Chase was challenged to connect with the pads as Kyle called out which hand or foot he wanted Chase to use. Kyle ended that part of the demonstration by holding his left hand out at shoulder height and challenged his son, with a gleam in his eye, to hit the pad with his right foot. A look of determination crossed Chase's face, and he surprised his father by managing to do so in the form of a jumping reverse hook kick. The auditorium where the talent show was being put on erupted into applause.

Chase had intended to just end the show there, but when he turned his back to his father, Kyle flipped the shirt of his uniform inside out, changing the color from white to black, then pulled out a ninja mask and pulled it on. A small noise alerted Chase, and he acted entirely on instinct. The brief fight that ensued had the audience gasping as both men pulled out moves that seemed to be inhuman, and both were breathing hard from the exertion when Kyle pulled the hood off, and put up his hands in surrender, smiling from ear to ear. It wasn't until the next day, when everyone started treating him with the utmost respect, that he realized the special gift his father had given him by changing the ending of his demonstration in a way that made him show what he could really do if pushed to defend himself.

He might survive high school after all....

Chapter 1
Louisiana - mid June 2017

Chase Benton sighed as the big, rusty mailbox with the name "Boudreaux" in faded green letters came into view, slowing the truck and looking into all his mirrors to insure there were no other vehicles on the narrow dirt road before he began the task of backing his eighteen wheeler into his friend's driveway. It was a tricky business, but something he had done many times before, as his Uncle Jack always made sure that Chase had a couple of days to visit with the Boudreaux family whenever he was anywhere close to New Orleans. Although Cody, the youngest of the Boudreaux clan, was several years older than Chase, the two had become fast friends when Chase first started driving for Jack and Benny Trucking, and Chase had delivered liquor to the bar where Cody worked. Jack had noted the difference in Chase's tone of voice whenever he got to visit with Cody, as there was something about the little Cajun that made his intense nephew relax for a bit, so Jack was more than willing to give Chase a mini vacation in the south lands whenever he could.

Although Chase himself couldn't explain what it was about Cody that made him feel more relaxed, it was a feeling that even permeated the air around the little shack in the bayou that Cody called home. As soon as the truck was parked under the huge oak tree that was liberally festooned with Spanish moss, Chase felt as if a weight had been lifted off his shoulders. Blasting his air horn to chase away any snakes or spiders before he opened his door, Chase watched the shack's door for a couple of minutes to see if Cody was at home, but when there was no response, he grabbed his duffle bag out of the sleeper and locked up the truck.

Watching his feet to make sure he didn't disturb any fire ant nests as he crossed to the porch, he listened to the sounds of the bayou that Cody had insisted were like a natural symphony, meant to sooth a man's soul. There were the soft songs of several species of birds, a chirping of crickets, the croak of a big bull frog somewhere close to the back of the garage, and even a bellow in the far distance that Cody had once told him was a big bayou alligator looking for either a mate or a fight. By the time he was reaching for the hidden key to Cody's door, Chase was smiling.

After showering, putting on deodorant, brushing his teeth, and changing into a clean pair of jeans and a plain black t-shirt, he gave himself a very critical once-over in the mirror, trying to decide if he should shave before going into the bar in New Orleans, where Cody was no doubt doing what the

Cajun called "holding court". After a couple of minutes of making faces at himself, he decided that the couple of days of beard growth, and the hair that badly needed a trim made him look a little older and, perhaps, a bit more dangerous, so he just sprayed on a little Axe cologne, and tossed all his belongings on the bed in the room Cody always let him use. He carefully made sure to lock the door and replace the hidden key, knowing how picky Cody could be about such things.

On his way out toward the garage, where Cody let him store a motorcycle to use when in town, he took a quick detour to his truck to retrieve his leather jacket, as he hated the sting of bugs hitting his exposed flesh more than he hated the overheating that wearing the jacket sometimes caused. A button on his key chain opened the automatic door on the garage, also turning on a bright light that sent a couple of snakes slithering out the door, and glistened off the polished motorcycle that waited for him. The smell of wax in the air and the brand new helmet on the seat told him that Cody had been expecting him, and was hinting that he thought his young friend needed to protect his head. Although tempted to leave the helmet in the garage just for spite, Chase decided it might be nice of him to humor the older man, so he strapped the helmet on before peeling rubber, leaving a long black stripe on the cement floor, which he was fairly sure he'd be required to clean off before he went back out on the road at the end of the weekend. Pausing at the end of the driveway, he pushed the button on his key chain, and watched to make sure the garage door closed all the way before speeding off toward town.

Parking his motorcycle next to Cody's in a parking lot near the French Market, he tucked the new helmet under his arm and made his way to the bar a couple of blocks away, brushing his still-damp hair into some semblance of order with one hand. Several women tried to catch his eye as he walked by, and although he saw them, he totally ignored them, giving one exceptionally bold one who touched him a glare cold enough to freeze her to the spot before continuing on his way. He glanced back at her as he reached for the door and, although she watched him, she didn't make another move his way. Like his father before him, he was starting to find the attention he received for his looks to be almost an annoyance, and wondered if it was wrong of him to wish for a disfiguring accident so that women would take notice of him for his personality instead of just his looks for a change…

He pulled open the door to the bar and stepped inside, pausing to give his eyes time to adjust to the dim interior. Despite it being only 4 p.m., the bar was already hopping with locals and tourists, enjoying the drink specials and complimentary snacks that came with Happy Hour, but it didn't take Chase long to locate Cody. The wiry Cajun looked up from the bar and bellowed "Chase! Mon frere! Come on in and 'ave a seat!"

As Chase made his way over to a bar stool next to the waitress station, several of the patrons whom he'd met on earlier trips greeted him as well, and he did his best to remember all the names to greet them in return. Those whose names he couldn't recall were greeted with a generic "Good to see you" as he passed, and he settled himself on the stool feeling like some sort of local celebrity. When he set the helmet on the bar, Cody removed it, then set a drink in front of him before he had time to order, and Chase made a show of sniffing suspiciously at the innocent looking soda before taking a sip, finding that it was a liberally mixed rum and coke. Coughing as the rum burned all the way from his mouth to his stomach, he looked up at Cody, who was grinning from ear to ear.

"I t'oght you should 'ave one good strong drink, den da res' are just coke. I 'ave five hours before I can go anywhere, so I want to make sure you don't get too drunk to drive 'ome."

"Thanks!" Cody said in something between a hiss and a groan, making it sound as if the drink had burned a hole in his voice box, and all the patrons close by laughed. Cody just rolled his eyes, and hurried off to the other end of the bar to refill a drink for someone who was signaling for attention.

While Chase nursed his drink, the waitresses coming to the bar to order drinks and food for their assigned tables all spoke with him, and since many of them were related to Cody either by blood or marriage, they caught him up to all the news of the extended Boudreaux family while Cody was busy dashing back and forth behind the bar. It was Cody's petite cousin, Josette, who drew the most of Chase's attention, however, as she was working with a cast on one wrist, and kept glancing over her shoulder as if she was expecting some sort of trouble. She kept insisting that everything was fine, but her pale blue eyes had a haunted look, and even Cody was watching the patrons more intently than normal.

When the second bartender came on duty at 6, Cody was able to spend more time talking to his young friend, and insisted that Chase have some of the cook's award winning jambalaya for dinner. The plate had just been cleared away, and Chase was downing his second after dinner glass of straight coke, laughing at Cody's teasing that he wasn't a real man if he couldn't handle the spice from the jambalaya, when the bar door was yanked open with a bang and a large man came in, obviously already drunk, and announced his presence by bellowing for Josette. Although she went white as a sheet, she continued to take care of her customers as if nothing was happening, making her way back to the bar with a tray full of glasses to place the order for another round. The newcomer spotted her and stumbled his way over, but not in time to catch her at the bar. Undisturbed, he ordered a beer, and stood at the waitress station for her to return.

"Don't you be makin' any mischief tonight, Beau, y'hear?" Cody said as he handed the man his beer, but Beau didn't respond. He just leaned against the bar next to Chase's elbow as if he expected the youth to give up his stool. The look on Cody's face was all Chase needed to see to know that he was required to act like Beau's presence wasn't disturbing him, and to stay where he was.

Josette returned to the waitress station with

another tray of empty glasses just as Chase was nearing the punch line of a joke he was telling Cody. She loudly asked Beau to move out of the space so she could put down her tray, and he took one step back, but as she settled the tray on the bar, he leaned in, and asked her in a most impolite way if she was selling herself to any of the men she was serving drinks to. Cody, who was looking at Chase at the time, saw something happen then that he had never seen in his many years working as a bartender. He would later describe it to the rest of his family in these words: "One minute, Chase is smiling and telling me jokes, and de next minute, it's like someone flip a switch. I 'aven't seen a look that cold even in the eyes of a rattlesnake just before he make a try for you."

Turning his head to look at the man who had just insulted his friend's cousin, Chase spoke in a tone that was politely conversational even as his eyes turned to two chips of green ice.

"What did you just say to her?"

Never having seen such a cold look on Chase's face in the entire time she'd known him, Josette wisely took several steps back away from him. Beau, not realizing the danger, stepped even closer, leaning in to impress upon the boy that he was much bigger and much tougher.

"I'm calling a spade a spade, as if it's any of your business, punk!"

"Maybe it's time you leave if you can't be nice."

Chase's voice never wavered from that calm, conversational tone, but Beau took offense anyway, and Chase carefully moved his drink out of harm's way, pushing the bar stool back so he could stand as Beau gathered himself for the first swing. Just as Chase was expecting him to do, Beau threw a roundhouse punch that had always sent his opponents to the hospital.

As quick as that rattlesnake that Cody would later compare him to, Chase dodged the blow and, grabbing the back of Beau's neck to use his own momentum against him, slammed the bigger man's face down on the cleared space on the bar with a quick thrust. The force of the impact made glasses jump down the whole length of the bar, and when Chase let go, Beau slid silently to the floor without so much as a groan.

Chase watched him for a moment or two, but when the big man made no move to get up to continue the fight, Chase calmly pulled his bar stool back into place and sat back down. He leaned over again for another look, then grimaced.

"Do you have a mop somewhere handy, Cody?" he asked calmly, and Cody, shaking off the shock of what he'd just witnessed, came over and tried to peer over the top of the bar at the unconscious man.

"Why you need a mop? He bleedin'?"

Chase looked disgusted.

"No, he spilled his beer."

As if those words broke the spell that had fallen over the bar, people first laughed, then began talking loudly about what had just happened. Cody picked up the phone and called for an ambulance. Josette's sister, Beth, who was one of the other waitresses, came over with the mop to clean up the spilled beer, and gave Beau a hearty kick to the ribs on her way past. Josette, in a most unladylike gesture, spat on Beau's face and said loudly "That's for breaking my arm, espece de con!"

When the ambulance arrived and the EMT's saw who was laid out on the floor, they excitedly asked Cody for details of what had happened, as they had often been called to take people to the hospital after Beau started a fight, but had never seen the man himself with much more than a bruise or two. Cody, without even a glance Chase's way, calmly told them "He slip and bang his head on the bar. See here? I t'ink he even leave a dent!"

No one contradicted Cody, and when the EMT's had loaded the still unconscious man onto the stretcher and rolled him out to the ambulance, the bartender offered a round of shots on the house for their silence, which guaranteed that Chase wouldn't be in any trouble for sending the bullying son of one of the city's richest men to the hospital. Chase turned his shot glass over so that Cody couldn't fill it without saying a word, but continued to laugh at the other patron's teasing until it was time for Cody's shift to end.

Only Chase and Cody knew how much it bothered the young man to send Beau to the hospital, despite the circumstances....

Chapter 2

Kelly and Aloriah Starbird followed the rest of the ghost tour guests, bringing up the rear of the tour group so that they could get pictures of some of the areas they were walking through without having the other guests in the photos. The trip to New Orleans, and especially the ghost tour, was Aloriah's reward for buckling down and graduating with honors the week before, and she was having the time of her life.

Aloriah stopped suddenly and turned, aiming her camera down an alley and taking several shots without really knowing what drew her to do so. As such unexpected action was something the girl had done since early childhood, Kelly slowed enough to stay close, but continued to keep the group in sight. As soon as Aloriah had taken the pictures she wanted, mother and daughter giggled as they ran to catch up, acting more like sisters, not seeing the faces that peered out of the alley after them, faces which Aloriah hadn't noted when taking her shots.

As they walked along, pausing now and then to hear a story about New Orleans' gruesome past, Aloriah began to get more and more uncomfortable, feeling a strange current of animosity in the air, looking around casually as if just bored while trying to sense where the feeling was coming from. Kelly, too, was sensing something not quite right, feeling an odd tingling sensation that her grandmother in Nova Scotia had jokingly referred to as "her spidey senses" after Kelly had taken a liking to comic books like "The Amazing Spiderman" in her youth. As she had been taught by her grandmother, who was a strong empath, she allowed her feelings to reach out and test the air.

Catching Aloriah's eye to strengthen the silent communication that they had always shared, she heard Aloriah silently say *There* as her eyes pinpointed a small group of rough-looking men who were touching off the alarms in her daughter's senses. Stretching her arms over her head and faking a yawn, she was able to look at the group long enough to confirm that they were the source of the uneasy feelings she was having. She wasn't sure what they had done to catch the attention of such unsavory looking men, but she was certain there was trouble brewing.

By the time the tour ended, both women were getting extremely nervous about walking the dark street back to their hotel, so they hurriedly blended into the crowd and headed toward the Cafe du Monde for some coffee and beignets. Perhaps after they'd had a snack and sat for a bit, they could come up with another plan than the walk back to the hotel, which just a few blocks away, but on a dark street. Although they each tried not to do so, the feeling of animosity was so strong that they kept taking glances back, repeatedly confirming the presence of the group that was keeping them in sight.

As they rounded a corner and stepped into the darkness between two streetlights, there was a strong mixed odor of Axe, Old Spice and a soft under note of liquor before two men separated from the shadows, each claiming one of the women by slinging an arm over her shoulder. Kelly stiffened immediately, but Aloriah felt an overwhelming sense of protection from these two strangers and relaxed. The men who had been following them paused, and the feeling of animosity changed to momentary confusion. The small, wiry Cajun with salt and pepper hair who had claimed Kelly grinned, and gave a boisterous greeting that carried through the crowd, causing several people to turn and look their way.

"There you are, ma petite! 'Ow was da ghos' tour?"

Under his breath through his wide smile, he murmured "Play along. You bein' followed, as I suspec' you know."

Getting a nod from Aloriah that told her these men could be trusted, Kelly forced herself to relax and give the Cajun a smile, speaking almost as loudly as he had in hopes it would carry to the men who had been following them.

"We didn't have anyone jump out at us like in they do in the spook walks at Halloween, so Aloriah didn't have to punch anyone." she said brightly, and Aloriah did a convincing eye roll, made even more believable by the multi-toned hair, black lipstick, and dramatic eye shadow that gave her a Goth look.

"It was soooo booooring!" Aloriah whined in her best "beleaguered young teen" voice, causing the tall, green eyed stranger at her side to smile in honest amusement. The strong arm around her shoulder gave a gentle squeeze, and she felt nothing from him except for strength and comfort, which seemed to surround him like a cloak. This close, she could see the small scar left by a former lip piercing, but her attention kept getting drawn away from the handsome face to gaze into the clear green eyes, which seemed to assess every aspect of her being.

Something in those eyes told her that he liked what he saw, and that he was seeing much more than most men would have. He glanced down at the camera around her neck before his eyes quickly marked the men who had been following them. When he looked back down at her, she had the distinct feeling that he was the one who had somehow recognized that they were in danger, but when she opened her mouth to speak, he beat her to it.

"You know, the experts all say that you can catch things on camera that you might have missed with your naked eye." He suggested helpfully in a deep voice with no discernible accent. He didn't speak as loudly as his friend, so only the people closest to them heard him. "You may find that your boring walk actually produced something exciting."

Aloriah's eyes widened as she remembered

the strange urge to take a photo just before she started having that feeling that she was being watched. Something in the look in those intelligent green eyes, which watched her face so closely, told her that he suspected what she now did: she may be getting followed by those men because she was taking a photo in the right place at the wrong time. For those who were close enough to be hearing the conversation, she shrugged as if dismissing his suggestion, and wrinkled her nose as she responded in that same bored drawl.

"Probably not."

"You ladies ready for your coffee and beignets?" the Cajun asked, and they continued toward the Cafe du Monde as a group, the older couple taking the lead as the younger pair fell in behind, just as if this was something they had done a million times before.

Aloriah could still feel the animosity in the men following them, and she cuddled closer to the warmth of the man who kept his arm protectively around her shoulders. He tipped his head down as if he was going to kiss her cheek, and his warm breath sent shivers racing across her cheek as he whispered "My name's Chase and my friend there is Cody."

She tipped her head slightly to whisper back "I'm Aloriah. My mom is Kelly."

Then she made the mistake of looking up at him, and he looked deeply into her eyes again with a sweet smile, devastating her. Never had she had such a nice looking man treat her like he was treating her, and just as she was having that thought, he actually bent his head to touch her lips with a kiss as light as the touch of a butterfly.

"Pleased to meet you." he murmured as he drew back with a devilish smile. For just a moment, she was too stunned by his behavior to be able to sense the men behind them, and she didn't even notice that they had come to a temporary halt.

No one even a few feet back would have noticed the intensity in Chase's eyes as he took a seemingly random look at the people around them during that brief pause, but Aloriah could feel the tension in the muscles under his jacket and the intensity of his emotions. His beautiful green eyes narrowed slightly, and he smiled at her again as he started them walking again, whispering through his teeth "The four men who've been following you just got joined by a fifth, and all of them are looking uncomfortable as they're keeping their eyes right on you. Stay very close to me."

Chase punctuated his words with another squeeze, which backed up the feeling she was getting from him that he meant her no harm. She couldn't be sure how he had come to the conclusion that she and her mother needed protecting, as he didn't have anything about him that hinted that he was an empath like she was, but she wasn't about to look a gift horse in the mouth! Trying to connect to him as she did her mother, she tried to project the depth of her thanks as she whispered "Thank you so much for helping us!"

The genuine smile that made his eyes dance nearly took Aloriah's breath away! She was hard pressed to not just let herself fall into those dancing eyes and forget that he wasn't the lover he was pretending to be, and to also forget that her mother was walking just ahead of her. It would be so easy to just be carried away by the masquerade, and to make a spectacle of herself by grabbing onto him and kissing him the way she truly wanted to!

She felt a questioning presence in her mind, and when she looked at Kelly and met her eyes, a wordless communication went between the two women about whether to trust these two strangers who had come to their rescue. Kelly nodded and smiled as if in response to something Cody said as she looked at Chase, sensing the strength and comfort that Aloriah had sensed earlier, but having taken self-defense classes, she also noted the way he carried himself.

As she turned her full attention back to Cody to continue their lively conversation, she smiled with true joy for the first time since that odd tingling of her senses. Cody was the type of person that Kelly had always labeled as a terrier, small, fierce and very protective, but limited in how much damage he could inflict on his opponent. Chase had the air of a tiger that was ready to pounce the moment his prey came within range, seemingly relaxed, but lethal. Although she had no idea how the two men had decided that they were in trouble, she was quite glad that Chase and Cody were there to help her protect her daughter.

On reaching the Cafe du Monde, they were seated almost immediately at the last open table, and both of the men seated the ladies before taking their own seats. Chase carefully chose the seat that allowed him to watch the front door while Cody kept his eye on the entrance from the kitchen. When it became obvious that the unsavories who had been following the ladies weren't going to be able to come in and overhear the conversation, Chase started the serious questioning.

"Where do you ladies need to go this evening?" he asked bluntly, his eyes going back to the door as a couple left. He watched until another couple was seated, and Kelly smiled when those strikingly intense eyes came back to her for the answer. She gave him the name of the hotel, and was a little surprised when Cody snorted.

"That not a secure place to be, chere. They let jus' anyone in at all hours an' don' have a single security guard to come he'p if you done did get attack'd."

Aloriah tried hard not to smile at the way the Cajun talked, but Chase saw her twitching lips, and rolled his eyes, pretending to be upset by her reaction even though his eyes were gleaming with amusement as he copied Cody's accent. "Don' ya'll tell me you come to N'awlins an' din' 'spect to hear no Cajun."

Aloriah allowed her smile to show, and Cody gave her a wink before he pulled out a cell phone. "There gots to be somewhere safer for y'all, even if it be with my fam'ly in the swamps. How much you can spend?"

Kelly gave him a figure, and Cody started making calls, alternating between English and French, depending on who was on the other end of the phone.

A waitress came through while Cody was

talking, and Chase placed their order, once again watching carefully as another group left and a new group was seated. Once again, it wasn't the men who had been following the ladies, and once again, Kelly watched the way Chase tensed, then slowly relaxed. When Cody dropped the phone onto the table with a disgusted snort, all eyes turned to the thoughtful look on his face.

"Not a single place at dat price, chere. Look like we gon' have to give dese ladies a ride, mon ami, and take a long way aroun' so those baddies don' know where they stayin'." Looking from one woman to the other, Cody gave them a smile. "Y'all like motorcycles?"

Aloriah responded with a heartfelt "Yes" right away, producing an amused chuckle from Chase, but Kelly looked uncomfortable.

Cody reached over and patted her hand.

"No worries, chere. You ride with me. I take it easy on you." Cody gave Chase a very meaningful look as he continued. "We stop back at the bar anyway for your brain bucket. I t'ink I have an extra or two dere."

"If not, I'll let Aloriah wear mine." Chase swiftly volunteered, an evil gleam in his eye, and Cody's glare turned menacing.

"I din' buy you no helmet so's you can ride widdout!" He growled, but Chase seemed unfazed by the threatening tone. He leaned slightly toward Aloriah and tipped her a wink as he continued to tease his friend.

"Cody thinks I should protect a brain that I clearly don't have."

Both Aloriah and Kelly tried to hold back snickers as Cody cut loose with a stream of French, which was most likely not very politically correct from the looks on some of the other patrons faces nearby. Shaking his finger, he switched back to English to growl, "You lucky I can't reach you, boy. You need a good cuff upside that brainless head!"

Chase pretended to look scared, and the ladies couldn't hold back their giggles despite the glares that Cody threw at both of them. Cody picked up his cup to drain the last of his coffee from it while shaking his head.

"Now you jus' encouragin' him!" he grumbled, but a quirky grin was twisting up the corners of his lips as he set the cup back down.

The others at the table followed his lead, and finished their beignets and coffees, then Chase leapt up to pull out Aloriah's chair for her. Kelly felt her daughter's confusion at having a man actually treat her like a lady, and almost laughed as Cody did the same for her, leaning in before she started to rise to whisper "Dat's why I hang out wit' this boy. His mama done teach him right."

As Chase waited for everyone to be ready to move, he twisted his head around as if working out a kink, but Kelly noted the sharp look in the green eyes that belied his seemingly innocent movements. When he caught her watching him, he gave her just the slightest hint of a smile, then cut his eyes toward the door, where a single man was talking to the hostess as if he was innocently flirting. As Kelly marked him and returned her eyes to his, Chase gave the slightest hint of a nod, indicating it was one of the men he had marked earlier as being in the group that was following them. Like her daughter, she wondered what the young man saw that made him realize they needed help, but she was most grateful for his assistance, and she felt nothing threatening in his emotions or demeanor, at least not in terms of how he felt toward the ladies.

Toward those men following them, however…

As when they had entered the Cafe du Monde, each of the men tossed an arm around a lady, and as they passed the man at the door, Chase looked him directly in the eye, smiled, and nodded in greeting as if he knew him. The startled look on the man's face would have made Kelly laugh if she hadn't been so frightened. They strolled a couple of blocks to a bar as if they had nothing else on their minds, but Chase's occasional glances back as if making sure that the older couple was still keeping up confirmed that their followers were back in place. He held the door open for the other three to enter in front of him, and as soon as the door closed, his expression changed drastically.

"We may want to slip out the back, if it's okay with you, Cody. They seem to have picked up a few more friends since we last saw them." He said, barely loud enough for the four of them to hear, and Cody led the way into the back room while greeting co-workers and patrons with his normal jovial attitude. As soon as the swinging door to the back room closed behind them, however, Cody stepped up the pace, going into his office at a near run and popping back out in less than five minutes with three helmets in his arms, looking very disgruntled.

"I t'ought I had one more, but it mus' be at my house." Cody grumbled, and Chase took the newest helmet out of his hands while trying not to smile. When he started putting the helmet onto Aloriah's head, however, Cody's eyes narrowed. "I got dat one to protect your head, boy!"

Chase turned briefly to Cody, feigning innocence.

"But she's younger than I am, Cody! She has more brain cells to protect!"

Inside the helmet, Aloriah giggled as Chase's fingers went about their business of securing the chin strap, and Kelly fought a grin. Cody rolled his eyes like a long-suffering parent, handing Kelly one of the remaining helmets, and giving Chase time to finish what he was doing before leading them all toward the back door. As Cody punched in the code that would prevent the alarm from sounding when they opened the door, Chase again took the lead, taking Aloriah's hand to keep her close. Sensing that Cody's alarm code would only give them a set amount of time to slide through the door and let it close again, Aloriah reached back and took Kelly's hand.

At a nod from Cody, all three slid out the door and, following Chase's lead, the women flattened themselves against the wall in the dark alley while Cody joined them. Chase then slowly led the way through the shadows toward the parking lot. Pausing for a deep breath at the end of the alley, he leaned out to spot the men they were trying to avoid all standing and watching the door of the bar. With a smile, he slipped out with Aloriah, getting to his motorcycle and getting them both settled on it before Cody and Kelly followed suit. While the older couple got settled, Chase pulled a set of goggles out of a pocket on his leather jacket and put them on, then zipped up all the way so his collar protected his neck. When Cody was settled, they started their engines together.

It wasn't until both engines roared to life that the men in front of the bar turned and spotted their prey, giving a shout as they ran toward the motorcycles. Before they could get there, however, Chase and Cody were both out on Decatur Street, and heading toward Canal Street as if they were leaving of the city instead of just going down a couple of blocks and doubling back. Aloriah saw Chase's smile in one of his mirrors, and then was able to read the curse that he muttered when the light turned red, even though the motor was too loud for her to actually hear him. As Cody pulled up next to him, Chase gave a hand signal: *Follow me.*

Before the light had a chance to change to green, two cars containing the men they were trying to avoid pulled up just a car length behind them. Chase and Cody behaved as if they didn't know they were being followed. When they got into the faster two lane traffic, Chase spotted a group of other motorcyclists. Taking one hand off the handles, he reached down to squeeze Aloriah's bare arm, and for the first time with anyone other than her mother, she actually heard his thought as a soft whisper in her head.

Please hold on tight! his voice said, and she

wrapped her arms a little more securely around his firm waist, again seeing his smile in the mirror just before he set his hand back on the handle, then sent them careening out around several vehicles to slip in with the larger group of motorcycles. Aloriah felt her mother's panic as Cody followed suit.

With a skill well beyond his years, Chase carefully worked his way up through the other motorcycles so that they were toward the center of the long queue, yet close to the edge of the road. Cody stayed right behind him, matching him move for move. No one in the larger group of motorcycles took any special notice of them until Chase spotted a truck stop up ahead and gave a low hand signal to Cody, preparing his friend to leave the group. Because of the number of motorcycles in the group, the two cars were forced to stay almost a quarter of a mile behind them, and Chase took a deep breath, hoping it was far enough back for his newly hatched plan to work.

Shooting out of the queue without any directional to mark their departure, Chase and Cody went around behind the building to where the big rigs were all parked. Two matching tractor trailers were parked nose to tail right at the back of the restaurant with the lead trailer's nose only a few feet from a pair of dumpsters. With another quick hand motion to warn Cody, Chase slowed his bike, and slid between the trailers and the building, almost glancing his handlebars off the side of the big rigs a couple of times where the wall stuck out a little. He finished by shutting off his motor, thereby killing his lights, and sliding in behind the dumpsters, coming to a halt squarely behind the furthest one. In seconds, Cody had copied his move and was sitting squarely, totally silent, behind the second one. Then they just sat and waited for a few minutes.

Headlights cut into the parking lot behind them, and then a single car came slowly around the back of the building. Reaching one long arm back around Aloriah, Chase leaned forward, pulling her down with him to make sure her head wasn't in sight behind the dumpster. Seeing what he was doing, both Cody and Kelly followed suit, ducking as low as possible to make sure they weren't seen.

Aloriah felt the emotions of the men in the car, wanting to cry when she could confirm it was the group she had inadvertently taken a photo of when she followed her instincts. As they drew closer, it became evident that their windows were down, and they were arguing among themselves. When they drew even with the dumpsters, a scrap of the argument could be clearly heard.

"...and I swear I saw two motorcycles come back here!" said one man, his voice adamant, as if he was trying to convince the others that he was trustworthy.

"And I swear you ain't got the brains God gave a 'gator!" came a second voice with a heavier drawl, obviously angry with the first speaker.

"What if all she got was a dark alley?" a third voice piped in. "We was way back from the street!"

"All I wants is to see the pitcher." number two's voice came again, and Aloriah was certain he was the boss of the group. "If she din't catch nothin', she can go back wherever she came."

The car rolled beyond their hearing then, and Chase listened until he heard the engine gun and gravel being spewed, then turned his head slightly, whispering to Aloriah so softly that she could barely hear him, not entirely sure he understood why he even asked.

"Do you think they're gone?"

Reaching out with her emotions, Aloriah felt the men getting further and further away.

"I believe they are." She responded, just as softly, and felt strangely bereft when he removed his long arm from around her, allowing her to sit up straight again. When he reached down in the darkness to make sure her legs were out of the way before he restarted his engine, however, there was something intimate in the touch that brought her a strange sense of comfort. She still had some time before he dropped her at her hotel, and she was going to enjoy every minute of being pressed against that strong male back for the trip back into New Orleans.

Chapter 3

When they arrived back at the hotel where Kelly had rented them a room well in advance of their trip, more concerned with cost and nearness to the things they had wanted to see than anything else, Kelly pulled off her helmet and gave a long, disgusted look around. The hotel was barely a two-star, with the non-smoking room she was in with her daughter stinking of long-dead cigarette smoke. To save a few dollars in order to be able to have more fun with her daughter while here, she had chosen a place with a front door that was open 24 hours a day, and that had no security cameras or guards on duty to insure the protection of those foolish enough to rent rooms there.

Feeling her mother's despair, Aloriah reached over to place a hand on her shoulder, and that contact opened up the mental doors that allowed them to share a silent conversation about the predicament they found themselves in. Despite

Aloriah's feelings on the matter, Kelly's logic won out when it came to whether or not to continue to involve the two men. They couldn't continue to endanger the lives of two strangers who happened to step in at just the right moment. It was time to say goodbye to Cody and Chase, thank them for their help, and send them back to their normal lives with the hope that whoever was after them wouldn't recognize either man.

As she faced Chase, however, and looked up into the intelligent green gaze and half-smile, she had a horrific premonition. If they stayed in this hotel, they wouldn't survive the night. Looking back at Kelly's face, she saw that the premonition had been shared. Kelly was ghostly pale. Aloriah turned her eyes back to Chase and mustered a shy smile.

"You did say you knew of other hotels with better security, didn't you? I have a very bad feeling about staying here, and suspect we might be able to come up with a little bit more money if we really had to."

The smile went all the way across his face in an instant, making her think of a rising sun. One moment her world was dark, and the next, she had a savior who would see to her safety before he rode off into the sunset. Chase took a step forward, turning her toward the hotel even as he slid his arm back around her shoulders to accompany her.

"Let's get your things together while Cody makes a few more phone calls. He knows all the best places, and is friends with most of the reputable hotel managers. I'm sure we can get you in somewhere if we tell them the whole situation."

Kelly pulled out the room key, and went ahead of the young couple while Cody brought up the rear, pulling out his cell phone again, pausing only to look up at Chase and give a quick hand signal that the women didn't understand. The hand signal was a way of asking *Who pays?*

Chase responded back with another hand signal: *Me*

Cody smiled, knowing that the Benton's could have easily afforded any of the mansions in the Garden District. Well before they reached the elevator, he was in an animated conversation with someone in French, telling the other person "Security is the top priority. Spare no expense."

As the elevator doors opened to reveal an empty, albeit shabby interior, Cody smiled.

"All arranged for you, mes petites."

Both Aloriah and Kelly suspected they had missed something involving those hand signals, but for the moment, Aloriah couldn't read anything but pleasure from Chase. She watched him closely, frowning slightly when he didn't seem at all uncomfortable about being stared at, until he turned to her, opened his eyes wide in feigned innocence, and opened both hands in a gesture she'd used herself many times.

"What?" He asked, and Cody bit his lip, trying not to laugh.

Kelly covered her mouth with her hand, her dark eyes sparkling as she recognized that routine. Aloriah just looked even more frustrated, but didn't say anything, much to her mother's surprise. She was usually so much more aggressive, but didn't seem to know what to do with the handsome young man who seemed so determined to help them.

Getting to the room with little more said, the ladies packed quickly while Cody called a cab, since carrying the bags on the bikes would prove too difficult. Chase stood at the window, staying out of everyone's way while watching the street, making sure that the men who had been after the ladies hadn't found them yet.

During the ride down the elevator, Chase seemed outwardly thoughtful, but Aloriah could feel the inner gathering of strength as he prepared to defend the ladies, if necessary, on the way to the taxi. It was only then that she took a good look past the handsome face and stunning eyes to really touch his emotions, finding the warrior that her mother had already taken note of. The way he held himself as the elevator descended, the way his eyes began a sweep of the lobby the moment the doors began to open, and even the way he held her back for just a moment so that he could step out first reminded her of the fierce primal man. Sensing the concern that made him behave that way, she allowed him to take control, following behind him without a word, and watching as Cody made sure that Kelly was with her in the middle of the group while he took up the rear guard.

As they stepped out onto the sidewalk to watch for the ordered taxi, no one paid attention to the large man standing in the shadows, smoking a cigarette, at least, not until he spoke in an obviously fake British accent.

"What's all this then?" he rumbled, and

Aloriah gasped at the speed Chase displayed when he spun around, putting himself between the ladies and the stranger, his arms up in a traditional martial arts defense posture. The only outward sign of alarm he displayed was a narrowing of his eyes as he tried to identify the person. When the big man put his hands up away from his sides and stepped forward into the light, however, Chase let out a snort and barked out the first truly offensive thing the ladies had heard him say.

"Dammit, Bear! Don't you ever learn anything?"

The huge, grey haired man gave an unapologetic grin.

"At least I knew better than to touch you!" he responded, and he rubbed one wrist where there was a surgery scar. "I really can't afford to have my arm pinned back together again, and I'm not about to tell your dad that I was that stupid again so that he'll pay for it."

Chase sighed, looking disgusted, as Cody greeted Bear, then Chase introduced him to the ladies as a long time friend of the family, one of the oldest truckers on the road (which earned the younger man a playful punch to the arm), and gave Bear a quick run-down of the situation. Bear smiled, promising to watch for anyone who came in looking for the ladies so he could give the illusion that they were still in the hotel and being watched. Aloriah stood watching the big man as his face registered the pleasant emotions she could feel from him, but underlying all else was a respect for the younger man, the kind of respect one earned through deeds.

She made a mental note to ask Chase about the comment about the man's arm later, but then the cab pulled up, and she wondered if there was going to be a later. She couldn't help but smile, however, when the huge trucker took her hand in a ham-sized fist and told her it was a pleasure to meet her. He did the same to Kelly, who also smiled and returned the compliment. Then he slapped Chase on the back hard enough to make the young man stagger and said "Say hi to Superman and Lois Lane for me."

Bear walked away, not seeing Chase make a comically exaggerated look of pain, stretching as if he was readjusting his spine from the man's goodbye "pat". Looking to make sure the old trucker was far enough not to overhear, Chase moved closer to the others and whispered "Never tell that man he looks like he's getting weak, even jokingly. He reminds you each time he sees you that he's not weak, and never will be."

While Cody spoke to the driver in rapid French, Chase loaded the bags into the trunk and got the ladies settled. Aloriah admired the fine back view, her first really good look at her erstwhile rescuer when her mind wasn't distracted by other things, as he went over to his bike. He threw his leg over and stopped to look back at her and smile. She found herself blushing, her first thought: *Shouldn't it be illegal to be so sexy?*

With a playfully horrified look, knowing she was watching, Chase picked up the helmet she'd been wearing and brought it toward his head. Just before putting it on, he mouthed "Goodbye, cruel world" and closed his eyes, sliding it over his head like it was going to kill him to wear it. Aloriah couldn't hold back a giggle, and Kelly smiled as she took her own look at the young man over her daughter's shoulder. A very nice young man in a good looking package with a hero complex. They could have done worse.

A muffled whistle came from beneath Chase's helmet and Cody looked up, seeing that he was holding things up. He finished his conversation with his uncle in the taxi by telling him "I'll see you at Maman's next Sunday."

Pulling on his helmet, he jumped on his bike, then he and Chase started them simultaneously. The cab pulled out, and the motorcycles fell in behind, like a mini motorcade. As the events of the evening suddenly caught up with them, Aloriah and Kelly held hands and discussed the next move.

"First, I want to look at the photos you shot. Then we can figure out how to stay hidden until the flight home."

Cody's uncle, having been secretly filled in to what the ladies had been through, looked up into the rearview mirror and pulled a card out of his pocket, passing it back with a smile. "You fin' you need a ride to the po-lice, you call me."

Aloriah smiled at the way he drew out the word "police", and took the card, looking over her shoulder at the two motorcycles. She had never thought herself particularly lucky, but tonight, she had hit the jackpot when it came to finding helpful people in a crisis. Looking down at the camera that she still had around her neck, she turned her best puppy eyes on her mother.

"Since none of my friends will ever believe this happened, can I get you to take just one picture?"

Kelly laughed, knowing exactly what kind of photo her daughter wanted.

"Of course!"

Arriving at the hotel, Chase and Cody both quickly agreed to pose with Aloriah for the picture in front of the fancy hotel doors, then they escorted the ladies inside. The reservations were made under Chase's name with the excuse that it would be safer that way, and when Kelly tried to hand the concierge her credit card, he politely refused. "It must be the name of the person the rooms are booked under, just in case they know how to trace your credit card."

Kelly was frowning as she put her card away, and Aloriah was too lost in her own dismal thoughts, so they both missed the sly smile the concierge shared with Chase. Cody had explained the situation to him as well. The price mentioned aloud was for the cheapest room they had, and was entirely to prevent Kelly from causing a scene. What was really going on the credit card Chase presented was one of their finest suites, which was only accessible to those who held key cards to the two suites on the top floor. The women were more secure in this hotel than they would have been in a police safe house.

The time had come for them to part company, but neither Aloriah nor Chase felt ready. To extend the time with her, Chase pulled up an empty contact screen on his phone and handed it to Aloriah.

"If you have a cell phone, program it in. Otherwise, I'd appreciate having a home phone so I can check and make sure you made it back home safe."

Smiling, Aloriah opened her own contact screen and handed her phone to Chase for him to do the same. When they both finished and he couldn't think of anything else, Chase kissed her hand, and gave Aloriah a smile that tried to be cheerful, but failed.

"Thank you for a very entertaining evening, my lady."

Aloriah looked skeptical for a moment.

"Entertaining? You're kidding, right?"

"It's not every night I get to pretend I'm in an action film." His smile was a bit more real, and somewhat infectious, and as Aloriah smiled back, Chase stepped closer and tipped her head back with a finger. "Seriously, thank you for trusting me to help you. I hope things work out well for the rest of your stay in New Orleans."

He gave her a parting kiss that should have been indecent for a single night that couldn't even be considered an official date, then stepped back and urged her to go with the bell boy and get settled. "Call or text me when you know what's in the picture."

As the door to the elevator closed, blocking Aloriah's view of the handsomest man who'd ever kissed her, she sighed sadly. It wasn't until she was safely behind a doubly locked door, looking out the window at the nearly silent city streets, that Aloriah realized she hadn't asked about Bear's arm comment.

Looking at her phone with a smile, she decided she would have to call and ask about that. But later. Right now, she had to hook her camera up to her laptop and see what all the fuss was about.

It didn't take long to back track from the very nice picture of her between the little Cajun and the tall, handsome truck driver to the ones that she took on a whim. The first one made her blood go cold. It was a group of startled faces: the men who had followed them and later chased them.

The one just before that made her run for the bathroom. Those same men had a man in a police uniform held against the wall, and one of them had cut the officer's throat, sending a spray of blood across the alley that they were all professional enough to avoid being sprayed by. Wondering what had made Aloriah race for the bathroom, Kelly took a good look at the screen, and turned white as a sheet. It all made sense now.

Picking up Aloriah's phone, she made a phone call to the police to see if they would come to the hotel, if they wanted the photo sent to them, or if they should bring the memory card in to the police station. They asked her to email it to them so that they could have a look at it, but for the sake of using it as evidence, they would also need her to bring in the memory card once they had taken anything personal off it.

Then she called Chase, who didn't pick up his phone as he was still in transit to Cody's house, and left a message that they had found out what was on the camera. In the calmest voice she could manage, she simply told him "Aloriah took photos of a murder in progress".

Chapter 4

Chase parked his bike next to Cody's and followed his friend inside, pulling his phone out of his jacket pocket as they sat down at the table to have one more beer and discuss the evening before going to bed. Frowning when he saw that he'd missed a call, he smiled when he saw there was a message, and who it was from. The smile swiftly left his face as he listened to the message, then he played it a second time after hitting the speaker button so Cody could hear it, too. Cody's eyes grew wide and he stared at Chase for a long, quiet moment.

"We done did a good t'ing by getting them into another hotel." Cody finally said, then, instead of drinking any more of his beer, Chase stood up and started to put his coat back on. Cody looked alarmed as he jumped up to get between Chase and the door. "Whoa, whoa, whoa! Where you goin'?"

"Back to New Orleans to post a guard outside the hotel."

Cody didn't often put his foot down when it came to Chase, but this time he did, standing firmly between his friend and the door.

"You out your mind, boy? Those men got a good look at bot' of us as well as the women! If they see you on the street, they'll know where de women is at, and you'll be their next victim!"

Cody made sense, but something in Chase still wanted to go to protect Aloriah until she and her mother were safely on the plane that would take them home. Seeing the flustered look on Chase's face, Cody looked at his watch and made a face of his own. It was 11:30 p.m. in New Orleans, which put it at 12:30 a.m. in Maine. "I would tell you to call your father for advice, but I don't t'ink you should wake him up for this."

Looking at his own watch, which he kept set to Maine time, Chase got a very thoughtful look on his face.

"It might be too late to call, but I can leave him a text." Grinning at Cody, he took his coat back off and sat back down, picking his beer back up as he thought about how to best ask for the advice he wanted without alarming anyone. He settled for the simple method, typing in "I need your advice. Call when you get this message."

He set the phone down on the table and picked up his beer, trying hard to relax until his father got back in touch in the morning even though he still wanted to throw on his jacket, jump on his bike, and ride back into New Orleans. Both he and Cody almost jumped out of their skins when the phone rang just a few minutes later, and he picked it up to see his father's face smiling at him from the screen before he answered the phone.

"Dad? What are you still doing up?"

Kyle's voice sounded almost annoyed.

"Angela came home from a school picnic with food poisoning. We're at the hospital waiting for the doctor to decide whether or not we can take her home."

Cringing, Chase debated whether or not he should add to his father's worry, but then Kyle asked the all-important question, and Chase wasn't the type to lie to his parents about something so important.

"What's going on that you'd text me in the middle of the night?"

With a deep sigh, Chase told his father about the women who'd had the shady men following them, the way he and Cody had stepped in, the motorcycle chase, and the phone message he had just received about the photograph that had caused it all. "I want to go back to New Orleans to protect them until they can get the photograph into the right hands, but Cody thinks that the men who are after them got a good enough look at us to recognize me."

There was silence at the other end of the line while Kyle absorbed all that he had been told, then there was a soft chuckle.

"Like father, like son, it seems, eh?"

Chase chuckled as well, having heard about the murder his own mother had witnessed and his father's part in helping her put the perpetrator behind bars. Much as he and his dad got on each other's nerves at times, it was truly helping him to hear the old man's voice and get some advice from someone who had lived through the same kind of problem he was having now.

"So, have you found out if the ladies are bringing the photo in or emailing it, or is this just your gut reaction talking at the moment?" the elder Benton asked, and Chase almost cursed himself out loud. He hadn't even thought about the fact that the police might only need the emailed photo, keeping the ladies within the safety of the penthouse hotel room.

"Reacting purely from the gut." he admitted, and Kyle's soft chuckle at the other end of the phone made him feel worlds better.

"Just don't hit any walls, or Cody, if you get mad at yourself."

Chase smiled.

"I won't, Dad, and thanks for the advice. Tell Ang to get better soon."

Kyle's voice softened.

"Take care, kiddo, and let me know how things work out."

They hung up almost simultaneously, and Chase immediately dialed Aloriah, pleased when she picked up right away, but not liking the hoarseness of her voice. She sounded as if she had been crying, and his heart clenched in sympathy.

"Hey, it's Chase. I got a message from your mom about the photo."

"Yeah, it's rather... graphic."

She swallowed hard during that pause, and he almost heard the click in her throat, suddenly understanding that the hoarseness of her tone wasn't from tears. She had been vomiting. It must be quite the photo to get that reaction!

"Have you been in touch with the police?"

Aloriah gave a short snort of a laugh.

"Mom emailed the picture to them, but they want us to bring in the memory card in the morning to make sure that there's no question about the chain of evidence. I'm trying to pull off all the photos that might identify us in any way so the perps can't find any of us."

Chase thought about that last photo that had been taken, just outside the hotel doors, and he smiled. It shouldn't have, but it gave him a warm feeling when she included Cody and himself as part of the "us". There was a slight pause on her end, then he could almost feel the tears in her voice.

"I'm so sorry I got you and Cody mixed up in this, Chase. I should learn to control my impulses." She ended on a sniffle, and he could picture her with a tissue in her hand.

"Well, I'd accept that apology, but as I recall it, Cody and I got ourselves mixed up in this." Across the table from him, Cody snickered and added his own comment in a loud voice.

"Y'all got mugged, sugar. We just din't take nothin' off ya."

Aloriah heard Cody and laughed softly.

"Tell Cody I didn't see it as mugging. More like a couple of knights coming to the rescue before the damsels had a chance to get taken by the dragons."

Chase related her comment to Cody, who preened and winked at Chase.

"You do not want to know what Cody's doing right now." he told her with a laugh, then got serious again. "So what time are you and your mom going into the police station?"

There was a pause as she covered the phone, then her voice was back clear again.

"They told her to bring it in at about 9 a.m. so the Commander can be there to take it personally. They also told her that this is the safest place we could be in New Orleans, and she's really mad at you for not telling her what the room really costs."

Chase sighed, having hoped to avoid the revelation about his father and the family money, but…

"Tell her it's courtesy of KB Enterprises, otherwise known as my dad's business."

There was dead silence for a moment, then he heard her passing on the news with awe in her voice. Cody watched the pained expression on his young friend's face until Aloriah laughed at whatever her mother had said.

"She says she's not mad at you anymore. We just won't tell my dad where we stayed or who paid for the room."

Chase let out a breath that he hadn't realized he'd been holding. While at Cafe du Monde, it had come out that the ladies were visiting from Maine, and that he was a driver for a trucking company from Maine, but he hadn't said anything about which company he drove for. It was bad enough to be Kyle Benton's kid when in Greenville, but to admit that he was the heir to the owner of the prestigious company that had bailed out most of the smaller businesses in Northern Maine when out of the small town wasn't something he usually did. He even had Cody looking at him with exaggerated shock on his face!

Changing the subject, he continued to talk soothingly to Aloriah as Cody pushed a note over to him with a question written on it: "What time do they need escort to the police?"

He passed the note back after writing "9" and winked at Cody as the Cajun started making phone calls, gathering a larger entourage to make sure that the ladies would make it safely to the police department with the memory card. When Aloriah sounded calm and collected, Chase wished her a good night and hung up, putting his cell on it's charger before he and Cody also called it a night.

Cody went into his room and promptly went to sleep, exhausted from all the excitement. Chase, however, tossed and turned, finding himself still staring at the ceiling as the sky began to lighten. Finally admitting that he wasn't going to sleep, he got up and went into the bathroom, looking at himself in the mirror for a long time before going back into his room to pull out an old film canister that he carried in his overnight bag. With a gleam in his eye as he thought about Aloriah's Goth look, he pulled out the lip ring that he kept there, then went back into the bathroom to force it back through the partially healed piercing. It became a test of his ability to put himself through pain without crying out before he accomplished the task, and he was really glad that Cody wasn't awake to witness him wiping tears from his eyes from the strain.

Returning to his room, he applied fresh deodorant and cologne before pulling on his clothes, opting for a red, white and blue plaid shirt instead of another t-shirt. As he turned to leave the room while buttoning the shirt, he realized that Cody was up and leaning against the door frame, watching him while blinking the sleep out of his eyes.

"You know she say they go to the police at 9."

Chase sighed.

"I couldn't sleep."

Cody just shook his head, and as he headed for the bathroom to wake up with a hot shower, he called back. "Jus' be careful, you. I don't be the one who wants to call your father and tell him you be dead."

Chase smiled and finished dressing, grabbing his phone on the way out to the garage. Grabbing the new helmet as well as one of Cody's older battered ones, which for some reason were kept instead of being thrown away, he strapped the new one onto the back of the bike and pulled the battered one onto his own head. Rolling the bike out into the driveway before starting it, he looked up to see Cody, with a towel around his waist, watching out of the bathroom window. Giving a quick salute that brought a smile to the Cajun's face, Chase headed out to New Orleans, knowing that Cody would be following with the rest of the group he had gathered in a couple of hours.

Chase pulled up in front of the hotel just as traffic was starting to pick up in the city. Pulling his motorcycle into one of the special parking spaces that the hotel provided for motorcyclists, he took a short walk to a coffee vendor's cart, then walked back to the hotel to lean against a lamp post and light a cigarette. Even though he didn't smoke, he really didn't want to be arrested for loitering, so he mostly stood sipping on the hot cup of black coffee, putting the cigarette up to his lips whenever he saw a police car coming his way. Had the officers driving by been more observant, they would have noted that he didn't blow out any smoke, but after a friendly nod of the head, they all drove on without paying close attention to the young man leaning against a post enjoying a morning smoke with his coffee at a proper distance away from the doorways of all the businesses.

In between sips of coffee and faking that he was smoking, he stood leaning his head back against the lamp post, watching the windows at the top of the hotel where he knew Aloriah was. When the door to the hotel opened at 8:30 and the two ladies he was watching for came out, the cigarette was burned down almost to the filter and the coffee cup was long empty, but still in his hands for the sake of the patrolling officers.

Getting rid of his props, he stepped forward with a cheerful greeting, wanting to laugh at the look of pleasure on Aloriah's face and the obvious gratitude on Kelly's. Pulling the younger woman into a hug and giving her a kiss on the forehead, he sighed, very glad that he hadn't waited for Cody.

"You have an escort on the way, so we need to stay here for a little longer." he told Kelly, who gave Aloriah a look that clearly said *I told you so* even though the words never left her mouth.

"So what are you doing here?" she asked instead, and Chase grinned.

"I couldn't sleep, so I came in early."

Noting the lip ring that had been absent the night before, Aloriah turned to her mother with a mischievous grin. She was wearing less dramatic makeup this morning and her colorfully dyed hair was pulled back into a ponytail to make her look as ordinary as possible. "Considering that my escort has his lip ring in, can I go back up and put on my normal makeup."

Kelly's glare answered the question without her saying a word, and both Chase and Aloriah chuckled. Any further conversation was interrupted, however, as a distant roar of motorcycles drew their attention. As they turned to see the group approaching, Kelly's jaw dropped to find Cody leading in a group that was fifteen members strong. They drew up in front of the hotel, forming a semi-circle around Chase and the women, and as soon as all the motors were shut off in unison, Cody pulled off his helmet with a huge grin.

"Bon jour, mes petites! I bring you protection for your trip to the police."

Both Kelly and Aloriah wore bright smiles as Cody introduced them to the members of the group, which consisted of several members of his family and their friends, almost all males. The few women in the group, all built like either Kelly or Aloriah, looked tough enough to take on any challenge, and left Aloriah gasping when they shook hands. Once again, Kelly and Aloriah found themselves very thankful for the two men who had stepped in to help them in their hour of need.

While Chase went to get his motorcycle out of

its parking space, a cheerful argument began over who got the honor of having the ladies ride with them to the police station. Kelly was laughing over the banter as Chase rolled his motorcycle into the group, but he settled who Aloriah was going to ride with without ever saying a word. He simply walked over to her to put the helmet over her head, then took her hand and led her over to settle her behind him while waiting for the argument to finish.

Seeing what he'd done, one of the biggest men, a fellow named Antoine whom everyone called Tony the Tiger, did the same with Kelly, making her laugh over the exaggerated pout on Cody's face, which got him a lot of teasing as everyone settled onto their machines. All the motors started in unison, and the group pulled out as if they had rehearsed for this impromptu parade for weeks.

As they traveled, the column of bikers kept shifting around the two women they were protecting, making it nearly impossible for anyone to get a clear shot at them should anyone be wanting to try. When they pulled up in front of the 8th District Police Station, all the motors went off in unison, and the two women were surrounded by leather-clad bodies until the door to the station was opened. Just Chase, Kelly, Aloriah and Cody slipped inside, leaving the remainder of the escort milling around the door and watching for anything odd.

Chase took up a station next to the door to be able to identify any of the men who had been tailing Kelly and Aloriah, while Cody escorted them to the officer in charge of taking care of complaints. Kelly took over, beginning by telling him that she had emailed them a photo the night before and had been told to bring by a memory card. The officer immediately smiled and nodded, then escorted the two women to see the Commander, who greeted them quite warmly and took their statement himself before accepting the memory disc into evidence.

"Thank you for bringing us the nails for this gangs coffins. We've been investigating them for a while, and the officer that you caught photos of them murdering had a thick file in his desk full of evidence against them for various crimes." With a sad sigh, he admitted that the toughest part of the whole situation would be locating the body so that they could give their comrade a full military funeral. "We've already distributed the photos you emailed to all the stations throughout the district. Every officer on patrol right now is searching for these cop killers, so we're hoping to have them and all of their known associates under wraps in just a couple of days."

"We're due to fly home the day after tomorrow. Should we hole up in our hotel just to be safe?" Kelly asked, and Aloriah's eyes narrowed as she read discomfort from him that he hid behind a cheerful smile.

"This gang does their dirty work after dark. You should be perfectly fine during the day, but make sure you're back in your hotel before dark."

Kelly thanked the Commander, but as they walked back out to Chase and Cody, she reached over to touch Aloriah's hand and knew, as her daughter did, that they wouldn't be safe from this gang until they were on the plane heading home. Putting on a fake smile, they both made their way back across the lobby, but withheld the details of the conversation until they stepped outside the doors, and were once again surrounded by the biker escort. That was when Kelly told them all what had been said as well as what she and Aloriah feared.

Cody looked around at all the assembled bikers, and then he grinned.

"You come wid' us, chere. We show you barbecue Cajun style."

The bikers all cheered, and sensing that they meant to make sure that she and her mother would arrive home safely, Aloriah smiled and winked at Kelly. Before another argument could ensue about who would ride with whom, she took Chase's hand, laughing when Kelly chose to ride with Cody this time. Once again, all the motors were started at the same time, and this time, the two ladies were put in the center of the bunch as they all rode out of the city and out into the bayou.

Their ride took them from the highway, down dirt roads, and past cypress swamps, where they passed under trees liberally festooned with Spanish moss. At the end of their ride, they came out into a small area where several small houses, many outwardly looking like shacks that were about to tumble into the nearby swamps but sturdy enough to survive another hundred years or so, gathered together in a rough circle around a dry, open field.

At the edge of the field was a roadhouse, with a large front porch where there were musicians jamming even at this early hour, and a huge area inside for socializing and dancing should the weather turn foul. Since it was warm and sunny with barely a cloud in the sky, there was a fire already going in an outside pit, and a couple of people already tending to what would eventually be the lunch and dinner menu.

As the motorcycle entourage pulled up in front of the roadhouse, people came out of the various buildings to see what was happening. In moments, the group they had arrived with had swelled to almost triple its number, and the two ladies from Maine were being introduced around as if they were royalty. Once again, Chase laid silent claim to Aloriah by placing his arm around her waist, keeping her close to his side as he greeted many in the crowd like they were long-time friends.

Cold drinks were brought out, both alcoholic and non-alcoholic, and Chase made sure that he and Aloriah got tall glasses of cold sweet tea before they went and settled at a picnic table in the shade. He didn't get long to sit down, however, before Cody started telling the story about Beau coming into the bar to start trouble, and how fast Chase had sent him to the hospital with a concussion. Looking as uncomfortable as the internal emotions that washed over Aloriah, he stood to accept the thanks of several of Josette's relatives for protecting her from her former fiancé.

When he was allowed to sit back down next to Aloriah, he oozed discomfort from every pore. Hoping to ease some of the tension she could feel from him, she reached over and placed her hand over his, her voice soft and soothing as she spoke to him.

"It sounds like you did a very good thing. Why would that upset you?"

A little surprised that she could tell he was upset, Chase sighed deeply and gave her a little half smile.

"It's nice that all my years of training in martial arts can prevent an innocent from suffering at the hands of a bully, but it still really bothers me to send anyone to a hospital." he returned in a voice soft enough that no one would overhear.

Feeling him relax a little, she smiled at him and gave his hand a little squeeze.

"It's nice to know that you're here to protect me and my mom from all evil doers. Can I know the name of your hero self since I know your secret identity, or would that mean you have to kill me and feed me to the 'gators?"

That made Chase relax even more, and he laughed as he turned the hand under hers so he could squeeze her hand back.

"Well, since my dad's nickname was Superman when he still drove trucks, which made Bear decide that mom was Lois Lane, I guess that makes me Superboy."

Frowning slightly and looking around, she teased "Where's Krypto, then? We could use a good super dog."

That brought out a short laugh, and she felt the tension leave him again, at least until Kelly came over to sit with them and mentioned his behavior at the bar.

"So, my instincts were right when I thought

you reminded me of a big cat waiting for its prey to show itself. How many years of martial arts training have you had?"

Chase's nose wrinkled at the question, but he relaxed again as he answered.

"I came home with my first bloody nose in second grade, and Dad, who does martial arts himself, decided it was never too early for me to start taking classes. I have black belts in Tae Kwon Do, Jiu Jitsu and Karate, but I also do Tai Chi for stretching and Yoga for calming whenever I can."

Kelly, who had only taken a few self-defense classes while watching some of the students in the more advanced forms of martial arts, whistled to show how impressed she was. Chase smiled at her, his eyes very serious.

"You don't need to worry about getting on your plane safely. I don't intend on letting anyone get anywhere near you while I still breathe."

Feeling her eyes tear up at the declaration that she could feel resonating deep within his soul, she smiled back.

"Thank you for coming to our rescue, Chase. I won't ask what cued you in, because I suspect you probably can see things normal humans would never take note of, but I am very, very glad that you and Cody stepped in when you did. I haven't convinced my husband to let Aloriah take self-defense classes, and would have been *way* outclassed if it came down to a fight."

Aloriah felt those words touch him deep in his soul, and the genuine smile on his face said everything he couldn't put into words. Kelly, too, felt that she had managed to touch his soul, so she gave him a wink and blew him a kiss as she got up to go over to ask the cooks some questions about Cajun cooking.

Chase and Aloriah sat for a little while like that, just holding hands and not talking, and she couldn't figure out for the life of her why she felt like she'd known him for most of her life, even though she knew next to nothing about him. It was as if, when he'd stepped out of the darkness to drop his arm over her shoulders, it had been planned like that forever, fate taking over her life the moment she had made the decision to follow her instinct to turn and just take a picture down a dark alley without ever looking through her viewfinder to see what it was that she was taking a picture of. Their quiet camaraderie was short lived, however, when Cody's brother, Henri, came over to ask Chase to show him some more moves "just in case".

Chase pulled Aloriah's hand up to his lips to give it a quick kiss, stood up to remove his leather jacket, and took Henri out into the middle of the field. They started with a typical forward assault, with Chase talking the older man through how to disarm an assailant. For the purpose of the lesson, Henri had a short stick to represent the knife that the assailant was using.

At first, Henri was the assailant with Chase talking him through the moves, going a little faster each time until the move was done at the normal speed Chase would use to disarm someone. To all watching, it was almost like seeing a dance rehearsal.

When Henri was sure that he understood the maneuver, they switched parts, with Chase holding the stick and Henri disarming him. Once again, they did the moves slowly at first, then sped things up until Henri was certain he would be able to disarm a real person.

Before Chase could rejoin Aloriah at the table, Cody hollered "But what if there be more than one? How many was they followin' you last night, Miz Kelly?"

"Four." Kelly responded with a smile, wanting to see what would have happened if they had been forced to fight off the whole pack of gang members.

Chase just smiled, stretched, and rolled up his sleeves, waiting calmly while four of the men picked up short sticks and surrounded him. The ensuing skirmish, with everyone trying to be careful not to really hurt each other, resulted in four "injured" attackers and Chase, despite breathing hard, still standing with barely a "scratch".

Still instigating, Cody pointed out that, by the time they had reached the Cafe du Monde, the attackers had been joined by a fifth man. Putting up one finger to indicate he needed a minute before taking on five, Chase sauntered over to the table where Aloriah watched, unbuttoning his shirt as he walked to reveal a lightly furry chest and a nipple ring in the right nipple. Reaching past her to grab his cup of tea, he took a long swallow while her senses were overcome by the scent of Axe cologne that clung to him, then he removed the shirt with a grin meant only for her.

"Hold onto this for me?" he asked as he put the shirt into her hands, then he bent and gave her a quick kiss on the cheek. "Thank you."

Finding it a little hard to catch her breath as he sauntered back out to what had become an impromptu battlefield, Aloriah looked away from that sexy hunk of man to see her mother grinning at her. Kelly mimed fanning herself, and Aloriah rolled her eyes before turning her attention back to the demonstration.

The savage dance began again, with the fresh men playing the five assailants thinking that they had the advantage because Chase should have been feeling tired. He surprised them with his speed, however, disarming three of them in short order, and causing the two that still held short sticks to step back and reassess their "prey".

It was just then, however, that one of the children, not comprehending that it was just a game, ran up from behind with a large branch, and swung at Chase as one would take a swing at a baseball. His attention on the two in front of him, Chase was taken entirely by surprise, and the sound of the branch breaking against his back made all those watching gasp and flinch in sympathetic pain. The child's mother's voice echoed in the silence that followed, and the fact that she used his full name even had Chase smiling despite the pain on his face.

"Alphonse Guillaume Thibodeaux! How dare you!"

Several people, many of them young women, rushed forward to assist Chase, but he thanked them and made his way back to the table where Aloriah was standing, tears in her eyes and her hand over her mouth. Cody hurried over with a roll of paper towels, seeing blood seeping around the hand Chase had pressed to his lower back. When he got the table, Chase turned so that Aloriah could press paper towel to the injury and inspect it to see how bad it was.

As she wiped away the blood, she was pleased to note for Cody that it just appeared that a knot in the wood had broken the skin, leaving a wound no larger than the end of her thumb that wasn't very deep, but because of the bruising around the area, had bled pretty profusely. As she held a wad of paper towel over the spot and applied gentle pressure, instinctively reaching within herself to ease his pain, Cody started off to find peroxide and a bandage. One of the older women beat him to it, even setting down a small container of Bag Balm on the table next to Aloriah.

After tending the wound, Aloriah looked up at that muscular back, and was startled to see a scar on his left shoulder that looked like he'd had some kind of stitches at some point in his life. When she reached up to gently touch it, he turned to look at her over that shoulder and, strangely, she knew right away that he had been knifed.

"One of those bullies I told your mom about. It was a four against one before I had truly learned to disarm first, then neutralize." he told her quietly.

He pulled his shirt back on, but didn't button it so that the cool breezes could finish drying the sweat off his body, sitting next to her to drink his tea. As soon as her mind was off the damage he had sustained, Aloriah felt the anger directed her way by several pretty young women. Clearing her throat while Chase took several gulps of sweet tea, she aired a thought that the other women's anger brought to mind.

"Not that I don't appreciate spending this time with you, but there are several much prettier women here who seem to be a little upset that you aren't paying any attention to them. Did they do something to make you mad at them?"

Chase looked up as if just becoming aware of the numerous eyes that were watching him with Aloriah. On most of the faces those eyes belonged to, he was able to read the question she hadn't asked. Why would he be giving all his attention to a chubby girl when there were so many pretty, skinny girls all but begging for him to notice them? He snorted softly and looked into Aloriah's light brown eyes that almost appeared golden. How could he explain about the disgust he felt when looking at those girls who reminded him of the stuck up cheerleaders in school?

"If you look at them closely, they all appear to be cookie cutter girls."

At the look of confusion he got, he smiled. "All of them are so skinny that you could count their ribs at fifty yards and act like they expect every man in existence to bow to their whim just because they have pretty faces. If a mold existed, they could have all been put through the same one. I really detest the skin and bones type who think that, just because they're skinny enough to be fashion models, all men should fall at their feet to be walked on."

Looking her over with a very appreciative gaze, he continued. "You, however, have some very delicious looking curves."

Aloriah felt the blush that heated up her cheeks and tried to turn her head away to hide it. Chase gently lifted his hand and turned her face back, leaning forward almost as if he intended to kiss her again, and giving her a smile that started fires in other places than her face.

"Give the bones to the dogs, give the meat to the man is my motto."

If she hadn't been able to feel his emotions, she would have sworn that he was lying to her despite the steady way he looked deeply into her eyes while declaring that he liked her more ample form, but being an empath, she could feel the truth in his statement. He truly liked her even though she thought herself too fat to appeal to any man! How could this even be possible?

Their conversation was interrupted by the cooks, who rang a triangle to announce that the meal was ready to be served. Giving her a smile, Chase jumped up and offered her his hand to help her to her feet, slipping his arm around her waist as they joined the line to get some food. When they reached the table where the food was set up buffet style, he made sure she had her plate and utensils before he got his own, then explained what the various dishes were, getting a nod of approval from her as he served up a dollop of each for her to try. When they reached the huge metal pan full of barbecued pork ribs, she stopped the cook at one small three-rib rack, insisting she had plenty of food on her plate.

As she walked back to the table and started talking with Kelly, who had chosen to eat with them, Chase got a couple of the larger racks, as the cook and Chase both agreed that she didn't have enough on her plate to keep a gnat alive.

He set his plate down and offered to go refill their glasses with sweet tea, grinning as he walked away from the table at the look on both Aloriah's and Kelly's faces when they saw the pile of food he had collected on his plate. When he got back and sat down, they both looked at him from the top of his head to his toes, especially the flat stomach displayed by his still unbuttoned shirt, and Kelly was the one who made the comment they were both thinking.

"Ok, I really have to know. Where do you plan on putting all that food?"

With an innocent look, Chase said "I'm a growing boy with hollow legs!"

Tony, who was on his way over to the table to join them and heard the comment, snorted as he sat down. "I t'ink you just take after your papa. He put away dat much and den some when he join us for de barbecue."

The mention of Kyle started a lively conversation around the table, starting with Chase telling those who knew the elder Benton from his time on the road what he was up to these days. They moved on to stories about the Boudreaux and the many other families who were related to them around the area. Then came the old stories about the area, both spooky and comical.

Caught up in the tales and laughing at the

many amusing anecdotes as she ate, Aloriah wasn't paying close attention to her plate, at least not until she accidentally dropped her fork and happened to look down. Strangely enough, although she remembered getting just three ribs, there were six rib bones on her plate, and she looked at Chase with suspicion evident on her face.

Feeling her eyes on him, Chase looked over at her, trying his best to appear innocent and pretending that he thought she was looking at him that way because he had barbecue sauce on his face. As he wiped his face vigorously with a paper towel, he tried to avoid looking at Kelly, who had caught him sliding extra ribs onto Aloriah's plate, but had simply smiled at him and kept her mouth shut. She was biting her lips to avoid laughing, and he was quite sure the jig would be up if their eyes connected.

Aloriah was still glaring at him when he finished wiping his face, however, and, without a word, slid her plate out of his reach. That got Kelly giggling, and he did his best imitation of big puppy dog eyes, hoping that Aloriah wasn't too mad at him for making sure she got plenty to eat. Despite wanting to laugh at his antics, Aloriah did her best to keep glaring as she softly growled at him.

"You are a sneaky little booger, aren't you."

"Me?" he asked, still doing his best to play innocent and seeing the corners of her lips twitch before Aloriah turned her eyes on her mother.

"And you were in on it."

Kelly grinned, unabashed.

"I don't want you to waste away to nothing

before we go home. Besides, those were really good ribs."

Finally unable to hold back her own grin, Aloriah admitted "Yes, they really were."

Chase playfully put his head on Aloriah's shoulder and batted his eyes at her.

"Am I forgiven?"

Aloriah laughed and pushed him away. "Ok, you're forgiven, but only just this once."

As Chase grinned and went back to cleaning up his plate, Kelly found herself hoping that he would stay friends with Aloriah after they left New Orleans. It had been a long time since Aloriah had found someone she could fully trust apart from her mother, and Chase was one of those genuinely nice people who Kelly had the feeling would think twice before callously hurting her daughter. Add to that the fact that, in the less than 24 hours since he had stepped out of the shadows, he had made Aloriah smile more than anyone else had throughout her high school years, and Kelly could easily become his greatest fan.

With the meal taken care of and the tables cleared off, someone brought out a guitar, someone else brought out an accordion, and some fine zydeco music soon filled the air. Despite the warmth of the afternoon, dancing ensued, and after watching Aloriah tap her foot to the beat for a couple of songs, Chase started trying to talk her into dancing with him, getting excuse after excuse as to why she wouldn't. When he finally succeeded was when he told her, "Oh, come on. It will help you to work off the extra ribs I slipped onto your plate."

Kelly watched as they joined the crowd of dancers, and started to snicker when, after dancing properly for just a couple of minutes, Chase obviously attempted to get a smile out of a very stern-faced Aloriah by dancing like he had no clue what it meant to dance to a beat. When all he got in response was the slightest twitch at the corners of her lips, he got even more ridiculous.

Eventually, Aloriah couldn't resist any more and laughed, a rich sound the likes of which Kelly hadn't heard in years. The sound almost brought a tear to Kelly's eye, because it was the kind of laugh that used to happen all the time before Aloriah started school and realized that she was different from the other children because of her ability to feel what they felt.

It made her realize just how much tension there was at home as well, where Bruce Starbird was always yelling at his daughter for something, whether it be that she had neglected to do something major that he had requested, or some minor infraction such as not putting her shoes in the exact spot he thought she should have when she removed them on entering the house.

It was the constant badgering that had made Aloriah turn to binge eating, causing her weight problem, which caused more badgering, which caused more binge eating. It was a never ending cycle of self-destruction where her daughter was concerned. It was one of the reasons that Kelly had suggested this trip as a reward for Aloriah's good grades at school instead of just giving the girl the money she had been saving for her daughter her whole life. It was also the reason that she had insisted that Bruce remain at home in Maine, so that Aloriah could enjoy the trip without being constantly badgered.

She was in serious debate within herself as to whether or not she was going to give him any of the details of this trip when they got home, as she knew her husband far too well. If she tried to just give a general statement, like "it was a blast", he would badger her for specific things they did that they had enjoyed. If she told him about the things they did, he would push for all the details as to how they had come to be in the bayou at a barbecue. If he found out about the photograph that Aloriah took, he would never let her forget that she had inadvertently put herself and her mother in danger because of an urge that he had never experienced, and could therefore never understand. Perhaps she would just tell him it was boring and pretend none of this happened.

The band started playing a slow dance number, and Chase pulled Aloriah into his arms for some dirty dancing that would have made Patrick Swayze proud. Kelly suddenly found herself smiling. What might happen should the handsome young man show up at the door asking to see Aloriah? The thought that it might shock Bruce enough to cause a heart attack for some reason struck her as funny, especially considering the way the young man was treating the girl who Bruce constantly put down. With a sigh, she decided that she almost hoped Chase *would* appear at the house, because it might do her husband good to see someone treat his daughter like she was special.

As the slow dance ended, Cody drew everyone's attention with a loud whistle, looking at his watch as all eyes turned his way.

"I need to go back to N'awlins to start my shift. Would the ladies like to go back now, or will the escort bring them back later?"

Many of the people who had formed the escort also looked at watches, and expressed regret that they, too, had to think about getting back. Standing up on her seat at the table, Kelly cleared her throat.

"Before we go, I would really like to thank everyone here for making my daughter and I feel so welcomed. We've had a great time being introduced to your marvelous food, people, and music." She gave a huge grin that was reflected on most of the faces around her. "You are all welcome to visit us in Maine if you ever get the urge to freeze your tails off!"

That brought a round of laughter and a smattering of applause as she stepped down to make sure that she had everything she had brought with her. She was a bit surprised when those who wouldn't be riding with them came over to thank her for coming and give her hugs, telling her that she was welcome to return at any time. Chase and Aloriah got the same treatment, although several who knew Chase from previous visits chose to jokingly tell him he was only going to be welcomed back if he brought the ladies back with him.

On arriving back at the hotel, Chase found that he really didn't want to leave, even for the much needed sleep that his body was calling for. He would never be able to explain to anyone else, but there was something about these two ladies that brought out the need in him to protect them until the point that he could watch them get onto the plane to go back to their home. He stood watching with a slight frown as Cody said his goodbyes, confirmed that he expected Chase to be sleeping when he arrived home after his shift at the bar, and left.

Left alone in the lobby with Chase, both Kelly and Aloriah could feel that he was tired, but still unwilling to leave them. Kelly's mothering instincts came out.

"Are you okay to drive yourself to Cody's, or do you need to nap first?"

Chase recognized the tone of voice and smiled.

"I'm fine to drive, thank you, but I was wondering..." his tongue played with the lip ring as he tried to think of a way of asking without insulting Kelly. "What are your plans for tomorrow?"

Kelly tried hard not to smile, sensing that he was fishing to see if there was any way he could join them for their final day in New Orleans. She seemed to think for a moment, then listed the things they had wanted to make sure to do while visiting.

"Well, let's see. When we came here, we had five things that we wanted to do. We wanted to take a tour of the French Quarter, which we did right after getting settled at the hotel the first day. We wanted to tour the Cities of the Dead, and do a ghost tour." She smiled at Chase. "Which as you know, we accomplished with a little extra excitement tossed in at the end. We wanted to do a tour of the bayou, which wasn't exactly as the New Orleans Bayou Tours does it, but close enough. So all that we have left is a tour of some of the mansions in the Garden District."

Chase held his breath while Kelly prolonged his agony, turning so she could link eyes with Aloriah to ask silently *Shall I ask him to come with us?*

Aloriah didn't answer in any way except with a smile, and that smile was like the rare bit of honest laughter when she was dancing. It wasn't just a stretching of the muscles like she gave to everyone but her mother. This was a smile of purest happiness.

"Would you care to join us in the tour group tomorrow just to make sure we make it back without meeting any gang members?"

Chase didn't even need to give her a verbal answer. His smile and the happy gleam in his eyes said it all.

Chapter 5

By the end of the walking tour of the historic Garden District, Kelly and Aloriah were of the opinion that it would have been a pretty boring two hour hike if they hadn't had Chase along. Although he was quiet during the tour guide's stories about the mansions they visited, he would add his own stories, sometimes factual and sometimes outrageous fabrications, as they walked to the next stopping spot. At first, they got strange looks from the other people taking the tour with them, but at the end, several of their fellow tourists stopped to thank the young man for his colorful tales. Having only meant to entertain his companions, Chase was actually a little embarrassed by the attention, which Kelly found the most amusing part of all.

With nothing else planned for the trip, Kelly was at a loss as to how to spend the remainder of their time, only knowing that she didn't want to just wander the streets and risk being spotted by any members of the gang they had photographed.

Chase, with his most engaging smile, made an excellent suggestion.

"We could take a paddleboat tour and enjoy a lovely dinner on the water. It would be my treat, since you lovely ladies gave me something to do with myself rather than just hanging around with Cody." With a gleam in his eyes, he added, "Nothing against him, but since Cody is here all the time, his greatest form of entertainment is hauling me around to visit with all of his numerous relatives."

As with the walking tour, Chase did all he could to entertain the two ladies, but as the paddleboat started steaming its way back toward the pier, Aloriah became more and more withdrawn. When Kelly used the excuse of locating a restroom to leave the two young people alone for a bit, Chase took Aloriah to a quiet spot near the rail and, without preamble, asked her what was wrong.

"The plan for tomorrow morning is to get up, get our things packed, and take a taxi directly to the airport because it's going to take most of the day to fly home."

Although she tried to hide it, there were tears in her eyes, and Chase understood what she wasn't saying. Once he left them at the door to the hotel, she was afraid she would never get to see him ever again. With a smile, he asked her for her cell phone again, and scrolling to the contact box where he'd given her his cell phone number, he added in his land line number, his parent's land line number and his address, handing it back to her when he was done editing the entries.

"There. All the information I can give you short of revealing where my birth mark is."

Stunned that he would do such a thing, she looked at the entry before absently asking "And where might this birth mark be?"

With a playful grin, he responded, "What birth mark? I don't have a birth mark."

Pulling his own cell phone out, Chase had Aloriah edit her information as well, and before Kelly located them again, he had promised to stay in touch, sealing his promise with another of those sweet kisses he seemed so fond of giving her. Kelly felt the difference in her daughter's emotions the moment she joined them, and smiled at Chase from behind her daughter, sure that whatever he had said or done was the reason behind it.

The cab ride back to the hotel was made in silence, and even Kelly was feeling a little sad when they got out and went into the lobby to say goodbye before sending Chase out to his motorcycle. He offered Kelly a hug first, and she suddenly realized just how tall he was when her head barely reached his shoulder. As he backed away, she thanked him again for all that he had done, from stepping in when he had realized that they were being followed by some shady characters, to paying for the hotel, and keeping them company for the past two days.

"It's nothing I wouldn't want someone to do for my mom and sisters." he responded, and gave her a parting kiss on her cheek.

Smiling, Kelly went over to the elevator, keeping her back toward them as Chase pulled Aloriah into his arms for a goodbye hug and a much more thorough goodbye kiss than the one he had given her mother. With his hand on her cheek, he placed his forehead against hers and looked deeply into her eyes.

"Remember what I said. I promise to stay in touch with you, and if you'd like, I'll come and visit the next time I'm home for a few days."

With a sigh, Aloriah nodded, then watched as he walked through the door and out of sight before joining her mother to go up to their room for the night.

The next morning, Kelly and Aloriah were just settling into seats to wait for the boarding call when Aloriah's phone rang.

"Hello?"

"Hi." Chase said. "Did you make it to the airport okay?"

Aloriah smiled, and Kelly knew who it was right away.

"We just got through security and are waiting to board the plane. What are you doing up so early? I thought you were planning to sleep in."

Chase laughed, a warm, rich sound that awoke a sensation in Aloriah that she didn't want to think about.

"My uncle just called and told me one of our drivers is out of commission. I've been asked to pick up a load of shrimp in Biloxi, Mississippi and deliver it to Louisville, Kentucky. They're already loading the refrigerated truck, so I'm just making sure you're safe before I bail and get my fuzzy butt on the road."

She laughed at the image that "fuzzy butt" brought to mind, then wished him a safe trip.

"You have a safe trip, too." His voice was so soft and warm, it almost brought tears to her eyes. "I'll call you as soon as I can."

When he hung up, Aloriah told Kelly what he'd said.

"So it's a good thing we're going home today, huh? We would have been left in New Orleans without our protector." Patting her daughter's arm and giving her a smile, she soothed her the best she could. "Maybe he'll get to come back to Maine with a load soon."

Having spent the past several days feeling totally accepted by those around her, especially the handsome young man who had stepped out of the shadows at the time when she most needed a savior, Aloriah sat looking at the tips of her multi-colored hair, wondering why her father couldn't seem to accept her that way. When the boarding call came, she put her phone in her pocket and picked up her carry-on bag, but was still deep in thought until she was seated next to her mother and buckled in.

"Do you think if I let my hair go to its natural color that Dad would start treating me like a human again?"

Kelly looked at her daughter and sighed, unsure of what to answer.

While they were getting settled on the airplane, Chase was standing with Cody in the front yard saying his goodbyes to his friend.

"You sure the gang isn't going to come after

you?" Chase asked, and Cody laughed, but the light in his dark eyes was cold.

"The officer they kill was Antione's brudder. He show us the picture the police have that Aloriah took, and two of them, I know they mama. They best be hopin' the police get to them befo' the Bayou Boys do, 'cause they be gator bait, we catch 'em."

Chase tried to pretend Cody was joking, but he knew that the motorcycle gang that had ridden with him wasn't a group a sane person would mess with. They had been pleasant the day of the barbecue, but he was very glad that the Starbirds hadn't been witness to their dark side.

He climbed into his truck with the form of goodbye that had become a tradition for leaving the Boudreaux residence.

"I'll come back when I can't stay so long!"

Chapter 6
Early August, 2017

"Eight weeks." Chase repeated aloud as he hit what his father called "the sweet spot" on Route 15, where one topped a hill and saw Moosehead Lake and the town of Greenville laid out below. It was almost eight weeks to the day since he had met a nice young lady in New Orleans, and he had finally convinced his uncle to let him have a week long furlough at home so that he could see her again.

He had made it a habit to call her to chat at any time that his loads had been dropped early enough to allow them to do so without getting her into trouble with her father, but he was dying to wrap his arms around her and kiss her sweet lips again. Turning onto the private road that would bring him to his house, the wheels of the truck seemed to sing those words like a litany. *Eight weeks, eight weeks.*

At the driveway to the farmhouse that had

once belonged to Helen "Gram" Godfried, but that was now his, he turned in and pressed the button that would open the door on the modified barn that now served as the parking space for this truck. He still was a little dumbfounded that none of his older cousins had wanted the place, but since they had all turned it down in order to move out of Greenville after they graduated, he had moved in two years ago even though he was seldom home. As the garage door dropped into place behind him, he turned an expert eye to the sky, frowning slightly at the rain clouds coming in from the west before turning to look east toward Old Town, where Aloriah was. The sky didn't look any more promising in that direction, so he was debating what he could suggest they do for the evening as he started a pot of coffee and hopped through a shower before calling her.

He was padding back to the kitchen in nothing but a pair of blue jeans when his phone rang, and he pulled it out of his pocket to see that it was the very young lady he was thinking of. With a brilliant smile, he answered with a cheerful "Well, hello gorgeous! I was just thinking of you."

The soft sob from the other end made the smile disappear.

"Chase, I just wanted to let you know that this phone is probably going to be shut off before the end of the day. My dad and I just had a huge argument and he kicked me out."

Spinning on his heel, the coffee forgotten, he headed back to his room to finish dressing while growling, "Where are you?"

"I'm just crossing the bridge that takes you off

Indian Island. The nearest homeless shelters are in Bangor, so I'm going to try to catch the bus to go there and figure out what to do when I have somewhere to sleep tonight. I just don't know how to tell you to reach me, because I don't think they allow personal calls there."

"Don't get on the bus. I was just about to call you to tell you I just got back to Greenville this morning, and was going to see if you wanted to go out with me." A hint of the smile returned as he pulled socks and a t-shirt out of his drawer, then dug through the bottom of his closet for his favorite pair of sneakers. "If you don't mind living in the boonies, you can stay at my house until you figure out what you want to do. There's plenty of space and you can even have your own room." A little voice in the back of his head added *Unless you want to sleep with me*, but he didn't say that out loud.

A gasp greeted his offer.

"You don't have to do that!" She sounded truly shocked that he would make such an offer, and his grin widened as he balanced the phone on his shoulder while he sat down and pulled on the socks and sneakers.

"I know I don't have to. I want to. Now, is there someplace you can hang out for about 2 hours? I drive like a maniac, as you well know, but it won't do either of us any good for me to get pulled over, and it's a fair distance."

Astonishment was evident in her voice when she responded "You're serious!"

"Serious as a heart attack!"

There was a moment of silence during which

he could tell she was thinking of her options. When she spoke again, he could hear the relief in her tone.

"Most of the places around here have a rule against loitering, and the cops can be total jerks about it because of the mischief that the college kids get into if left unchecked. But if I head for the campus of UMO, I can sit out on the quad and no one will bother me."

"Good thinking. Stay on the main roads just in case it takes you longer to walk it than it takes me to drive it, and I'll plan on finding you on the quad at UMO if I don't see you before then. Be careful, okay?"

"You, too." He could hear the tears returning when she gave a very heartfelt "Thank you, Chase."

"I'll see you soon."

He hung up the phone and put it back into his pocket, muttering a curse about her father as he yanked the t-shirt down over his head and went back to the kitchen, pausing long enough to find a travel mug to fill with coffee for the ride. Assuming she might be toting some form of bag full of belongings, he bypassed the motorcycle keys, grabbing the key to the classic Mustang off the key holder instead. Putting on sunglasses as he locked the door, he took a couple of sips of hot coffee before setting his cup down in the garage to peel the cloth cover off the car that he thought of as his 'baby'. Snagging the coffee and tapping the button to open the garage door, he hooked up his seat belt before starting the car, enjoying the deep throated roar before putting it into gear and pulling carefully out into the driveway, making sure that the garage door closed behind him as he headed back toward the main road.

Throughout the long drive, he thought of questions he would have to remember to ask.

Did Aloriah have her driver's license? As much as he hated the idea of anyone other than himself driving his baby, he really didn't want to bring his lady out to the farmhouse and leave her stranded with no means of getting to town short of begging rides from his family.

Did she have a job in the Old Town area that she needed to give notice to? He didn't want her to lose a good job reference, because jobs were scarce in the Greenville area and anyone without a good job reference would have a hard time finding work.

And what about her reputation? Was she concerned that she might be labeled as a tramp for just moving in with him like this? Small town people could be cruel sometimes, and he didn't want to make her uncomfortable because he had some overblown hero complex.

As he got closer to the UMO campus and it started to drizzle, he started watching for walkers on the road, especially one with multi-colored hair and a chunky build. He had turned onto College Avenue and was nearing the campus when he saw a woman of the right build carrying a familiar looking suitcase, but she had black hair.

He slowed down anyway to get a better look, making the driver behind him honk his horn, and his eyes widened as she turned to look back. It was Aloriah, all right, and the raccoon eyes she was sporting from her mascara showed that she had been crying as she walked. Pulling carefully to the side of the road, he let several cars pass before opening the car door.

Aloriah heard the honk of the horn, and looked back at the beautiful classic black Mustang that was going much slower than the posted speed limit. Her vision slightly blurry from her tears, she couldn't tell what the driver looked like, and when the car pulled off to the side of the road, a frisson of fear went up her spine.

She was getting ready to drop her suitcase and make a run for it when the traffic finally cleared enough to let the driver open the door, but when a tall, lean form unfolded from the driver's seat, relief flooded her. She still dropped her suitcase to run, but toward the familiar figure instead of away from him.

In a few strides, Chase had his arms wrapped around her, pulling her into a hug so tight it almost squeezed the life out of her. The smell of his cologne enveloped her, and she decided that there was no smell better than that in the whole world. Letting out a sigh of relief, she started to lift her head to tell him how much she appreciated him doing this for her, but she didn't get the chance to say a word. His mouth covered hers, and all thought was banished by the sensations that overwhelmed her senses. When he withdrew and cleared his throat with an embarrassed grin, she smiled back at him.

"Sorry." he murmured. "This is probably not the best place for that. Let me grab your suitcase and get you out of this rain."

As soon as they were seated in the car, he

asked her the first of the important questions he had come up with, "Do you have a job you need to give notice to?"

Her snort of derision answered that question before she spoke.

"That was part of the argument. When I got back from New Orleans, I colored my hair back to its natural color and stopped wearing the Goth makeup. Mom helped me get a set of decent looking clothes, and I went out job hunting. I got a job doing dishes at one of the little restaurants in town, but I don't have a car, so Mom was dropping me off in town on her way to work, and I was hanging out at the library until my shift started. Since I worked until closing, Mom would come back out and get me. Dad kept griping about the cost of gas for her to come back out to get me, and even though I was giving her gas money, it wasn't enough. He went into the restaurant determined that he would get me a shift that ended when Mom was on her way home, and he got me fired. "

"Jerk." Chase commented, bringing a smile to Aloriah's face.

"I haven't been able to find another job, and now it's all my fault that I got fired." She sighed and looked out the window at the passing scenery, and her sadness was almost palpable. Chase let the silence ride for a few minutes, then changed the subject.

"Do you have a driver's license?"

Aloriah looked down at the stick shift between them and smiled.

"Yes, I do, but I'd need lessons on how to

drive this sweet beast. I've never driven a stick, and especially not one that's been made into a turbo monster."

Liking the way she referred to his baby, Chase made a mental note to give her lessons, certain that she would treat the car with the respect it deserved. Then he went on to the third question that was bothering him, his voice soft as he phrased it in the nicest way he could, trying not to offend her, but needing to hear her answer.

"And how do you feel about your reputation? Greenville is a small town, so when you start filling out job applications, everyone will recognize the address as my house. Since they know I'm not married..." He let the sentence hang, not wanting to put words to what some of the townspeople would surely think. The question brought a slow smile to her face.

"It's not *my* reputation I'm worried about. What will people think about you bringing a fat chick from Old Town to live with you when there are no doubt several pretty, unmarried ladies right there in Greenville who would gladly move in with you?"

Chase took his eyes off the road long enough to frown at her for that description of herself.

"We already discussed this in the bayou." he reminded her with mock ferocity. "I'm not interested in the cookie cutter skinny girls, and it's the very ones you refer to in Greenville that made me come up with that term. Besides, most of the unattached ladies in Greenville are more interested in my daddy's money and inheriting his barn house on the hill to be interested in li'l ole me and my ancient farmhouse."

Unable to believe that any woman would care more about his money than his sexy body and playful attitude, but feeling from his emotional state that he was absolutely positive that was all they wanted from him, Aloriah didn't respond, deciding she didn't want another argument today, and especially not with someone who had driven all the way from Greenville to Old Town just to rescue her.

After several miles of looking out at the farms and small towns they were driving through in silence, she asked if anything interesting had happened during his travels, and with a smile, he started off with "Well, in New Orleans, there was this really nice lady who took a photograph at just the wrong time."

Aloriah laughed, and the mood in the car lightened considerably. Wanting to hear her laugh again, Chase started telling her stories about some of the towns they passed through, which was something his father often did when they were taking long trips growing up. As when they were in the Garden District, a few of the stories were factual, but most were comical fabrications. He got what he wanted. She laughed more.

As they pulled into the Indian Hill Trading Post for some groceries, as he had admitted that she had called right after he arrived in town, Chase reached over and squeezed Aloriah's leg with a smile. "Don't you be shy about telling me what you'd like to eat. The only limit you have to work with is that you're limited to what the store carries."

Wanting to take a couple of photos to send to her mother so she wouldn't worry, Aloriah pulled out her cell phone, but when she looked at the screen, it appeared that her father had already shut her service off. With a shrug, she put it back into her pocket as Chase met her at the front of the car to slip his arm around her waist, giving her a kiss and a wink. "Are you ready to become the talk of the town?"

Still thinking he was exaggerating in the same way he had on some of the stories on their ride here, she just smiled and gave him a wink back. She was totally unprepared, therefore, for the reaction when they stepped through the door and the cashiers saw him.

"Chase Benton!" The one closest to the door yelled. "Long time no see!"

He laughed and greeted both cashiers by name.

"Hi Julie. Hey, Mrs. Brown."

"Mrs. Brown!" snorted the second cashier. "You're almost 21, whelp! I think you can start calling me Edith. And who's that lovely lady you're with?"

Chase looked at Aloriah with a wide grin and another wink.

"This is my girlfriend, Aloriah."

While she tried not to look at him in surprise for the term, the ladies both hooted with pleasure.

"Such a pretty name for such a pretty lady!" said the cashier who had insisted Chase call her Edith. Julie gave Aloriah a mischievous wink.

"I knew the gossipers who said you were gay

were way off base!"

Aloriah started to laugh while Chase rolled his eyes.

"Thanks, Jules. Just what I needed my new girl to hear. Not only is there going to be gossip about her being in my house, but there will be some who will insist she's a guy in drag."

Deciding to play along with the fun, she looked at him with fake concern and said, "Um, Chase, there is something I need to tell you..."

The two ladies laughed even harder while Chase face palmed.

"I like her." Julie said when she could catch her breath again. "Welcome to Greenville, Aloriah."

Releasing her long enough to grab a shopping cart, Chase gave her a wink as he came back up to her.

"Come on, princess, let's go shopping."

Aloriah was a little surprised at how frequently they had to stop to talk to the townspeople, and how easily Chase handled some of the nosier questions without lying, but without actually telling the entire truth, either. The nosiest of the bunch was a young man whose animosity toward Chase was so strong Aloriah was quite sure she would have noticed even without her ability to feel the emotions rolling off him. When he stopped them, Chase reached out and drew her closer, as if he felt she needed protection, before responding to the man's greeting.

"Hello Jason." Chase said in a more formal tone than he'd used with anyone else. "What can I do for you?"

With the most insincere smile Aloriah had ever seen in her life, Jason looked her over from head to toe and back.

"Well, you could start by introducing me to your lady friend so I can tell Cassie who it is that took her place."

Chase stiffened at the obvious attempt to make Aloriah jealous, but did the honors by simply saying, "Aloriah, this is Jason, who has never admitted that Cassie only had pipe dreams about dating me."

"Nice to meet you." She smiled as if truly glad to meet him, but ignored the hand he held out, slipping her arm around Chase's waist instead. Jason's nose wrinkled at the snub, but he looked back at Chase and continued to dig.

"What do your folks think about your new girlfriend?"

Aloriah felt like hitting the man, but kept the smile on her face as Chase answered.

"We just got in, so I haven't been out to the house yet to introduce her. We need to get settled, and catch some sleep in a real bed so we aren't overtired before I introduce her to dad." Putting in a little dig of his own, Chase added, "You know how he is."

Jason hid it well, but Aloriah's empathic talent picked up the frisson of fear that went through him at that. He was scared of Kyle Benton, and Chase knew it. The conversation ended there with Jason saying he had things to do, then he got away as quickly as he could without seeming to hurry.

Chase took a couple of deep, calming breaths, letting Jason disappear around the corner, before he muttered under his breath "He's still a jackass."

Taking a deep, calming breath of her own, Aloriah gave him a squeeze and asked "So why is he scared of your dad?"

A gleam of mischief entered Chase's eyes and he smiled.

"You'll see!"

Before she could ask him more, someone else came around the corner and hailed Chase, and by the time they finished their shopping, loaded the groceries into the car, and headed out to his house, the cryptic comment had retreated to the back of her mind. It came back to the forefront as, while carefully backing the car into the garage, he told her they really were going to settle in and get a good night's sleep before they went to the next house up the road to meet his parents.

"Is your dad really that bad?" she asked, and Chase snorted.

"Most of the town thinks he is." At the look of alarm on her face, he smiled and elaborated. "What the town knows about him is very few facts, but a lot of gossip and rumor, and some of the rumors he started himself."

As they got out and went around to the back of the car to get the food and her suitcase out of the trunk, she was intrigued, and she couldn't stop herself from asking "Such as?"

"Such as the rumor that says he knows places out in the wilderness around here where no one would ever find your body if you crossed him."

Grinning at her look of shock, he gave her the truth. "He really does know some pretty remote spots around here, but he's never killed anyone."

Since that didn't seem to ease her fear, he elaborated further.

"The biggest reason I like people to be very well rested before I introduce them to him the first time is because he's very smart, as in Sherlock Holmes smart. He not only listens to what you say, but how you say it, and what your body language says while you say it. In other words, even if you think you're good at lying, don't try to lie to him. He'll throw you out of his house and you'll never be welcomed again."

She smiled and said "Well, that explains it."

Looking confused, Chase asked "Explains what?"

"The way you answered people at the store. You didn't really come right out and say that you arrived this morning, and then drove out to get me. You just said that we just got in. Not a real lie, but not the whole truth, either. But why did you call me your girlfriend?"

He blinked, doing that innocent face thing of his that always made her smile.

"Well, you are a girl, and you are my friend, and you're going to be staying in my house." He shrugged. "Why do they need to know that you're sleeping in Gram's old room, and I'm sleeping in mine?"

Then his look became very sensual as he set his bags down on the porch to pull the key out of his pocket. "Of course, I'm game if you'd rather just share my bedroom and let the rumors be true..."

As tempting as that idea was when he was looking at her like that, she wasn't sure that he was really offering because he really liked her, or if he, like the guy who had gotten her drunk and stolen her virginity at a high school party, was just hard up. Rather than have her heart broken when she was already in emotional turmoil after the argument with her father, she sighed.

"Give me a couple of days. After this morning, I don't want to make any hasty decisions just because I'm an emotional wreck right now."

Chase considered that response as he turned the key in the lock. Trained by his dad on which body signals meant what, he had been reading her body language since their first meeting, and he was quite positive that she liked him. Every time he hugged or kissed her and she didn't pull away told him that she was liking his touch, but there was also something that sometimes showed in her eyes or on her face, like just now, that spoke of pain and embarrassment when she thought about going further than the occasional hug or kiss.

As he pushed the door open and let her walk in while he gathered up the bags he'd set down, he made a vow to let her have as much time as she wanted before he pushed again. He had already come to the conclusion in the past eight weeks since their meeting that she was a very special young woman, and he wanted to spend his time getting to know her, every part of her, but if she needed more time, he could be patient.

When he stepped through the door into the

kitchen, Aloriah was looking around with an exaggerated look of shock before she turned her eyes back to him.

"What?" he asked as he set his bags down and shut the door.

"I think I now know why the townspeople think you're gay."

Looking around the room that still looked like it did when he took the house over, all he immediately noticed was that everything was spotless. Maybe a little *too* spotless, considering that he was almost never home, but he could explain that.

"Okay, so maybe it's a little too clean for a bachelor pad, but my mom has a housekeeper come in now and then, so I don't have to waste my time cleaning when I come in off the road. Give it a day or two and it will look lived in again."

The corners of Aloriah's mouth twitched, but the gleam in her eyes didn't diminish. She looked pointedly at the windows.

"I was referring to all the frilly curtains." She looked at him with mock seriousness. "Is there something you're not telling me, Chase?"

He laughed and looked at the curtains himself. The walls and the countertops were all a soft beige, so Gram Godfried had added a splash of color with green lace curtains that had big flowers silk screened on them. He hadn't really thought much about them in the two years he had been living in the house, but Aloriah was right. They did look a bit feminine when one took a good look at them.

"Okay, so before I take you on a tour of the

rest of the house, I should probably explain that I didn't do the interior decorating. This house belonged to my dad's grandparents. My great-grandmother did all the decorating, but she passed away a few years ago and left the house to her surviving family. All of my cousins, who are older than me, didn't want to stay in Greenville after high school, so when I graduated and decided to drive for the trucking company, the house was given to me to use whenever I was in town for a while. It's partially to give me a place to call my own, but also partially because there's a lot of times that I get home in the middle of the night, so I don't wake everyone up when I pull in. I haven't been home much over the past two years, so I've just never redecorated to make it more manly."

Aloriah stood looking at him as if he'd just told her one of his tall tales.

"A likely story." she teased, and squealed when Chase grabbed her and pulled her close with a devilish look in his eyes.

"If you hadn't already turned down the idea of sharing my bed, I'd be showing you how *not* gay I am right now!" And he punctuated that sentence with a steamy kiss that left Aloriah's knees weak.

When he finally backed off and let her take a couple of calming breaths, she looked up at him with a smile.

"Okay, so you're not gay. I promise I won't say another word about the frilly curtains."

After they had put the groceries away, Chase picked up her suitcase and led the way through the house, pointing out a very formal looking dining room that he claimed he never used, a living room with a stand-up piano against one wall, and a door under the stairs that he said was small bathroom that consisted of a toilet and a sink. As they went up the stairs, Aloriah tried to look everywhere except at the blue jean clad bottom that was almost at eye level in front of her. Her hands were tempted to reach up and cop a feel, and she had to keep reminding herself that she didn't want to take the relationship to that level yet. Her hands were shaking as they reached the upstairs hallway.

Chase took a left turn to go into the room that was going to be hers to use so that he could set down the suitcase. Following him in and looking around the room, it was clearly evident that this was the master bedroom at the time that his great-grandmother had still occupied the place. The big, canopied bed looked very inviting, but if she had thought that the kitchen was frilly, this room was a frill overload, with ruffled curtains in all the windows and hanging from the bedposts along with a flowery bedspread with pink bows down both sides.

Looking at her face, Chase said teasingly "Yes, this is the master bedroom, and no, I have never spent a single night in here. Too much ruffled pinkness for my taste."

Before she could stop herself from saying it, the words were out of her mouth, and she blushed deeply at how forward the question sounded.

"So, where *do* you sleep?"

Chase grinned at the blush, but instead of answering, he just took her hand and led her down the hall to the right of the stairs, pointing out the large bathroom with both a big, claw footed tub and a shower stall in addition to the toilet and sink as they passed it. Pushing open the door at the far end of the hall, he said "Ta dah!"

This room was as masculine as the rest of the house was feminine. The walls were a pale blue, the wall to wall carpet was a rich navy blue, and instead of curtains, there were navy blue Venetian blinds on the windows. The double bed, covered with a thick maroon comforter to offset all the blue, had a dark mahogany sleigh bed frame that matched the no-frills dresser and nightstand. Smiling as she stood next to Chase in the doorway, Aloriah couldn't resist a deep sigh and another teasing comment.

"Okay, so I believe you. You really are a manly man."

Forcing himself to clamp down on the urge to pull her back into his arms and see if another steamy kiss would encourage her to sleep here with him for the night, Chase cleared his throat and suggested that they go make something to eat. The kitchen was safer when it came to his almost out-of-control libido.

Much safer.

Chapter 7

Chase awoke from a restless night with the pending meeting with his parents still foremost in his mind. Although he had heard the story many times about how his mother had been brought to Maine after a nearly fatal motorcycle crash in Atlanta, he was still nervous about how his parents might feel about him taking Aloriah out of Old Town without her parent's knowledge. He had called and spoken to his mother, telling her that he was in town and would be coming by with a friend that he wanted the family to meet, but he had carefully avoided getting into any of the details over the phone. He didn't want them to have a pre-formed opinion about Aloriah before they got to meet her face to face and hear the story in her own words.

Deciding to wait to hear what his parents might suggest on the situation with Aloriah's parents before he called Kelly and opened a can of worms, he got up and dressed in jeans and a t-shirt, then made his way barefoot down the hall to the master bedroom. Taking a deep breath, he knocked lightly.

"Aloriah?" he called softly, and was alarmed when all he got for a response was a deep, painful moan. As he started to reach for the doorknob, he heard movement and opted to wait a moment. The door was opened to him, but only by the tiniest margin before she moaned again, and he noticed that the curtains were closed tightly over all the windows so that the room was in semi-darkness.

"I'm sorry. I woke up with a migraine." She said, the pain evident in her voice.

Not understanding the level of her distress, Chase pushed the door wider, and was startled to see Aloriah back away, hissing in pain as she covered her eyes with both hands. She then turned ghostly white and unexpectedly dashed past him, making it to the bathroom and throwing the toilet seat against the tank with a bang only seconds before she dropped to her knees and started vomiting violently.

More familiar with vomiting than he was with migraines, Chase got a cool, wet cloth that he handed to Aloriah when her heaving had stopped. She thanked him in a voice that sounded nothing like her normal self and pressed the cloth to her face, hissing again when she opened her eyes to the brightness of the room. Unsure of what else to do, Chase knelt beside her.

"What can I do to help?"

Opening just one eye the barest crack to peer at him, Aloriah sighed.

"Gee, Mr. Wizard, can you make the entire world dark, maybe?"

Unscathed by the rampant sarcasm in her

tone, Chase smiled as he got up and grabbed a large bath towel out of the cabinet to toss over the window. He grabbed a second one that he gently put over Aloriah's head before helping her to her feet. From under the cloth came her next sarcastic comment.

"Ok, smarty pants, that *is* an effective solution to making it dark, but how do I get back to my room with this over my head?"

Wondering silently if his own sarcastic streak was this annoying, Chase didn't say a word, just picked her up into his arms, grinning as she gave a squeal.

"Put me down before you hurt yourself!"

"I'm not going to hurt myself if you don't squirm!" he insisted, trying hard not to laugh when she went stock-still.

"But I'm too heavy for you to carry!"

Finding it hard to ignore her perfume and her softer body parts that were pressed against him in this position, Chase couldn't resist arguing to get his mind off her and his long-starved libido.

"You're not too heavy!"

Aloriah snorted.

"I bet I weigh more than you do!" she persisted.

"What does your scale say when you step on it?"

Making her voice come out like a crotchety old person, she growled, "Hey! One at a time!"

Chase started laughing so hard he thought for sure he was going to drop her. Unseen beneath the towel, Aloriah grimaced as the noise of it caused her aching head to protest, but she also felt like smiling. It was actually refreshing to have someone laugh at her sarcastic comments instead of yelling at her for being "fresh".

She felt him move sideways as he got to the bedroom door, and felt a trace of disappointment that her time in his arms was almost at an end. It surprised her, therefore, when he set her on the bed, and instead of leaving right away, he sat next to her after she removed the towel from her head, brushing her hair away from her face in the dim room. Even in the near darkness, she swore she could see the concern in his eyes, and she was willing to bet that, if not for the migraine hindering her empathic ability, she would be able to feel it as well.

"Is there anything that I can do to make the pain go away?"

The concern that Aloriah thought she was seeing in his eyes was evident in his voice, and she sighed as she shook her head "no".

"The only thing that helps is to stay in the dark and sleep until it passes." Then she smiled as she realized the one thing she could ask of him. "Something like a glass of ice water might be helpful, though. I always wake up parched several times before the migraine finally goes away, and you've already witnessed what happens if I try to get a drink by myself and step into the light."

The smile that her admission produced seemed to light up the room, but not in a way that made the pain worse.

"You get comfortable, and I'll be right back."

By the time Chase returned with an insulated

5-gallon beverage cooler full of ice water in one hand and a glass in the other, Aloriah was sleeping, so he slipped in quietly and put his offerings on the night stand where she would see them when she awoke. It was his intention to just slip back out without disturbing her, but as he started to turn to leave, he paused for a moment to look at her peaceful face. Without any makeup, she looked almost childlike, and it was hard for him to remember that she had actually graduated high school just before the trip to New Orleans.

When awake, she almost seemed like she was older than he was, with all the worries of the world on her shoulders. Seeing her like this, he was almost overwhelmed with the desire to run his fingers through her hair, cup her cheek, kiss her... and his hand started moving forward of its own volition.

Aloriah startled him immensely when she suddenly sat bolt upright as if she felt his approaching hand, her eyes open, but unfocused. In a voice deeper than he'd ever heard come out of her mouth, she growled out something in French that almost sounded like one of the Cajun curses he knew, but he couldn't understand it. As soon as she finished speaking, her eyes closed and she dropped back onto the pillow, settling back down as if nothing had happened.

Worried that the strange behavior indicated that her headache was something more than she was letting on, he went and called his parents to let them know that she wasn't feeling well. He arranged to bring Aloriah by the next morning for breakfast, then returned and sat on the edge of the bed for a while, watching her sleep while he worried about her. After a point, when there wasn't a repeat of the strange behavior, he started to feel sleepy after his restless night, but not wanting to leave her, he stretched out on the bed next to her, draping his arm across her so he would know if she stirred.

Aloriah woke some time later and found a seemingly bare male arm wrapped around her waist, feeling a firm body pressed down the length of her back. She was unable to get her brain to make sense of it. What had she done while the migraine had her in its grip?

Lifting her head slightly, she glanced down at their legs and saw that, while she was under the covers, the blue jean clad male legs were on top of them. As she let out a soft sigh of relief and moved to put her head back on the pillow, the scent of Axe cologne made her smile, and she found she was able to identify the owner of the arm, legs, and bare feet. Chase!

As if thinking his name awoke him, his arm tightened around her, and his lips touched her ear in a kiss. Shifting slightly and turning so that she could see him, she was treated to the sweetest sleepy smile. Then he reached up to gently brush his fingers down her cheek, and in the dim light, she could see in his eyes that he was still very concerned.

"How's the head?" His voice was soft and slightly scratchy from sleep.

She thought about when she lifted her head to look at his legs, and the movement hadn't caused the pain to return. When she concentrated, she could feel his concern as well as an emotion she didn't want to try to decipher. Apart from being a little foggy, and very thirsty, she was able to think without pain as well. She smiled.

"Seems to be okay now."

Another soft smile touched his lips, and she realized that she could very easily get used to waking up to these beautiful sleepy smiles.

"No more urges to speak French?"

Aloriah looked at him in surprise for a moment, suddenly wide awake as dread raced through her, then came the closest she had ever come to saying a curse in front of him.

"Oh crap!"

Amused, Chase lifted an eyebrow.

"What's crap?"

She almost growled her response.

"I thought I outgrew that."

Chase said nothing, just continuing to watch her, trying not to show his amusement while she seemed so angry at herself.

"Let me guess. I sat up, said something in French, and then lay back down like nothing happened?"

Chase nodded. Aloriah gave a heavy sigh and looked pained, knowing she would have to explain the situation, especially since he was pushing for her to sleep in his bed. She had to come up with the words to let him know what he was in for if she consented to that next step, and especially now, when she knew it hadn't just gone away when she got older.

"You know how little kids do sleepovers?"

He nodded.

"I stopped being invited to those. The first time, I terrified three other girls by sitting up and growling something in German that no one understood. That tale went through the school like wildfire and no one wanted to let the witch into their house. Three years later, a new girl in town invited me over, and we slept on her living room floor. That time, I sat up and spoke Yiddish in front of her father, who had just stopped to make sure we were both asleep before going up to bed. He happened to be Jewish and said I told him in a growling voice that his grandmother was going to die. When she did two weeks later, no one else would *ever* let me come over to their house for the night."

Brushing his fingers down her cheek again, feeling sad that she had been ostracized for something she couldn't control, he murmured "Poor sweetie. Did anything evil happen after the German incident?"

"No, but did I say anything in French that you could understand?"

He smiled and told her the truth, which was that it had almost sounded like cursing, but was so garbled by the growling that he couldn't be sure. Wanting her to understand that he wasn't upset about the episode he'd gone through, he leaned over her and kissed her.

Before he could think to put a lid on it, his long-starved passions flared, and he deepened the kiss. When she moaned against his lips and didn't push him away, he moved to a slightly better position and continued to kiss her, thrilled when she also moved to a slightly better position and started kissing him back with some passion of her own. He felt her hands moving along his back and it was his turn to moan.

For Aloriah, the first part of the kiss was the same as the soft, sweet kisses he'd given her in New Orleans, and she could feel that his initial intention was to comfort her. Then she felt something change within him, as if the kiss had opened a door to something he was trying to keep in check. When he deepened the kiss, she was lost to the passion he inspired within her, moaning just before he shifted slightly and continued to kiss her. As if on their own, her hands had moved, wrapping around him to move across his muscular back, urging him on. Her heart soared when he also moaned.

It wasn't until he stopped, dropped his head to her shoulder, and let out a deep sigh that she realized something was wrong. He was upset about something, but strangely, she could tell that he wasn't upset with her. He was upset with himself.

"Crap" he murmured, and she smiled, remembering how he had responded when she said that.

"What's crap?"

He lifted himself up to look down on her with a slight smile. It amused him that she had imitated not only his words, but the tone he had used not too long ago.

"We're in the wrong room for this."

When she just looked at him in confusion, he indicated the room in general.

"My great-granddad died several years before my great-grandma, but she wasn't the type to have lovers. There aren't any condoms in *this* nightstand." She understood from the way he phrased that sentence that there were condoms in his nightstand up the hall, and she blushed. Seeing her blush even in the dim light, he kissed her again, gently, and as she searched his emotions, she was stunned to realize that what he had said to her at the barbecue in New Orleans was really how he felt. Even though others might consider her fat and unattractive, Chase didn't see her like that. He saw the inner person, and actually liked what he saw. When he drew back, she lay looking at him with confusion evident on her face.

"What's wrong?" he asked gently, and the tender look on his face made her want to cry.

"I just don't understand. For years now, I've been told that I'm fat, and ugly, and no one would ever think me sexy. And then you come along." She paused a moment, trying to find the right words. "I just don't understand what you see in me."

"Ree," Chase said gently, using the pet name he'd given her when he teasingly told her over the phone the week before that her name was beautiful, but too long, "Everyone who's been insulting you only sees that you don't fit the mold. You aren't what the media has brainwashed us to believe is the epitome of beauty. I see these wonderful, round, child bearing hips," she snorted as his hand brushed her hip, and he smiled as he moved his hand upward "and big, full breasts," his hand moved to her cheek, "and the most beautiful golden eyes that seem to look into my soul and see beyond what others can see."

When he looked deep into her eyes, and saw her confusion melting away as she felt nothing but the truth in his statement, Chase kissed her again, feeling his passion reignite. After a moment, he sighed and rolled onto his back beside her, pulling her into his arms so that she cuddled against his side.

With her head on his shoulder, she watched his face as he concentrated hard to control the passion she could feel still just under the surface. A devilish smile curved her lips, and she ran her hand across his chest, feeling the nipple ring beneath his t-shirt, smiling at his little hidden symbol of rebellion as she felt his heart start beating a little faster, and he groaned and gritted his teeth. He reached up with his free hand and made her stop playing with the nipple ring as he gave a little growl.

"You're playing with fire." he warned her, but she just cuddled closer with a grin, laying very still while he tried again to control himself. He was unlike anyone else she had ever met before, and she couldn't believe that it had just been sheer luck that he had been in New Orleans at the same time she was.

"So," she finally said when he seemed to have won his internal battle, "if I sneak into your room later and cuddle with you in your bed, we can maybe continue this?"

Chase laughed, pulling the hand that was on his chest up to his lips.

"If you sneak into my room later, I'll make

sure you walk funny for a week!" he promised, and Aloriah smiled, knowing that he meant that.

Chapter 8

Not wanting to be "walking funny" the first time she met Chase's parents, Aloriah made the decision to wait until after the meeting before she "snuck" into Chase's room, and when she worriedly told him that after he'd made them supper, he seconded that emotion, taking away her feeling of guilt. He did, however, insist on escorting her to her door to wish her a good sleep by kissing her until she almost changed her mind. Once assured that he would be on her mind even if he wasn't sharing her bed, Chase whistled as he sauntered to his door, glancing back now and then to make sure she was still watching him, then gave her a very sexy smile before he disappeared from her view. Still thinking that no man had any right to be that sexy, she smiled as she crawled into bed and had dreams of his sweet kisses.

The next morning, they each had only a glass of juice before loading into the car, as Chase insisted that his parents wanted them to be there for breakfast and, considering that his dad was former military, they really shouldn't be late. He seemed distracted, though, and as they drove to the house where Chase grew up, Aloriah could feel his worry, as well as his attempts to hide it from her.

Not sure what was causing him to be so worried, but wanting to offer what comfort she could, she reached over and placed her hand on his leg. Giving her his best attempt at a smile, he put his hand over hers and squeezed gently. Looking at her briefly, he smiled as his eyes took in how pretty she looked in a nice sundress, normal makeup, and the dark hair that made her gold eyes even more obviously unique before he turned his eyes back to the road.

"Have I told you how beautiful you look this morning?" he asked, and she smiled.

"Thank you, but you're making me nervous by being so worried. Are you afraid I'll say something untoward?"

Chase smiled as he realized that he had forgotten about the "special talent" she had told him about, impressed that she could tell he was worried when he was consciously hiding the body language that should have cued her in, and hurried to assure her that his worry wasn't about her.

"No, you'll be fine. I'm just worried about what Dad will say when I introduce you as the girl I met in New Orleans, and then inform him that your parents think you're in a homeless shelter in Bangor."

Aloriah smiled that it wasn't her behavior he was worried about, and assured him that she would make sure it was understood that she had been kicked out, and he had once again rescued her.

"You make it sound like you kidnapped me, so no wonder you're so worried." she teased, and she felt him relax, both under her fingertips and mentally.

As they neared the spot where the trees thinned, where she'd be getting her first look at the house, he gave her another glance and another smile.

"Are you sure you're ready for this?" he teased. "Last chance to back out."

With a deep breath, she nodded, thinking he was referring to the meeting with his parents, but as they came out of the trees and she got her first look at the house he grew up in, she gasped and realized that she really wasn't ready for the beauty before her. Apart from the swimming pool, which was encased in a room with glass walls and a glass ceiling to allow it to be used year round, the barn house looked exactly as it did when Chase's mother first saw it, but since Chase wanted to see her reaction, he hadn't told Aloriah a thing about what he called "the old homestead". Having never seen anything quite like it, she was speechless as her eyes took in every detail of the barn that had been converted into an extravagant house.

Glancing at her again, Chase waited for her to say something, but when nothing was forthcoming short of her gaping, open mouthed and wide eyed, he grinned and said "Well?"

"You were brought up in a barn?"

Chase laughed.

"Did I remember to mention that Dad is also known around town for being just a little eccentric? He wanted my sisters and me to be able to answer with a resounding 'yes' if someone asked if we'd been brought up in a barn."

Aloriah smiled and shook her head, thinking "a little eccentric" was an understatement from the way he'd said that, then she looked at Chase with a gleam in her eye and said "Moo".

When he answered her with a grin and a "Baa", she felt the last of his worry slip away.

As the car pulled up in front of the door, the door opened, and one of the most beautiful women Aloriah had ever seen stepped out, her long, chocolate brown hair showing just the first few strands of gray as the sun hit it just so. Her impatience as her son got out and hurried around the car to help his lady friend out would have been palpable even to someone without empathic talent. The smile on Teresanna's face and the emotions behind it didn't change even the smallest fraction when he put his arm around Aloriah's waist to bring her over to meet his mother.

The warmth reflected on Teresanna's face and in the hand she extended washed over Aloriah's empath senses like a wave, almost bringing her to tears. Like with Chase, it didn't matter to Teresanna what she looked like, she simply accepted that her son wouldn't bring Aloriah into his home if he didn't think her worthy. It was such a rare thing in Aloriah's world that she was at a loss.

"Welcome to our humble home." Teresanna said softly, her dark eyes alight with joy, then she turned to her son to give him a hug. "Come on inside. I was about to make coffee."

Following her through the door, Aloriah

stopped as soon as she was able to get a good look at the great room. Her eyes wide, she whispered "Wow", and then blushed when the whisper seemed to echo around the room. Teresanna laughed softly and put her arm around Aloriah's waist.

"I know, not so humble," and she gave her guest a wink, "But it's one of the most unique places you'll ever see."

Their conversation was interrupted by a bellow from upstairs.

"Angel, have you seen my green t-shirt?"

Rolling her eyes, Teresanna stepped away from Aloriah to spare her ears before yelling back.

"It was standing up on its own, so I put it in the laundry."

"But you said it was the one that matches my eyes!"

Teresanna shook her head at the whiney tone, reminiscent of a three-year-old talking about a favorite toy, and muttered "He's such a baby sometimes."

Chase, with a wink at his mother, hollered back "Why don't you wear the gray one. It matches your hair!"

The next bellow almost made the rafters shake.

"What did you say, boy?"

A man stepped out of the bedroom, naked from the waist up and hair uncombed, with what was supposed to be a frightening frown on his face, but he had forgotten that his son was bringing a guest. When he saw the stranger in the room, his expression changed to that of a small child caught doing something he shouldn't. That expression was immediately followed by a wide grin.

"Oh! Hi, young lady!"

Then he disappeared back into the room while Chase and Teresanna both laughed softly, trying not to let Kyle hear them. Aloriah, stunned by her first look at Chase's father, just looked from one to the other, thinking she had surely taken a look into the future. The son's resemblance to the father was uncanny.

"That was evil." Teresanna berated her son, trying to be stern but unable to wipe the smile off her face, "But funny."

Chase winked at Aloriah, proving that he didn't take his mother's rebuke too seriously, and changed the subject.

"So, you said something about coffee?"

Shaking her head and giving her boy a playful swat on the rump on the way by, Teresanna led the way to the kitchen, starting the coffee without waiting for them to join her. Chase put his hand on the small of Aloriah's back to follow, but they were stopped when two teenaged girls, nearly exact duplicates of their beautiful mother, came racing down the stairs with squeals of joy.

Laughing as he accepted their hugs of welcome, Chase introduced Lynn and Angela, who both welcomed her with grins and hugs. The girls, one her own age and the other just a couple of years younger, started asking her questions faster than she could answer them, but when she looked at Chase, he held his hands up, shrugged, and shook his head. They didn't seem to be expecting any answers, so she took his lead and just let them babble.

A loud clearing of the throat from the stairs made them all turn to find that Kyle, in a dark blue t-shirt with a picture of a moose on the front, was on his way down. The two girls sobered immediately, and when he looked at them sternly, they excused themselves to go back and finish cleaning their rooms.

"I expect those beds to be made and to find nothing hidden underneath when I come up to get you for breakfast." he warned, keeping the stern look until their bedroom doors were closed behind them. Then he grinned at his eldest and winked at Aloriah.

"I learned about that 'clean the room by hiding your toys under the bed' from the boy, here. Thanks to him, the girls can't get away with anything." he confided, and she giggled at the innocent face Chase tried to pull off, knowing his father was speaking the truth.

Chase took care of the formal introduction, and like Teresanna, Kyle greeted her with genuine warmth, playfully apologizing for being 'less than decent' when he first came out of the bedroom.

"I've seen worse when going swimming." she assured him, and he laughed before indicating they should go into the kitchen to join his wife. Looking closely at both Chase and Kyle, she reaffirmed her first assessment of the elder Benton. Despite the prominent grey streaks in his dark hair and a few wrinkles that were starting to settle into his face, Kyle was easily as handsome as his son with the same stunning green eyes.

Teresanna smiled as they came into the kitchen, asking Chase to bring cups, cream and sugar out to the table while the coffee finished brewing. She then asked Kyle to toss a pound of bacon into hot water to start it thawing while they talked. Both men jumped to do her bidding, and she gave Aloriah a wink.

"I trained them well." she joked, then, hearing the coffee maker make the "that's all the water" sound that indicated it was ready, she invited Aloriah to join her at the dining room table. As the two couples sat down at the table with their coffee, Aloriah, having noticed that Lynn and Angela were both very normal names compared to Chase, couldn't resist a simple enough question.

"Just out of curiosity, why did you name your son Chase?"

Kyle looked at Teresanna with a gleam in his eyes and tried to pull off a pout. On a younger face, it would have been believable, but on that all-too-manly face, it almost made Aloriah giggle.

"It was supposed to be a joke, but his mother and great-grandmother took me seriously."

Teresanna rolled her eyes and smiled at Aloriah.

"Funny man over there made the comment that, if his first child was a son who looked like him, he was going to be chased by all the girls all through school. He suggested we should just name him Chase. Kyle's Gram decided that Chase Andrew Benton rolled off the tongue very nicely." Teresanna shrugged. "I thought that, after raising Kyle, she deserved the right to name his first born."

Looking toward Chase, Aloriah saw him blush for the first time since she'd known him, and when he looked up from the close study of his cup, he gave her a shy smile, also a first.

"You're an empath. Dad's a psychic." He looked at his mother and gave a more normal smile. "I haven't figured out Mom's special talent."

Teresanna laughed.

"I'm an evil tyrant who wants to take over the world." she joked, making everyone laugh.

Leaning back and looking at Aloriah with an assessing gaze that suddenly made her uncomfortable, Kyle asked a quiet question with just one word.

"Empath?"

Thinking *oh crap, there goes my welcome to this house*, Aloriah explained about her ability to feel emotions and the fact that her mother's family had been able to do so for many generations. Kyle, watching her body language, let a hint of a smile touch his face as he revealed how much his son had shared about the happenings in New Orleans.

"So was that why you decided to take a photo down a dark alley during your ghost walk?"

Aloriah blushed even as she tried to make a joke about it.

"Yeah. Unfortunately, it's a talent that gets me in all kinds of trouble." Then she looked at Chase and a little half smile touched her face. "And it makes me meet the strangest people."

Kyle and Teresanna both laughed as their son looked shocked that she would call him strange, but neither missed the way his hand went under the table to squeeze Aloriah's leg when he gave her a wink. Taking the last sip of coffee out of his mug, Kyle gave his wife a similar wink and stood up, stating that the bacon should be thawed enough to meet the grill by now. Walking past Chase, he put his hand on his son's shoulder and said "I can use your help."

Chase opened his mouth to respond negatively, but Kyle slipped his arm under Chase's and pulled off a quite effective half-Nelson, forcing the boy to rise out of his seat whether he wanted to or not. As they disappeared into the kitchen in that unorthodox manner, Chase called back "I'm helping Dad cook bacon, so see if you can talk Mom into giving you a tour of the house."

Teresanna continued to sip on her coffee as if nothing untoward was happening, but Aloriah couldn't restrain a giggle.

"Are they always like that?"

Teresanna gave her a bored look that did well to hide the amusement Aloriah could feel beneath the surface, and said dryly "Unfortunately."

Then she brightened and smiled.

"Grab your coffee cup, and I'll show you my favorite place in this monstrosity my husband calls a house."

As they stood up and started to walk into the family room, Teresanna looked down and made a "tsk" sound when she saw the sandals Aloriah was wearing, which sported a slight heel.

"Let's lose the shoes first, as you really don't want to be climbing in those."

Mystified, Aloriah sat on the couch and did as instructed, pushing the sandals under the edge of the end table so no one would trip. Seeing that sign of consideration, Teresanna allowed herself a secretive smile. Having schooled her children on the belief that looks weren't everything, she was quite pleased to notice proof that her eldest had been listening. When Aloriah stood and picked her coffee cup back up, Teresanna led the way into the silo library, pausing to flip open the secret panel and flip the switch that lit the recessed lights in the spiral staircase. Aloriah gasped in pleasure and Teresanna grinned.

"It's much more effective at night, but you get the idea."

When the older woman took to the stairs and started to climb, Aloriah followed, realizing by the time they hit the second floor and kept going why she had been asked to remove the heels. The stairwell itself was a good workout on the calves, but in heels, she would have been in pain.

When Teresanna slipped out of view at the top of the stairwell, Aloriah came to a sudden halt, thinking she must be dreaming. How could there possibly be stars up there in the daytime? A few more steps, and she realized the magic behind what she was seeing, smiling as she entered the circular room with twinkling lights in the pattern of the stars in the night sky.

Watching the young woman's face, Teresanna said softly "Did Chase mention that his dad is a little eccentric?"

"Only when we were on our way here this morning." Aloriah responded, her voice sounding as if she was speaking in a dream state.

Her eyes hadn't left the lights above her head, and she identified several constellations she recognized. Seeing her own reaction to the "starry sky" in the younger woman, Teresanna grinned, catching the girl's attention long enough to point out a couple of bean bags for them to sit on.

"Now, I'd love to hear your version of the story about New Orleans. It sounds like you had quite the adventure."

While Teresanna was hearing the story Chase had told them about New Orleans from a different perspective, and with a lot of detail that he had left out when relaying it over the phone, Chase was in the kitchen telling his father about the unplanned drive to bring Aloriah to Greenville. Having heard a lot of news stories about rapes, beatings, robberies, and even a murder in local homeless shelters over the past year, Kyle was very proud of his son for thinking of the young lady before he thought of his own comfort. When Chase ended his tale with a comment about the local gossips and how he feared they would see the situation, Kyle just grinned.

"It's a small town, kiddo. What else do they have to do with themselves up here?"

Chase sighed.

"I just don't want to see Aloriah hurt."

Kyle grinned, pleased to hear that the boy had been listening to the lessons they had tried to teach him from infancy.

"Have I told you lately that I'm proud of you?"

Chase made digging motions and Kyle laughed.

"No, it's not 'shovel the crap' time. After hearing the way you and Cody risked your lives to get Aloriah and her mom out of a dangerous situation, and now this, I can see that you took the lessons your mom and I taught you to heart. She's a very nice girl, from what I've seen so far, but not everyone would have done the same." Puffing up his chest, he teased. "I raised me a good kid."

Grinning at his dad's antics, Chase imitated the puffing up of the chest.

"Yes, you did."

As the smell of cooked bacon wafted its way up to the top of the silo, Aloriah's stomach growled, making Teresanna laugh at the embarrassment the noise brought to the young woman's face. With a wink, she got gracefully off the bean bag, then suggested they go down and see how things were going.

"I'll follow you down in just a moment." Aloriah said, and waited until Teresanna's head had disappeared before she struggled to get out of her own beanbag.

"Why did I wear a sundress?" she muttered as she ended up having to roll out onto her hands and knees in order to stand up.

Pausing on the second floor of the library, Teresanna heard the mutter and struggled to control her amusement, really liking this young lady who had caught her son's eye. She had just managed to gain full control when Aloriah came gracefully down the stairs to join her, then the two of them went to collect the other girls before heading down to breakfast. Aloriah tried not to smile when

Teresanna went into both rooms and peeked under the beds, more because of her husband's threat than her own belief that the girls would actually disobey, confirming that her daughters had done as their father had asked before allowing them out of the rooms.

Prepared for the kind of solemn, silent breakfasts that her father had insisted on in her own home, Aloriah found she wasn't prepared for the Kyle-inspired insanity that was breakfast in the Benton home. After putting a couple of eggs and a couple of pieces of bacon on each plate before sending them in via his son to be placed in front of each occupied chair, he sat at the head of the table with a plate of Pillsbury rolls that Chase had prepared and asked who wanted one. Each one who responded positively was then expected to "catch" as he lobbed the roll their way.

Keeping her mouth shut as she watched this display, trying hard not to show the shock she was feeling, she found herself at the center of attention when Kyle turned mischievous eyes her way after everyone else was "served". Sounding very concerned that she might be missing out on the most important part of the meal, he leaned toward her.

"Are you sure you wouldn't like a roll with your breakfast, Aloriah?"

"No, thank you." she said shyly, then some little demon on her shoulder made her add, "I'm trying to watch my girlish figure."

Kyle grinned and gave her a wink, then asked the girls for details about a trip they were planning with their friends for the next day. As Lynn and

Angela took turns talking about all the fun stores they were going to shop at, the movie they were going to see, and whose house they were going to end up a with multiple questions, some serious and some silly, asked by Kyle, Aloriah ate quietly and read their emotions.

Angela was just excited about being able to spend time with her friends, Lynn was looking for any excuse to get away from the house, and Kyle wanted to make sure they would be under adult supervision the whole time, concerned about the safety of his girls in the city. Teresanna was listening for anything she might need to discuss with the parents who would be picking the girls up in the morning.

As she reached her hand down for a second piece of bacon, Aloriah, who had already eaten her eggs, encountered something that was definitely not bacon. Looking down, she found that a roll had mysteriously appeared on her plate. Clearing her throat as she recalled the last time food had mysteriously appeared on her plate, she looked over at Chase, who was studying the ceiling as if he'd never seen it before.

The clearing of her throat had made everyone else notice her, and as she looked from Chase to the roll to Chase again while he was a little too obvious about trying not to look at her, it didn't take long for the others to figure out what had happened. The girls both started to giggle, and Kyle leaned back in his seat to see how Aloriah would handle it. Teresanna, trying hard not to join the girls in laughing, covered her mouth with her hand. As if he was just realizing that everyone was looking at him, Chase looked at Aloriah, trying hard not to smile.

"Didn't we already go over this at the barbecue in New Orleans?" she asked, and he tried to play innocent.

"What?"

While tempted to take the roll and tuck it down his shirt, she took it off her plate and put it back onto his. A pleased smile crossed his face.

"A roll? For me?"

Kyle snorted as his son took the roll and ate it, seemingly not noticing the scathing look he was getting from his lady friend, and Teresanna got enough control over the urge to laugh to look at her husband in mock seriousness.

"He's definitely your son!"

With the same attempt at an innocent look his son had just worn and the same tone of voice, Kyle looked at his wife and said "What?"

Teresanna responded by just rolling her eyes.

When Kyle gave her a grin and a wink before asking what Chase had planned for the rest of the day, Aloriah felt as if she'd passed some strange family test. She felt accepted here, something so lacking in her own home that she actually relaxed, at least until Chase washed the last of the roll down and was able to answer his father's question.

"I'm taking Aloriah into town so we can get her a few more clothes."

When Aloriah tried to object, he just smiled at her.

"You only have one suitcase, Ree. You're going to need more clothes than that around this crazy bunch."

Kyle leaned toward her, his left eyebrow lifting even though he sounded extremely serious.

"I'd suggest letting him buy you some clothes." He paused for effect. "He drools." Then he wrinkled his nose. "A lot."

As he leaned back in his chair again, Aloriah couldn't help laughing at the pseudo-serious look on his face while Chase made a face and pretended to drool.

"Yup, Chase is his kid, drool and all!" Teresanna proclaimed from her seat with a grin, then stood up to start gathering plates. Aloriah jumped up to help, and when they got to the kitchen, Teresanna directed her to put the plates into the sink, then pulled her into a hug.

"Welcome to the family, sweetie. I promise to try to make them behave better the next time you're here to eat."

Aloriah grinned as she got released.

"Good luck with that. I have a feeling that would take a miracle."

Teresanna's only response was to roll her eyes and nod, grinning back.

Chapter 9

Back in the car heading toward Chase's house, Aloriah was arguing about the plan to bring her into town to buy clothes, as she felt that he had already done more than he should have done. He was just as adamant that he was going to take her shopping, even if the choices of where to shop in Greenville were limited, and they might have to plan a trip to a larger town if they didn't find the things she needed.

"Come on, Ree. I picked up your suitcase to put it in the car yesterday, so I know you don't have a whole lot stuffed into it. How much do you actually have to wear?"

She frowned at him for a moment before looking down at her hands.

"I have two pairs of pants, a couple of shirts and this dress, plus socks and underwear as well as the shoes I'm wearing and a pair of sneakers."

"So, in order to make a full load of laundry, you'd have to be running around the house naked." He seemed to think about that one, and an evil smile crossed his face just before he looked over at her, licking his lips as if he was thinking she would make a very tasty lunch. "Do you need to do your laundry today, by any chance?"

Aloriah snorted.

"No, I don't have to do laundry yet, and you're a very sick man." She sighed. "Maybe you're right, but I only agree to two more outfits. You shouldn't be giving me a place to live, feeding my fat butt, and buying tons of clothes when I don't even have the slightest hint that I'm going to be able to get a job."

Hearing something in her voice that made him think he was listening to her father talk, but feeling like he was at least making headway, Chase asked what he thought was the most pertinent question.

"What size do you take?"

There wasn't even a slight hesitation.

"Circus tent."

If he hadn't been driving, he would have glared her down for that, but since he couldn't fix her with a glare until she squirmed, he let his frustration show in his voice.

"I'm serious, Ree. Give me a number so I know whether we can find anything in Greenville or if I should drive someplace else."

With a deep sigh, Aloriah tried again to get him to understand why she hated to shop, especially for clothes that seemed to increase in size every time she had been brought to the stores.

"I'm serious, too, Chase! I feel fat enough without having to go into a store and have people look at me like they expect me to lift my skirt and let a midget walk out."

Chase sighed.

"You aren't fat. You're just right."

Unable to understand what he saw in her and feeling like she was going to cry, Aloriah looked out the window, watching the trees pass the window while silence fell within the car. She heaved a deep sigh that Chase thought must have come from somewhere around her toes, and finally gave him a number.

"The pants Mom bought me for job hunting are a size 18."

Chase tapped his fingers on the steering wheel as his driveway came into view, frustrated that she was fighting this whole idea, but still pleased that he finally had a number to work with. There was nowhere in Greenville that had much in the way of plus sized clothing, so he made a sudden decision.

"Do you need to hit the bathroom before we take a longer trip? I think I know where I want to take you shopping, but it's a little over a half an hour drive time."

Rolling her eyes, Aloriah shook her head "no", and the satisfied smile that crossed his face made her wonder what Chase was thinking. He was happy, but that was all her empathy was getting from him, which was better than the frustration he'd been feeling moments before. She went back to silently watching the trees pass by her window, hating the idea of shopping, but unable to dissuade him from his insistence that she needed more clothes.

After a few minutes, Chase sighed and tried to change the subject.

"So, when Mom took you on a tour of the

house, what did she show you?"

Aloriah smiled thinking about the silo library and the little room at the top.

"She brought me to the top of the spiral staircase so I could see the stars."

Chase grinned. He should have known. Whenever his mother needed a little peace and quiet for a few minutes, he would find her on a bean bag staring up at the lights that formed star constellations.

"So she didn't show you the exercise room, or the swimming pool?" Those were his favorite places in the house. When he needed to think, he would go and lift weights, and when he needed to clear his mind, he'd do laps in the pool.

"Why show a fat chick rooms she's probably never used?"

There was something in her voice that made Chase wonder just how much verbal abuse she had sustained to have such low self-esteem. Having met her mother and getting the feeling that she cared for the girl inside rather than the appearance of her daughter, just as he did, he had the distinct feeling that Aloriah would have been one of those people who would have been much happier to have been raised in a single parent home.

"You know, swimming is one of the best exercises you can do to start a weight loss program, if that's what you'd like to do. We can get you a bathing suit and you can go and swim every day. By Christmas, your family won't recognize that beautiful, svelte person as you."

Still unwilling to let him take her away from

the upsetting thought of shopping for clothes, she didn't even look his way.

"Bathing suits don't come in Shamu size."

Chase refused to let her dissuade him from getting her into the pool. He didn't know anyone who didn't love to swim, and the thought of having someone to swim laps with him was too appealing.

"How about a pair of shorts and a shirt until you get down to where you feel comfortable in a bathing suit?"

That brought her eyes back around to him.

"Why are you determined to make your family vomit? They seem like such nice people."

Chase laughed. He was really starting to like the never-ending sarcasm.

As they drove toward Dexter, where Chase thought he might have a better chance of finding clothing in the right size, he dropped the shopping references that seemed to be upsetting her. To entertain her, he starting telling her some of the unwritten rules at the barn house, should she choose to spend time with his family while he was away. Aloriah kept looking at him, slack jawed, wondering if he was being totally serious, but could find none of the emotional markers that would have hinted at a lie.

"Okay," he began, "you already know that Dad can be a little strange, so these are the important things for you to know before you spend much more time in Greenville. First: if you appear anywhere near a mealtime, you *will* be required to eat. Try telling Dad that you just ate, and he'll make you list off what you just ate, what time you ate it, and how big the portion was. It's much easier to just humor him and eat with the family."

Thinking of the breakfast they'd just had, she smiled, thinking it was much more fun to eat with the family anyway than to miss Kyle's shenanigans.

"Second: If you don't want to be forced into some kind of physical activity, always wear a dress or other such fancy clothes when you visit. He figures that jeans or shorts mean you aren't doing anything special when you leave, so it's fine to pick up a couple of bruises learning self-defense or to be tossed into the pool if you refuse the lesson."

That revelation was a bit of a surprise, but she could easily picture it. Chase's pushiness about something she could wear in the pool started to make more sense.

"Third, don't show up after 8 p.m. unless you've been specifically invited or have made arrangements to spend the night. Dad gets really cranky when he's trying to get the girls to bed and enjoy some quiet time with Mom, but he's stuck entertaining someone."

That made her laugh, as she was sure she would feel the same way. Unless she was having trouble sleeping, as when she was in New Orleans, she liked a fairly early bedtime herself. Looking over at Chase and thinking of bedtime, she was suddenly nervous. Wanting to make a good impression on his parents, she had put off that whole "sneaking down the hall to his room" thing, but would she be able resist the urge tonight? If she did go into his room, would he be pleased, or was part of his game to get her to embarrass herself?

Although he wasn't empathic, Chase heard the laugh fade away and saw the look she gave him out of the corner of his eye. Since he had just mentioned bedtime, it didn't take much to figure out where her train of thought had taken her. Thinking of how she had felt in his arms, he was hoping she was considering his offer to share a bed. As his father was fond of saying *There's always hope*, and maybe if they found some clothes she really liked, there would also be just a smidgen of gratitude.

He wouldn't be able to explain to anyone else why, but from the moment he had seen the heavy set Goth girl, so obviously worried about something even though she and the older woman she was with were trying to pretend nothing was wrong, he had felt a strong attraction to her. When he saw the four men acting strangely, following the two women, his protective side had come out. And when he had dropped his arm over her shoulder after pointing them out to Cody and forming the plan to act like they had been waiting for the ladies, he had found himself wanting to hug her, and kiss her, and take that sadness out of those beautiful golden eyes.

"Okay." He said as if there hadn't been that brief period of silence in the car when they had both thought about bedtime. "Shall I go over the things that Mom considers to be common courtesies to make her life easier?"

Smiling again and giving him an enthusiastic nod, thinking of the tiny woman who could make the men who towered over her jump to do her bidding, Aloriah listened as he went over the list. Most of them were things she probably would have insisted on if she were in charge of the house, such as taking boots off at the door in the winter to avoid making a mess of the great room floor. Other things were actually fairly humorous, because they hinted at things Aloriah didn't even want to think about, such as dropping the trap door over the top of the spiral staircase if making out with someone on the bean bags in the room they called "the star room".

"My first girlfriend." he said to that last by way of explanation. "Enough said?"

Aloriah blushed, remembering her own experience with his amorous tendencies, and the blush made Chase add a little more in a defensive tone that wasn't reflected in his emotional state.

"Hey, we were still dressed when Mom came up!"

Just the suggestion that it might have gone further deepened her blush, and Chase only managed to avoid laughing by biting his lip. By that point, Lake Wassookeag was coming into view and he changed the subject, pointing out that they were almost into Dexter. He offered her the choice on whether to visit the thrift stores or Reny's first, and when she voted for the latter, he drove there, parked, and raced around the car to open her door for her.

She took the hand he offered to help her out, looking at him strangely, as it was really not something anyone had ever done for her, but he seemed to want to make sure she was treated like a lady. Wrapping his arm around her waist as they walked toward the door, he winked at her, having properly read her body language without the aid of her empathic talents.

"Get used to it, baby. I plan on treating you like a queen." He punctuated his words with a kiss to her temple, and Aloriah was totally mystified, because he really meant it.

When they entered the store and went to the women's clothing section, Aloriah was surprised to find several items that she liked in the larger sizes. Finding her normal size in the styles she liked, she brought them into the fitting room while Chase pulled out some styles that he thought would look good on her even though he had just seen her ignore them.

When she came out with a grimace on her face, swearing everything looked horrible, he swapped the things she had chosen for the things he had picked out. He handed the clerk the things she had decided against, started looking for other clothes, heard her clearing her throat, and turned to see her in one of the outfits he had chosen. The colors worked well with her hair, skin tone and eyes, and he looked beautiful.

"See, nothing tent-like." he teased, but Aloriah just started at him like he'd grown a second head.

"I don't know how you did it, but you chose better than I did. Would you care to try a few more things?"

He smiled at her.

"I just picked out the colors I thought I'd like to see you in." He held up a coppery colored silk shirt he had just found. "Like this one, that reminds me of the color of your eyes."

She waved a hand at him in a shooing motion

after taking the shirt from him, and made him smile even wider when she responded, "Well, keep looking then."

By the time they left the store, she had liked four full outfits that he had chosen for her as well as a bathing suit that she swore didn't look as bad as she expected it to. She had allowed him to talk her into a pair of new sneakers and knee-high boots that looked really nice with the new pair of blue jeans tucked into the top. When he tried to talk her into more shopping, though, she put her foot down, and with a laugh, he turned them toward home, feeling like he had won a major battle.

Chase noticed an interesting phenomenon involving Aloriah on the way back to his home. The closer they got to Greenville, the more quiet and thoughtful she got. Thinking that perhaps she was feeling ill or something, he reached over to touch her knee to get her attention, and she jumped as if he had stabbed her.

"Ree? Are you okay? Do you need me to pull over?"

"Sorry, Chase. I was just thinking."

Concerned, he took a glance over at her, but instead of the white faced look that he would have expected if she was feeling car sick, she was blushing. The blush got even deeper when she glanced over at him and caught him glancing at her. Her odd behavior still made him think about pulling over, but she took a deep, sighing breath and spoke as if she was trying to get her attention off of whatever it was that was bothering her.

"So, what would you like me to make us for

lunch?"

The mention of food made his stomach growl, and he looked down at it as if it was an alien entity. The shared laugh that followed seemed to return her to her normal self.

Chapter 10

As they pulled into the driveway, Chase could feel the tension starting to build in Aloriah again. She was trying very hard not to let it show, but there were little physical "tells" that Chase was picking up on as she struggled to make small talk. In his peripheral vision, he could see her looking at him, a slightly worried expression on her face, but when he turned his head to glance at her, she would look out the window.

Her hands, folded in her lap, were in almost constant motion, the top hand rubbing the back of the bottom one as if her fingers were cold. She kept crossing and uncrossing her legs, as if trying to decide whether or not to be open to him. Last but not least, there was a strained tone to her laugh, and she kept biting her lower lip.

Pulling up to the porch steps, he unhooked his seatbelt to reach into his front pocket for the door key, giving her a sensual smile as he reached out to take her hand, touching the tips of his fingers to her palm as he placed the key there. She seemed to suddenly have a dry mouth and blushed profusely.

"Why don't you take your new clothes up to your room while I park the car and I'll meet you back in the kitchen."

She swallowed hard, and a little devil on his shoulder made him place a hand on her cheek and lean forward. She responded by leaning shyly toward him to allow the kiss to happen, and when he purposefully made it a bit more sensual, she at first responded, then suddenly withdrew. She got quickly out of the car, grabbed the shopping bags out of the back seat, and gave him a strained smile before going up the stairs, fumbling with the key chain.

Chase pulled the car toward the garage with a soft chuckle, certain he now knew what had been bothering his lady. She was nervous and unsure about taking their relationship to the next level, but wasn't about to tell him so.

When he walked into the house, Aloriah was just coming back down the stairs barefoot, but still in the dress she'd worn that morning. Following her lead, he slipped his sneakers and socks off at the door, padding around the kitchen on nearly silent bare feet. Watching him move, Aloriah once again was reminded of jungle cats.

Noting that it was now mid-afternoon, Chase suggested a slightly more heavy meal than they had discussed in the car, followed by something a little lighter and less formal in the evening if they actually got hungry again. To try make her relax a little, he made sure to mention that the evening "snack" could be something portable enough to enjoy in front of the television. Aloriah visibly relaxed at the thought that he wasn't planning to throw her over his shoulder and carry her to his room any time soon.

As he prepared a nice piece of haddock for the oven, he gave Aloriah the task of making some rice pilaf and steamed vegetables. While the fish baked, he set the table, and in the tight quarters, he "accidentally" brushed against her more than once, enjoying the way she kept blushing at the unaccustomed attention.

After their meal, he handed her an apron and set her to washing their dishes while he dried and put things back in their proper places. Once again, his chore was accomplished with a lot of "accidental" touching, and by the time she was hanging the apron up and he was pouring them each a tall glass of iced tea to take into the living room so that they could relax together on the couch, she was blushing less frequently and actually instigating some of the touching.

Carrying their drinks into the living room, Chase set them down on coasters on the coffee table, where he picked up the remote, then grabbed Aloriah's hand as he dropped onto the couch in a semi-reclining position, pulling her down so that her bottom was between his legs. Before she could protest, he had pulled her upper body down so that she was laying against his chest, at which point he sighed in pleasure and gave her a kiss on the top of the head.

"This is very nice!" he murmured, and as she let herself relax against him, she had to silently agree. He was, perhaps, a little too muscular to be a totally comfortable pillow, but it was very pleasant to have his body wrapped around hers in this fashion.

He flicked through channels, pausing now and again to ask her opinion as to which form of "mindless entertainment", as he liked to call it, that she wanted to look at, and when he had found a station they both agreed on, he dropped the remote onto the floor and wrapped his arms around her. With the exception of the television droning in the background, it got very quiet and peaceful, and Aloriah found it hard to keep her eyes open.

Closing her eyes and drifting in a netherworld somewhere between being fully awake and fully asleep, Aloriah would have been hard pressed later to recall exactly when Chase went from passively holding her to gently running his fingers over her skin. At first, it was just a butterfly soft touch across her cheek and one side of her neck, moving to brushing across her hair and playing with its silky length. A slight tug at the ribbon she had used to tie her hair back into a ponytail came next, then the fingers were pulling her hair forward to drape it across her upper chest. When the soft touch ran down her bicep and slipped down to trace the line where her dress covered the upper swells of her breasts, she couldn't hold back a soft moan.

Feeling soft kisses touching her hair just above her temple, she tipped her head back, allowing access to her cheek and eyes. Beneath her, Chase shifted slightly, and she accommodated without opening her eyes, shifting herself and tipping her head back a little more to allow access to her mouth. The hand continued its explorations, first cupping her breast, then sliding down to her stomach and hip while the lips set fire to her lips before tracing a molten path down across her chin to the section of her neck that the hand had already explored.

Another shift, and she felt his leg slide out from under her as she shifted again to accommodate. She found herself caught between the back of the couch and that muscular frame as he moved down to allow him better access to her mouth and neck, but she didn't feel at all trapped there. His lips and fingers were making her feel like she was drifting in a world of pleasure, and when he started to touch her a little more firmly and kiss her a little more deeply, she reacted with a deep throated moan.

When the hand on her hip slid the skirt of her dress out of the way and she felt the skin on skin contact, she moaned again. He took the moan away from her with his kiss, leaving her breathless as his tongue played at the edge of her lips and his hand pulled her hips closer to his. She opened her eyes as she felt the foreign hardness pressing against her and looked into the most sensuous gaze that she had ever seen. A very sexy smile touched his mouth as he possessed her lips again, and when he withdrew, his voice was soft and husky.

"We have more room for this upstairs if you'd care to join me."

She didn't know where the nervousness she had been feeling earlier had gone, but she smiled as she nodded. It all felt so natural, so right, and when he slid off the couch and offered his hand to help her to rise, she took his hand and only paused long enough to grab one of the glasses of tea to take along. He smiled at her thoughtfulness, then led the way up over the stairs and down the hall to his bedroom, allowing her to set the glass on the coaster on his nightstand before wrapping his arms around her and pulling her close to allow him to continue kissing her.

As they kissed, he gently moved her backward until the bed behind her knees forced her to sit, but he didn't let her just drop. His strong arms eased her down, and when she was fully seated, released her to allow him to lean over her, gently turning her so that her head ended up on his pillows without breaking the contact of their lips. When he was fully on the bed, he eased himself down beside her before his hand on her hip turned her to face him. It was only then that he let them both have a moment to breathe.

His eyes delved deep into the depths of hers as he approached the subject that had been bothering him, looking for the truth.

"I don't want this to hurt you in any way, shape or fashion, but I really need to know. Have you ever gone all the way with anyone before?"

He saw her flinch at a painful memory, and she bit her lip before she answered.

"It was just once, and I don't remember much about it. I was really drunk at a party and woke up in the bushes with my jeans around my ankles and blood on my thighs. I only found out who it was when the comments about being a whore started."

There was a moment of pained silence, then Chase pulled her close, soothing her with his gentle touch while his emotions ran the gamut from anger to pain, and then back to desire when he bent to kiss her neck, breathing in her perfume. When he pulled back to look at her face again, there was a mischievous gleam in his eyes and a sensual smile on his lips.

"Oooohhhhh!" The single syllable was drawn out, making Aloriah smile. "So you don't know how much pleasure you can take yet."

Her mouth dropped open, but not for long. Chase placed another one of those soft-as-a-butterfly kisses on her lips and returned to the gentle exploration of her curves, making tingles everywhere he touched, and she wanted to purr with pleasure. He was very thorough, and before he backed away to remove his t-shirt, everything from her knees to the top of her head tingled from his gentle touch. With a provocative look that, in itself, seemed to add to the tingling she was already feeling, he crawled down to place himself between her bare feet where he started again with the gentle touch he had already lavished over the rest of her, determined to make sure that she wanted him from head to toe before he reached for the nearby drawer where his condoms were kept.

As he moved up her legs and started bringing his mouth into play, kissing the places he had already sensitized with his hands, Aloriah drew her breath in as a gasp and released it as a long moan. With her eyes closed, thoroughly enjoying his deliberate attempt to build her pleasure to fever pitch, she didn't see the smile that touched his face at her reaction, but knew from his emotions that she was making him very happy.

As Chase worked his way up Aloriah's body, he pushed her dress up out of his way. He was a little surprised when she squirmed, but when her squirming resulted in her dress being wiggled out from under her body and deposited to the floor with his shirt, he smiled before continuing with what he was doing. His hands and mouth paid homage to the luscious, ample curves that he had admired when they first met and that were now almost bare beneath him.

As he worked his way up to the full breasts that overflowed his hands, Aloriah couldn't resist the urge to touch him, but it was almost his undoing. Drawing in a gasp of his own as her fingertips moved on his broad shoulders and down his muscular back, only stopping at the waist of his jeans because they were a little tight for her to be able to slide her hands in, he felt a little bit of what he was doing to her when her fingertips set his skin to tingling. He traced his lips up to kiss her mouth before moving back down to her upper chest and throat, forcing back his own pleasure in order to continue to pleasure her. When her fingers slid between them to trace the line of hair from his chest down into the top of his jeans, he had to grit his teeth to fight the urge to just throw off his jeans and take her like an animal.

Aloriah let out a little sound of disappointment when Chase caught her hands and drew them up over her head to hold them against the pillow while he ran his tongue around the outside of her lips, then kissed her deeply while pressing his jean covered firmness against her softer womanliness. Feeling her fight to free her hands so that she could continue to touch him, he couldn't resist a teasing question.

"Is there something wrong?" he asked, his voice soft and very sensuous.

"Yes," she responded, her own voice not sounding normal to her ears, as she was almost mewling. "I'm in my bra and panties and you still have your jeans on."

If a smile could give a girl an orgasm, Aloriah would have sworn that was what happened next. Chase's eyes, a slightly darker color than normal, looked deeply into her eyes and the most passionate smile she'd ever seen lifted his lips. Releasing her hands, he unbuttoned and unzipped his jeans, but it was her hands that pushed them down over his hips, almost taking his briefs with them. With a devilish wink, he made sure those stayed in place.

"Not yet, sweetie. I'm not done playing with you yet."

Aloriah groaned, which only succeeded in making the grin wider. As he pushed the jeans off the bed to join their other clothes on the floor, he returned his attention to her bra encased breasts. While what he was doing with his mouth was very nice, Aloriah found herself distracted by the sensations caused by the light furring on his chest brushing against her bare belly, and even more so, by the thin line of that same furring that ran down the center of his belly rubbing through her thin panties. Her fingers ached to touch that very masculine chest and belly, but she didn't want him to hold her hands down again, so she gripped onto the blankets to each side of her hips.

She was so distracted by all the unfamiliar sensations that she didn't notice Chase had managed to undo the clasp on her bra until he reared back, and she had to let go of the blankets to allow him to pull it off her arms. Yet another item was dropped onto the growing pile on the floor.

This time, when Chase returned to continue to kiss and fondle her, he allowed her to touch him in return, and Aloriah was fascinated by the play of muscles under his skin as he moved. When he drew himself up against her to place another kiss on her lips, her super-sensitized skin noted every inch of the hair on his chest as well as the coldness of the nipple ring, and she had never felt such intense pleasure. Feeling faint, she found herself begging for something, but she wasn't entirely sure what, so all that slipped out were two words.

"Oh, please....."

Smiling, suspecting he knew from the tone of her voice what she wanted, Chase kissed her and leaned close to nuzzle the tender skin under her ear.

"Please what?" he whispered, his own passion about to send him over the deep end. Her answering moan brought a response from deep in his own body.

"Please....end this."

He kissed her once more before rolling off to get into a position to reach the drawer, and when his briefs hit the floor, Aloriah didn't think she could ever get enough of looking at that beautiful male body. Her own panties were gone before he turned to look back at the bed, and that sexy smile that she was coming to love reappeared as he slid back to the place that they both wanted him to be.

He captured her lips as he slid home for the first time, and Aloriah thought for sure that she was going to faint from the pleasure of it, able to feel not only her own pleasure, but his as well. When he drew back and thrust back in, she moved to meet him, shuddering. They both moaned as the pleasure grew, taking them higher and higher, and when Chase finally shuddered and collapsed, spent, Aloriah welcomed his weight, shuddering with her own unexpected reaction to his love making.

When he was able to catch his breath and rolled away to dispose of the used condom, Aloriah thought that was the end of it. She was just gathering her wits to get up and get herself dressed when he rolled back to her side and wrapped her in his arms. A soft kiss and a sigh followed as he made himself comfortable, silently encouraging her to put her head on his shoulder and get comfortable herself. Another sigh, and he looked at her with a dreamy smile on his face.

"You are the most magnificent lover I have ever known." he told her, giving her another deep kiss that restarted the fires of her passion. This time, instead of pursuing it, he closed his eyes, just enjoying the feel of her naked body pressed close to his.

Confused, but very satiated, Aloriah followed his lead, rubbing her hand across his hairy chest, briefly touching the nipple ring that always made her smile, as it was a little hint of his rebellious spirit that most people would never know existed. Her eyes got heavy, and soon she was asleep, held comfortably in strong arms. When he heard her breathing slow and even out, Chase lifted his head for just a moment to look at her sleeping face, a self-satisfied smile crossing his own face before he totally relaxed and joined her in slumber.

Chase awoke to a distant ringing sound, but it stopped before he was fully awake, so he settled back down, pulling Aloriah a little closer. She stirred slightly, blinking her eyes to look up at him, and smiled sleepily.

"Hey." she whispered, and Chase smiled back at her.

"Hey." he whispered back, and started to tip his head to kiss her, but his cell phone in his jeans pocket started to ring. The way he wrinkled his nose made Aloriah laugh, but she moved so that he could slip away from her and grab his phone.

"Hello."

He listened for a moment, a dark frown replacing the smile on his face.

"But Uncle Jack, I was supposed to have a week off." Looking toward Aloriah, who was sitting up on the bed and pulling a blanket around herself, he added. "I have a guest."

Again, he listened, and again, he frowned.

"Well, can I take along a rider? I'm sure my guest would rather be riding with me across country than sitting here bored in Gram's house with no way to go anywhere unless my folks take pity on her."

A look of surprise crossed his face.

"Really? I just need Dad's okay?"

The smile slowly returned, and he reached over to run his hand over the arm that Aloriah had laying on top of the blanket. His emotions were soaring, and she felt like she couldn't wait for him to hang up the phone to find out why he was so ecstatic. He gave her a wink as he responded to whatever his Uncle Jack had just said.

"Oh, we'll talk him into it. Trust me. He already likes Aloriah. I'll call you from Dad's tomorrow so he can confirm it for you himself. Later, Uncle Jack."

As he hung up the phone, he leaned toward her, and she felt his intent to collect the kiss the cell had interrupted before he could collect. She leaned forward to let him take it, then as he leaned back, his eyes danced with the excitement he was emoting.

"So, what do you think of the idea of traveling all over the country in my truck with me?"

Chapter 11

When Aloriah opened her eyes the next morning, Chase was no longer in the bed, but her bathing suit was in the space he had been occupying. Remembering the "rules" he had told her about, she laughed and brought it with her into the bathroom, almost sad to be washing his smell off her, but wanting to be sure not to offend the man who would be holding her future in his hands. Still not 100% sure she liked the way she looked in a bathing suit, she went into her room and pulled on a pair of jeans and a t-shirt, then grabbed her new sneakers and padded barefoot down the stairs.

Chase had coffee brewed and was making waffles with strawberries and whipped cream, and as she stepped into the room, he frowned.

"Did you forget the rule?"

With a grin, she lifted her shirt to show him the bathing suit, and he smiled and pulled her close for a quick kiss, then handed her a plate of waffles to bring to the table and asked her to pour him a coffee.

"How do you drink it?" she asked, finding

which cupboard held the cups.

"Black." came the answer, and she wrinkled her nose, which made him laugh and tease. "Must be a girl thing to ruin it with cream and sugar."

When they had finished breakfast, and washed and put away the dishes, Chase handed her a backpack and asked her to put in a couple of the large beach towels that he kept on a shelf above the washing machine. At her look of confusion when she looked at the backpack, he gave her a grin.

"We're taking my other mode of transport today." was all he would say.

When they reached the garage, he handed her a helmet and smiled, then grabbed a second helmet and walked past the car to a beautiful black motorcycle. Following him to get a closer look at the motorcycle, which had "Moto Guzzi" emblazoned on its gas tank, she was so obviously impressed that he couldn't help bragging just a little.

"It's Italian, made by the oldest motorcycle manufacturer in Europe. Really nice machine."

When he started to put on the helmet, she stopped him.

"I thought you didn't like helmets."

His look was incredulous.

"After meeting my mom, do you honestly think I'd ride into her yard without one?"

Aloriah thought for just a moment about his mother. Teresanna appeared to be a full foot shorter than her husband and son, but even though she hadn't sensed a mean bone in the woman's body, when Teresanna said "jump", both men said "How high?"

Not wishing to find out how the tiny woman had earned such respect, she put on her own helmet and strapped the backpack on before joining Chase on the beautiful machine.

When they pulled into the drive and parked the motorcycle out of the way between the house and garage, Lynn and Angie were outside on a bench next to the front door. Getting off the motorcycle and leaving their helmets, they approached the girls.

"Mom and Dad here?"

"In the weight room." Angie looked up from texting to reply.

Chase closed his eyes for just a moment, making Aloriah frown at his sudden discomfort, then he slipped his arm around her waist.

"Shall we?"

In the weight room, Kyle was doing his Tai Chi stretching, but picking on his wife, who had left him sleeping alone to get up and make breakfast for the girls.

"The girls are going to go shopping, so you leave your poor husband to fend for himself, and then he finds you in here lifting wimpy amounts of weight." He glanced over his shoulder to see if she was feeling sorry for him, but she just smiled.

"The weights aren't wimpy just because I'm not trying to be a big, bulky man, like you. I need muscles that are smooth and sexy." When she said the words "smooth" and "sexy", she put special emphasis on them. "Men who want big and bulky use heavy weights and low reps. Women who want smooth and sexy use smaller weights and more reps."

Looking at her and licking his lips, Kyle walked over and swung his long legs over her, putting his hands on the bench press bar to prevent her from continuing to lift.

"Okay, you're right. I *really* like smooth and sexy."

As he bent and gave her a kiss, she sighed, remembering several other workouts that she hadn't finished when his amorous tendencies had come out to play. Today, however, there was a bellow from the great room.

"Hark, hark! A child approaches!"

Kyle growled, but with one more kiss, he went back to his spot and started stretching while Teresanna, her count disrupted, started her lifting again at one.

As Aloriah and Chase came to the door, she was murmuring something to him about not having to announce themselves like that, at least until she felt the residual emotions in the room. She stopped at the door, and Chase grinned as he saw her eyes widen already starting to recognize when she was getting a *feeling*. Trying not to let her reaction show to his parents, Aloriah looked at the floor and shook her head to rid herself of the emotional overload, then looked up with a smile only to have her senses bombarded again by the visual shock of seeing Chase's parents in their workout gear.

Teresanna, in a tank top, yoga pants and sneakers, with her hair pulled up while she did bench presses was shocking enough. She was very lean and very much in shape, with muscles that moved like those of a big cat. It was Kyle, dressed like his son was beside her in karate pants, a muscle shirt and sneakers, who really took her breath away, because the outfit did more to highlight just how massive the man was than to hide anything.

If she were to compare the two men, Chase would have been like a thoroughbred, muscular, but more built for speed. In comparison, Kyle was muscled like a Clydesdale, a real work horse. And when he turned as if just noticing their arrival to give a slow, lady-killer smile...

Aloriah was tempted to fan herself, but didn't want to offend Chase.

Seeing his son's guest in jeans and a t-shirt, Kyle got a mischievous gleam in his eye as he turned and started walking toward them. Chase smiled, but whispered through his teeth "Be ready to show the swim suit."

"Good morning." Kyle greeted, a little too cheerfully. "Have you come to work out with us?"

Aloriah felt like she was about to swallow her tongue, intimidated by that all too male body in such close proximity, but she lifted her shirt the same way she had done for Chase and squeaked "I came to swim."

An expression of exaggerated disappointment crossed Kyle's face, then he grabbed Chase's head and gave him a noogie, growling "Well then, *you* need to choose a weapon because you took away my chance to throw one of your friends in the pool by sharing the house rules with her."

Laughing, Chase gave Aloriah a wink, then

suggested she go stand with his mother to be out of harm's way. He walked over to a display on the wall and chose a long bo staff. Kyle followed to get his own bo staff, then made sure the ladies were well back before going into the middle of the clear floor space with his son.

As Aloriah approached her, Teresanna stood up and grabbed a nearby towel to wipe away some sweat, then showed the younger woman where to stand to be able to watch the pending battle without ending up with a staff to the head. Seeing the look of concern on Aloriah's face, she smiled.

"Don't be too worried. They do this all the time, and Kyle really needs the workout." Taking a swig of water from her water bottle, Teresanna continued. "The girls and I know self-defense, but Kyle won't spar with us because he's afraid he'll hurt us. Chase is the only one he lets loose with."

While his wife was talking, Kyle had lifted the staff to his shoulders and stretched, smiling when Chase mirrored his move, then they both bowed before taking traditional defense postures to begin. The first strike happened with lightning speed, and Aloriah gasped as it looked like Kyle was going to split open Chase's skull, but with the same lightning speed, Chase blocked and responded with an attack of his own.

Aloriah stood watching with her mouth dropped open, as she had thought she had seen a good example of Chase's skill in New Orleans. That demonstration had barely brushed the surface of what he was capable of when he had an opponent of his father's skill level. By the time the men stopped, sweating and sure to be sporting some bruises from the missed blocks, she had decided that she was going to have Chase teach her self-defense while they were on the road. That is, if his father gave permission for her to ride with him.

While Chase put both bo staffs back in their places, Kyle grabbed his own towel and water bottle, then the men approached the ladies, both panting and sweaty from the exertion. Teresanna offered her son her towel to mop away some of the sweat when he stopped next to Aloriah, and he took it with a smile, wiping his face while he got enough breath back to speak.

"I'm going for a glass of water. Would you like one?"

Aloriah smiled, still a little stunned at what she had just watched.

"No, you go ahead, but I want to learn some self-defense whenever you get the chance to start giving me lessons."

Chase responded with a brilliant smile, then handed the towel back before heading for the kitchen. Kyle, having caught his breath enough to continue the conversation, looked at Aloriah with interest.

"Do you know any self-defense?"

Her lip curled slightly as she responded.

"My mom wanted me to learn when I started junior high, but I had already developed the binge eating problem. My dad said there was no use wasting the money when any man in his right mind wouldn't want to rape someone who looked like me."

Both Kyle and Teresanna looked shocked, then as Teresanna put a comforting arm around Aloriah's waist, Kyle's face contorted into a fierce snarl.

"Your father had better hope I never meet him without people around to protect him."

A little startled by the anger she felt behind those words, Aloriah remembered one of the rumors Chase had told her about, and she found she couldn't resist a little teasing.

"Yeah, I've heard a rumor that you know places around here where no one would ever find a body."

The snarl morphed into an evil looking smile and there was a gleam in Kyle's eyes.

"He could be the first person to prove that rumor true."

Aloriah joined Teresanna in a laugh at that, then Teresanna suggested she start her education with the first rule of self-defense. When Aloriah looked at her with a confused frown, the older woman smiled.

"Has Chase shown you the scar on his shoulder?"

"Yes."

Teresanna nodded sagely.

"That was because he forgot the first rule."

Aloriah remembered what he'd said about that, and got a laugh out of Kyle when she was able to say the rule in unison with Teresanna.

"Disarm first, then neutralize."

With a little encouragement from Teresanna, the two ladies stepped out into the cleared space with Kyle close behind, and as Teresanna acted as the "attacker" with an invisible knife, Kyle first showed the move, then had Aloriah practice. She was, at first, a little nervous when he would touch her to make a correction, but she soon found that she could ignore the touch and concentrate on what they were trying to teach her. As when Chase had done his demonstration in New Orleans, they went through the moves slowly the first couple of times, then sped up until the moves were accomplished at normal speed.

Aloriah was so intent on the lesson, she didn't realize that Chase had come back and was watching until he started to applaud when she had succeeded "disarming and neutralizing" his mother. From her spot on the floor, where she had dropped to demonstrate how a real attacker would fall if Aloriah was successful in her technique, Teresanna smiled up at her son.

"She's a fast learner! If you bring her here every day, we can have her trained to watch your back when you go back out next week."

The uncomfortable look that crossed Chase's face alerted both his parents before he started to speak.

"Yeah, about when I go back out."

He gave his mom a moment to be pulled back to her feet by his dad, then looked from one to the other while he spoke.

"Uncle Jack called last night. He's had to fire Brian."

"Now what did that sh....." Kyle looked at Aloriah before the rest of the foul word made it out of his mouth, and modified what he was going to say. "...jerk do?"

Trying not to laugh at the obvious change in terms, Aloriah took a deep breath and keyed in on the older couple's emotions. Both were somewhat upset, but waiting patiently for the explanation.

"He violated the three strike rule. It was the third time he'd started a fight with another trucker that resulted in damage to the truck."

Kyle rolled his eyes while Teresanna shook her head in disgust, then she asked the question that was most important to them both.

"How soon does he want you back on the road?"

Chase cleared his throat and tried not to look at Aloriah, as he hadn't even shared this part with her, afraid of what it might mean to her if his father turned him down.

"Tomorrow morning. The load is in Malden, Mass and needs to get to Orlando, Florida as soon as possible." Then he caught Aloriah's eyes. "I'd really love to have Ree come with me, but Uncle Jack says you need to okay that."

He stood quietly, his tongue playing with the place where his lip ring would have been if he had put it in, and waited to see if there was going to be an explosion. Kyle saw Aloriah looking at him and gave her a wink, sounding for all the world like he was serious even though his left eyebrow was flying high.

"Well, gee son, I don't know. What can she bring to the table other than making sure you don't fall asleep and wreck my truck?"

"Well, she *is* empathic, so she can probably keep us out of mischief by reading the emotions of the other truckers and getting us out of there if any of them want to start fights."

Kyle got a thoughtful look on his face as he stared up at the ceiling, and Teresanna seemed to be studying the view out the window while Aloriah played along with the game and looked worried. She mimed a circus strong man and gave Chase silent encouragement to suggest that she could help with the loading and unloading, but he shook his head. Kyle fought a smile as he saw them in his peripheral vision, and by the time he looked at his son again, he was all seriousness.

"Well, if you promise to teach her self-defense so that she can come back and defend herself against a real attack from me..."

Chase was nodding enthusiastically and a grin broke across Kyle's face as he grabbed his son and hoisted him up onto his shoulder.

"And if you let me throw you into the pool!" Kyle bellowed, and went to the deep end of the pool to follow through by actually throwing Chase in, fully dressed. Chase came up sputtering, but was soon laughing.

"Thanks, dad!"

Winking at Aloriah and patting her shoulder as he passed her on the way back into the weight room, Kyle went through to the house to go upstairs for a shower and a change into his own bathing suit. Teresanna paused to smile at the younger woman.

"Make sure to call us if you two start getting on each other's nerves, okay? We can always fly you back and bring you to Chase's house if the truck cab turns out to be too tight a space for you. Not everyone is cut out for traveling in a sleeper."

"Thank you." Aloriah said, then, with a grin, peeled off her jeans and t-shirt to cannonball Chase, hearing Teresanna laugh as she went back to weight lifting.

Chapter 12

After a morning mostly spent swimming, followed by one of Teresanna's healthy, filling lunches, the two couples went out onto the screened porch to enjoy the breezes coming across the valley while Kyle went over some of the things he expected from Aloriah if she was to represent Jack and Benny Trucking. Chase sat beside Aloriah with his arm along the back of the bentwood love seat while Kyle and Teresanna sat in matching bentwood arm chairs across from each other, Teresanna next to Chase and Kyle next to Aloriah. Kyle had promised that he would just hit the "high points" and let Chase teach her all the little details as they traveled.

"For a trucking company like ours, image equals money, so the big three that I'm going to go over with you are the most important things for you to remember, okay?"

Aloriah nodded and took a deep breath, feeling the seriousness of the moment.

"First is how you look. How you showed up today is perfect. You looked ready to work and reasonably clean cut."

"No nipple rings." Chase interjected from beside her, and Aloriah elbowed him. Kyle grinned, knowing about his son's piercing, and amended that thought.

"Tattoos, nipple piercings, that kind of thing are okay, but they need to either be tasteful or easily hidden under your clothes."

"I can get a tat?" Chase sounded surprised, but Aloriah could tell he just wanted to see how far he could push his dad.

"It's your body, but if it's on your face, it had better be the Jack and Benny logo."

It was evident that Kyle wasn't going to let his eldest child goad him as he continued. "Second is that you need to be punctual for the pickups and drop offs. Jack is careful to give a 'range' for when you're going to arrive to make allowances for traffic conditions, but if you run into delays, like a break down, accident or some such, you need to call Jack so he can call the customer and keep them informed."

"In other words, Uncle Jack is the bullshit artist when it comes to delays so that we don't have to be." Chase interjected, and Kyle pretended to wipe something out of his eye with his middle finger. Teresanna grinned and took the third most important rule.

"Third is, no matter how tempted you are to do so, you don't make hand signals, like the one my loving husband just demonstrated, in front of the customer. Clean language and clean hand signals, at least in the customer's presence."

"But once we're out of their sight, you can say whatever you want and make whatever hand signals you want." Chase added.

Teresanna revealed her playful side then by faking a cough that was actually her saying "asshole". Kyle looked shocked.

"Teresanna Lee Benton! Is that really necessary?"

It was her turn to fake the wide, innocent eyes.

"What?"

"You know what!" Kyle said sternly. "And I know where you sleep!"

She seemed unfazed by that threat and responded with "And I know where you're ticklish."

"Nowhere!" Kyle said between clenched teeth. "I'm not ticklish. Not at all."

Teresanna rolled her eyes.

"Yeah. Okay. You're not ticklish." Under her breath, she added, "And the Pope isn't Catholic."

Both Chase and Aloriah shook with suppressed laughter while Kyle fixed her with a mock glare. She looked back with mock innocence until he shook his head, and then went back to what he'd been talking about.

"Now then, we've gone over proper dress, promptness and proper attitude. Since Chase isn't of age to drink until November and you aren't of age until..."

"Two more years from next week."

Kyle looked at her with a surprised smile. "Really?"

She nodded.

"Well, Happy Birthday a little early." He cleared his throat. "Do I need to tell you that I won't be happy if either of you are caught drunk or doing drugs in the truck?"

Chase started to open his mouth for a wise crack, but Kyle's glare stopped him. However Teresanna wasn't as easily controlled, and she leaned forward to stage whisper.

"Make sure you leave the flask in your suitcase at the house. You can pick it back up the next time Chase gets a few days off at home."

Kyle playfully face palmed, but Aloriah felt a little sorry for him even though she could tell he wasn't really upset at the silliness of his family.

"Yes, sir." she said respectfully, and Kyle peeked over his hand.

"Sir. I like that. I think you'll work out just fine."

Chase was suddenly overtaken by a huge yawn, and his father looked at him with his eyebrow raised.

"Am I keeping you up past your nap time, boy?"

"No, but I didn't sleep as well as normal last night."

Remembering how Chase had gotten her to go back to sleep after Jack's call the night before, Aloriah blushed deeply. Kyle noticed, but didn't say anything, at least, not right away.

Chase stood up.

"We probably ought to get back to the house. We have to pack, and get supper, and knowing Uncle Jack, our ETA will only work if we get into and out of Malden when it's not rush hour."

The older couple seemed to accept that excuse for them leaving so early, and walked them to the door to be able to say goodbye. When Chase yawned a second time, Kyle seemed concerned, putting his arm around his son's shoulders.

"You know, if you're unsafe to drive home right now, you two can cop a nap in the guest room upstairs and go back to your house later." Leaning in so that Chase would be the only one who heard the next comment, he whispered "I even put in soundproofing when I redid the walls last year."

Chase shot his father a glare and poked an elbow into the older man's stomach, but Kyle didn't even flinch. Instead, he laughed, his eyes gleaming with mischief.

"Do I even want to know what that was about?" Teresanna asked, and both men looked at her with wide eyes.

"No!" they said in unison.

Putting her arm around Aloriah's shoulders, Teresanna sighed.

"I'm so sorry, sweetie. I had control of the kids for nine months, but once they came out, they were under the influence of their dad."

Aloriah laughed, feeling much more comfortable with this unorthodox family than she had ever felt with her own.

Chapter 13

After getting hugged and told she was loved by Chase's parents as they were leaving the barn house, Aloriah was very glad they were on the Guzzi for the ride back to his house, as she was all choked up and very sure she would have cried if they had been in the Mustang and Chase had looked at her. She had just managed to gain control when he pulled up to the door to let her off, taking her helmet in exchange for the house key, asking her to toss the wet towels and her bathing suit into the washing machine while he got the Guzzi and the Mustang under their dust covers.

As she finished the task he had set her to, getting into clean clothes and throwing in her jeans and t-shirt as well, since they also smelled of chlorine, he came in, announced that the garage was "locked down", and stripped naked to throw his clothes in before starting the machine. Giving her a kiss with a devilish smile, he padded naked through the house and up the stairs while she started their supper.

While they ate, Chase went through the list of

things they needed to do before going to bed, which included making sure that they had enough clothes put away into the storage bins in the sleeper section of his truck to last for several days. By law, he explained, he could be on the road for eight days before he needed to take a couple of days off, but Jack always made sure that the longest his driver traveled was six days, and then got a minimum of two-and-a-half days to rest. In addition, they could only be on the road a maximum of eleven hours straight before he needed to take a mandatory ten hour rest period, but if they stopped for lunch and supper, he could work a total of fourteen hours per day before the rest period.

"I'll show you how we keep track of that in the log book tomorrow. Those are federal laws, so we can't break them, or Uncle Jack and Dad will both nail my butt to the wall. And just so you know, it's not just Dad who doesn't like drinking and drugs in the trucks. Federal law allows us to be pulled over and tested at any time for the safety of the other drivers on the road."

"What about that 'three strike rule' you and your dad were talking about?"

Chase smiled, finishing his bite of food before answering.

"On everything except the federal restrictions, Uncle Jack will let you goof three times before he gives you your walking papers, but he is pretty lenient about it. For instance, say we stop at this first stop and you get out of the truck in a tank top with no bra on..."

"Like I ever would." she interrupted, but

Chase smiled, ogling her breasts until she blushed.

"I'd enjoy it if you did, but chances are good that a lot of the customers would report you to Uncle Jack for inappropriate clothing. He'd call you and give you the first warning and tell you that was strike one. If you make sure to wear a bra and t-shirt for at least six months with no other complaints, he'll wipe that off your record and start again with strike one the next time he gets the complaint call about inappropriate clothing. If you just keep wearing the same clothing, you'll be allowed two more complaints before you're let go."

"I see." Aloriah said thoughtfully. "If you take the warning and correct the problem, he rewards you. If you don't, bye bye baby."

"There you go."

Aloriah thought carefully.

"So this Brian guy had been warned twice for starting fights and did it again?"

Chase smiled, but shook his head.

"He wasn't just fired for the fighting. He was fired for starting fights that caused damage to the truck three separate times. The trucks are expensive enough to maintain with just the normal stuff that can go wrong. Uncle Jack gave the warnings because of having to pay garages to take out dents and replace lights and windows when the damages were perfectly preventable if Brian had just learned to keep his mouth shut."

With supper ended, Aloriah washed, Chase dried, and then she switched the clothes they had washed to the dryer while they went upstairs to pack. Chase had left a duffle bag in her room that held more than her battered suitcase, and she smiled as she found she could put in everything she had and still have room for the her clothing that was in the dryer. By the time she had finished, Chase was leaning in the doorway watching her with a little smile, his own duffle bag, which hadn't really been fully unpacked after his arrival home, and what he called the "shower bag" on the floor at his feet.

"It has towels, wash cloths, soap, and shampoo. You know, the kind of things you need to carry into a truck stop shower if we don't happen to make it to a hotel before we have to do the ten hour rest break."

After bringing her out to the truck and showing her where to store their gear, Chase went back in and collected the laundry from the dryer, then made one more look through to make sure everything that had to be in the truck made it out there. He handed up all the things he had collected, then ran a check of all the truck's systems, making sure that all the internal fluids were at proper levels, it started normally, and that the windshield was clean both inside and out while he had a tall stepstool to get the outside properly clean. Aloriah, who had only seen him when he was relaxed, was fascinated with watching the side of him that she secretly named "Business Chase".

When everything was ready, Chase helped her down, then wrapped his arm over her shoulders as they walked back into the house. He was back to the relaxed Chase she'd gotten used to, and when he kissed her on the temple, he was smiling.

"Are you ready for bed?"

She looked up at the still-bright sky, then back at him with a confused frown. He laughed.

"To make it into Malden before rush hour traffic, we need to leave Greenville at about 3 a.m."

Aloriah groaned, and Chase turned her so that he could look into those golden eyes he was becoming so fond of. As he leaned in for a kiss, he murmured "You just have to get out to the truck and climb into the sleeper. I'll take care of all the driving."

The kiss took Aloriah's mind off the early departure and made her eager to hit the sheets, but as they walked into the kitchen, Chase groaned.

"I forgot about the food."

Looking at him strangely for a moment, she followed him over to the refrigerator, where they went through all the food they had bought. Anything that could be frozen went into the freezer, and the vegetables, eggs and the small amount of milk left over brought about a quick call to his parents to let them know what they needed to stop by and pick up to use at their house. Once he'd hung up the phone, he looked at Aloriah with a grin.

"I forgot to do that my second trip out, and had to replace the refrigerator when I got back because it was so nasty. I'd rather call Mom and let them use the food than have to do that again."

"How long were you gone?"

Chase wrinkled his nose.

"Six months."

Imagining what the food in a running refrigerator would look and smell like after six months, her own nose wrinkled, making Chase laugh at her funny face.

"I appreciate that you remembered to do that." she told him, then stood on her toes to kiss him and show him how much she appreciated it. Chase groaned as she reminded him where he was going before he thought about the food, and when she backed away, he threw her over his shoulder and carried her upstairs. Aloriah squealed that he was going to give himself a hernia, but he just laughed, not setting her down until he dropped her onto the bed and threw himself down beside her to show her, in no uncertain terms, that carrying her up over the stairs hadn't hurt him at all.

Sometime later, when they were both too lethargic to move and drifting closer and closer to full sleep, Chase breathed a sigh against Aloriah's neck and whispered into her ear.

"I love you, Ree."

With a smile, she hugged the arm that was wrapped around her waist and whispered back.

"I love you, Chase."

Chapter 14

2 a.m.

Chase woke to his alarm, forced himself to push away from the soft warmth that was Aloriah, and padded naked to the bathroom for a long, hot shower. Getting out feeling more awake and ready to go, he carefully shaved and left the towel hanging so it would dry properly. Chances were good that his mother would get the sheets and towels washed before he made it back home again, but just in case, he always made sure to leave his damp towels so they wouldn't get moldy.

Turning on a light when he got to his room to be able to see where his clothes were, he smiled when Aloriah groaned and pulled a pillow over her face. He took pity on her, dressing himself before sitting beside her on the bed to gently urge her out from under the pillow.

"Come on, sweetie. Time to get up and get dressed. Remember, you can climb right into the sleeper if you want."

Aloriah groaned again, but sat up yawning,

accepting her clothes as Chase handed them to her. He helped her out by hooking the back of her bra and, when she was fumbling with the laces of her sneakers, tying her shoes for her. When she stood up, he dropped his leather jacket around her shoulders and gave her a gentle push down the hall, telling her "Make sure to stop in the bathroom, because it will be a couple of hours before we stop anywhere. I'll make the bed and be right along."

She was coming back out of the bathroom when Chase came down the hall, and he pulled her into his arms for a quick hug before guiding her down the stairs. She stood on the porch waiting while he locked the deadbolt, glad that she had his jacket over her shoulders to keep her warm in the cool night, then they went out to the barn together.

Ensuring that she was safely in the cab before going around to the driver's side, Chase climbed up to find that she had already slipped off her sneakers and was sliding beneath the covers. She pulled his jacket up to her face, unaware that he was watching her, and breathed in the scent of Axe that clung to it, smiling as that smell surrounded her as she drifted back to sleep. With a smile of his own, Chase started the truck, backed out of the barn, and started down the road.

A little over an hour later, as Chase was pulling into a parking space at the Irving station in Newport for a coffee, Aloriah stirred and yawned. Looking back at her, he asked "Are you ready for a coffee?"

She shook her head, rolled into a more comfortable position, and went back to sleep. After making sure the doors were all securely locked, Chase made his way inside, chuckling as he walked. Obviously, his traveling partner wasn't an early riser, but even with her asleep in the bed behind him, he felt better having her along rather than leaving her behind at the house.

Just after they had crossed the border into New Hampshire, Chase heard a sound behind him. Aloriah slipped into the seat and buckled her seatbelt, then looked at the signs trying to figure out where they were without a word. Chase, ecstatic to have someone to talk to, gave her a smile.

"Good morning, sleepy sweetie!"

"You're awfully daring to be so cheerful when I haven't had coffee yet." came the gruff response, but Chase just continued to smile.

"So I take it you won't object if we pull off and get some breakfast?"

Aloriah didn't get the chance to answer, as the rumble from her stomach echoed in the cab. She blushed while Chase fought not to embarrass her more by laughing, then she said softly "I'm not much of a travel companion, am I."

"You're doing really well for a newbie who had a 2:30 a.m. wake-up call." he assured her, and she looked at him in confusion.

"I thought you said we were leaving the house at 3."

Chase grinned.

"We did. But I had to wake you up early enough to get you dressed and make sure you had a bathroom break before I loaded you into the sleeper."

Looking at him with a sudden suspicion, she couldn't resist asking the question.

"And how long before you woke me up were you up?"

Peeking at her over the top of his sunglasses, he thought truth was best.

"I got up at 2 so I could wake myself up with a shower first."

"Geesh. Now I feel like a real heel for sleeping while you drove."

Putting his hand on her knee, he squeezed gently.

"You'll get used to the weird schedules. Before long, you'll be getting up first and making us coffee before you wake me."

With a smirk, she responded, "Don't hold your breath waiting for that day, because you'd look really funny as a Smurf."

Chase snorted, but didn't respond. Instead, he turned on his blinker for the next exit, pulling into a restaurant just off the interstate. Reaching into a pouch on the right side of his seat, he pulled out a clip board with current log book page uppermost, showing her the way they kept track of how much time he was behind the wheel, how much time he was on duty, but not driving, how much time he was in the sleeper, and how long he was on rest breaks.

"Here's where we were in bed in Greenville." he showed her. "And this is when we left." He looked at the clock and marked the time for the beginning of their breakfast break, drawing a line through the "driving" section for the three and a half hours he'd been on the road. "I'll have you start keeping track of the log so you can warn me when we have one hour left before we hit eleven hours in the driving column. That way we can get off the road and, hopefully, into a comfortable sleep situation."

"I thought the sleeper was comfortable enough." Aloriah teased, and Chase leaned forward to give her a steamy kiss.

"Not for what I have in mind for part of the rest period."

Much to Aloriah's chagrin, her stomach growled again. She wanted to punch herself in the stomach and let Chase keep kissing her, but he withdrew with a smile.

"Let's go see what we can do to stop that noise for a while."

After locking up and climbing down on her side, Aloriah went to the front of the truck and met Chase, who took her hand and led the way in. Inside, he greeted several other truckers he knew, introducing her to everyone as *my girlfriend and new riding partner*. When they were seated, he gave her suggestions as to what meals were good and what meals weren't worth the money. When their food was brought out and she playfully barricaded her plate with the menus that she hadn't let the waitress take away so that he couldn't slip any extra food on her plate, he laughed and solemnly swore to not do that to her for the duration of their trip.

After breakfast, when she climbed back into the truck, Aloriah proved how fast she could learn by taking the log book and marking the end of their meal, drawing the line across as Chase had done.

She gave him a wink and put the log book back where he kept it as he started the truck, and they continued the drive to Malden.

A trailer had been left when Brian's tractor was damaged in the fight, so the load was ready to go when they pulled into the factory. Getting out, speaking to the factory owner to confirm what was in the load and where they were to deliver it, Aloriah found herself feeling uncomfortable for the first time since she had been picked up by Chase in Orono. The people moving around this parking lot weren't judging Jack and Benny Trucking by the driver, but by the company he kept, so after a quick stretching of her legs, she silently climbed back up into the truck, and waited for Chase to finish his business.

After the trailer was properly attached and Chase rejoined her in the cab to begin the journey to Orlando, he noted aloud that she was awfully quiet, but Aloriah just gave him a sad smile and didn't want to discuss it. Rather than returning to I-95, Chase asked her to bring up the internet on his I Pad and give him directions to I-84. When she questioned, he smiled at her and told her that, considering the time, it was the best way to avoid bumper-to-bumper traffic through New York, Philadelphia and Washington, DC.

"I'm one of those really grumpy people who'll want to start pushing cars out of the way if I have to sit too long in traffic." he confessed.

"But according to these maps, it takes more time to go that way."

Chase grinned.

"Remember meeting Bear in New Orleans?"

Remembering the huge man with the scar on his wrist, she nodded.

"He and I were both doing southern runs and bumped into each other in a restaurant in Portsmouth, New Hampshire. He bet he could take I-95 and beat me to a hotel in Savannah, Georgia where we were both planning on staying for our off duty days. On paper, his route saves you about 2 hours, but traffic was horrible through all three cities, and he got stuck in bottlenecks at toll booths more than once, so I pulled in almost a full hour before he did." A devilish smile crossed his face. "He doesn't bet with me anymore."

Aloriah was going to make a comment about him also not sneaking up behind Chase any more, but Chase's cell, which he was carrying in the pocket of his shirt, started to ring. Pulling it out to glance at who it was, Chase answered with a smile.

"Hey, Uncle Jack. What's up?"

"Hi kiddo. Just a couple of questions for you about the customer in Malden."

"Ok, fire away."

"What is your new partner wearing today?"

Chase frowned, glancing over at Aloriah.

"A plain black t-shirt, jeans, sneakers."

"And she doesn't have any piercings, tattoos, anything like that showing?"

Chase snorted and answered his question with a question.

"Do you honestly think Dad would have let her come along if that was a problem?"

While Aloriah looked out the window at the passing scenery and tried not to listen in, she started frowning, reacting to Chase's underlying frustration at being questioned without being told why. Catching on to that frustration from his nephew's tone of voice, Jack sighed and explained.

"The customer called and reported that she was inappropriately dressed. He told me he wouldn't do any more business with Jack and Benny Trucking if she continued to ride along."

Chase's jaw clenched.

"So are you going to tell me that I have to send her home?"

Jack laughed.

"Nope! This guy just violated the three strike rule." Aloriah looked over as Chase's emotions went from anger to confusion, seeing the emotion reflected on his face before his uncle continued on the other end of the line. "The first time we picked up for him, he reported that the driver was sloppy and unprofessional. I figured he just didn't like that John has a beard, so I sent Brian. He reported Brian was rude. That one I believe, but nonetheless, the third complaint about our third employee? I trust your opinion more than his as to whether or not your lady is dressed as your dad suggested."

A grin broke across Chase's face like the sun coming out from behind a cloud, and his voice reflected his relief.

"Thanks, Uncle Jack. She's a really good companion, and is already learning how to help me keep track of my log book. I appreciate your trust in me."

Jack laughed softly.

"The day I believe some guy in Massachusetts

over my own nephew is the day I need to retire. Now how about you let me talk to your lovely companion for just a minute while you get back to concentrating on your driving."

"Okay. I'll talk to you later."

Chase handed the phone to Aloriah just in time to see the one mile warning for their turn. She lifted the phone to her ear, her tone questioning, as he checked all his mirrors and switched into the proper lane.

"Hello?"

Jack's voice at the other end was a little higher than the Benton men, but just as friendly.

"Hi there. I understand from my brother-in-law that your name is Aloriah."

Smiling herself, feeling his acceptance even over the cell phone connection, she responded in her friendliest tone.

"Yes, but if it's easier, you can call me Ree, like Chase does."

'Good enough, Ree. Welcome to Jack and Benny Trucking. My only request is that you keep that nephew of mine in line for me, okay?"

Looking over at Chase, knowing that he was listening, she pretended to be worried about that directive.

"Keep him in line? That's an awfully tall order for my first time out, isn't it?"

Jack laughed, deciding even without being able to see her that he really liked his nephew's latest girlfriend. She had the same sense of humor as the rest of the family and should fit right in.

"If he gets too wild, just yank out his nipple

ring." He joked.

It was Aloriah's turn to laugh, and after thanking Jack for letting her ride with Chase, she hung up and handed him back his phone, feeling like her life might finally be turning around. Putting his phone back in his pocket, Chase got them onto the right road, and then cleared his throat, suddenly understanding her odd behavior in Malden.

"So, I take it your empathy told you that guy in Malden was a bit of a jerk?"

She blushed.

"And I should probably share that with you next time?" She asked shyly.

Chase just gave her a glance over the top of his sunglasses, confirming her belief that this might be the one man who she might be able to trust with all her secrets, including what her strange gift was telling her.

Later that evening, she informed him he had an hour and a half left before he had to be off the road, and then yawned. Smiling over at her, he suggested that she could go back into the sleeper, but she was determined to stay awake, and insisted she would stay in her seat. Her body won out, though. When Chase looked over at her a short time later, her head was leaned back against her seat and her eyes were closed.

Just as he was starting to watch for the next place where they could pull off and sleep, however, he glanced over to see her eyes open, staring straight at him with no sign that she was actually seeing him. As at his house, the voice that came out of her mouth was much deeper than her own speaking voice, but this time, there was no growl in the tone, so he was able to understand perfectly the southern accented warning that came out.

"Don't stop at the first place you see. Go on to the next truck stop."

Her eyes closed and she sighed, shifting slightly into a more comfortable position. The first truck stop, with several trucks already pulled into the spaces provided for the sleeper trucks, appeared within a couple of miles. Opting to trust whatever it was that spoke through her, he continued on, and Aloriah opened her eyes as they pulled into a little truck stop with just a few trucks around the back, a small restaurant, and no showers.

Making the choice to not tell her about her seeming premonition, Chase teased that he wanted her in a smaller place where no one could hear her screams, winking at her when she pretended to be afraid. Despite the small space provided by the sleeper, he did manage to make her cry out in ecstasy a short time later...

The next morning, as they climbed into the cab after a nice breakfast, Aloriah flipped on the radio as the truck started, joking that she had talked herself out the day before. As she adjusted the volume, the announcer was saying ". . . police are asking anyone who may have seen a vehicle matching that description pulling away from the truck stop in Harrisonburg, Virginia to please contact the hot line."

The announcer went on to state the number twice, then repeated the most important part of the story.

"Once again, police are saying that a man in a white pickup truck with an automatic weapon drove through a truck stop spraying bullets through all the sleeper trucks parked there at about 2 a.m., killing one and wounding twelve others. . ."

As they repeated the message for anyone with any further information to call the special hotline, Chase sat with his eyes wide, his face ghostly pale, and his hand over his mouth. His shock was palpable even without Aloriah being able to feel his emotions, and when he turned the radio down and turned to her, she was truly frightened.

He told her about what had happened after she dozed off sitting up, and it was Aloriah's turn to turn pale and hold her hand over her mouth with wide eyes. Taking a deep breath, imagining how he would have felt if he had ignored the warning and she had ended up hurt or dead, Chase took both her hands and looked deeply into her eyes.

"If you happen to be awake when you have one of those feelings, you tell me right away. I'd rather listen to you and have nothing happen than ignore that feeling and wind up hurt, okay." Giving her a little grin, he tried to lighten the mood a little.

"Use the Force, Ree."

Feeling a little better now that he was no longer alarmed and was joking about her special talent, she grinned back.

"I will, Captain."

Chapter 15

Over the next several weeks, Chase taught Aloriah all the ins and outs of the trucking industry as they traveled back and forth across the United States. For her part, she started to trust her empathic impressions more and more, giving him insights on some of the tougher customers they encountered as they pulled into the various businesses to do pickups and drop offs, allowing him to adjust his treatment of them accordingly and getting them more and more favorable reports. Jack was ecstatic, teasing her more than once that he was going to put empaths in all his trucks. Even Aloriah didn't realize the extent of her empathic talents, however, until one afternoon as they were hauling a load from Georgia to Colorado.

They were halfway across Oklahoma when Aloriah turned white as a sheet and asked Chase to pull over. He did so, turning to her to find her shaking like a leaf.

"What are you feeling?" he asked, and she tried to smile at the way he phrased that, as he now correctly guessed it to be her empathy rather than illness.

"I feel a great disturbance in the Force, as if millions of voices are crying out it terror."

Chase grinned at her Star Wars reference.

"So what do you want to do, Obi-wan?"

As he spoke, he turned his head to look out at the road ahead, wondering where the next exit was in case they needed to take a brief break, and suddenly *he* turned white.

"Never mind that question. I see your disturbance, even if it is a tad late in the year for that, since I've always been told the season for those is late spring. We're going to pull the truck off to the side of the road as far as we can, and abandon ship."

Looking where he just did, Aloriah saw the huge dark cloud that seemed to be dragging a tail behind it and understood what she was feeling.

Tornado!

And it appeared to be heading right toward them!

As Chase pulled the truck over, she reached into the back for a blanket out of the sleeper to use as protection against flying debris. She could almost sense his plan as he seemed to be studying the space where the ditch ran alongside the road, and definitely sensed his relief when he saw what he was looking for

"That space up ahead that looks like a culvert coming out of the bank just above the ditch. We're crawling in there if you think you can make it."

She looked even as she was opening her door to climb out, nodding, hearing Chase's door slam shut while she began to run toward it. In what felt like only a heartbeat, he was there beside her, and together, they made their way to the hollowed out area that looked like a culvert, but actually more closely resembled a shallow cave. Using his cell phone screen like a flashlight, Chase confirmed that there weren't any wild animals already sheltering there before he took the blanket from her and urged her inside, putting his own body between her and the threat of the tornado. Knowing the risk he was taking, Aloriah ignored the creepy feeling of roots and spider webs against the back of her neck to press as tightly as she could to the back of their makeshift storm cellar.

Pressing himself in as tightly as he could against her, Chase draped the blanket around his back, making sure that it was protecting every inch of exposed flesh and filling in around Aloriah as much as he could as the wind stared to pick up. When he was certain that they were as protected as he could make them, he wrapped his arms as far around her as the tight space allowed, braced himself against the walls, and began to silently pray.

Despite the roar that sounded like a freight train boring down on them, she felt safe and secure in the dark space with Chase's warm breath against the side of her neck, the emotions of the distant people that she was feeling in the truck overwhelmed by the determination of the man beside her to keep her safe. In the self-imposed darkness under the blanket, they heard the roar of the tornados approach, and something that sounded like a metallic scream. When Aloriah tried to pull the blanket back to see what it was, Chase stopped her. When she tried to protest, he captured her lips with his own, causing a sudden surge of lust that made everything else fade into non-existence.

When the noise died down outside and the normal sound of bird songs started to fill the air, Chase carefully lifted the blanket, now embedded with dirt, bits of wood and metal, and muttered a soft curse. The truck, despite the fact that he'd set the emergency brake before following Aloriah, had been dragged a short distance from where they'd left it and was lying on its side in the ditch. Part of the side of the trailer was peeled back just as if some giant hand had opened it like a can of sardines, and parts of the load scattered around. Despite the damage, it was evident that they had gotten very lucky, as the truck hadn't been in the direct path of the tornado, but out on the outer edge of the zone that was scattered with debris. Their little hiding hole was a little further away from the damage zone than the truck, preventing them from meeting the same fate as the truck. Pulling out his cell phone to try to call Jack, Chase gave another soft curse before holding it out to allow Aloriah to see that there was no service available.

"Care to take a little stroll with me, love?" He teased gently, and won a smile in return.

"Yeah, I think I need to stretch my legs a bit." She responded, as if he was asking her to take a walk through the park rather than setting out on a long hike to safety.

Taking her hand to keep her close, still somewhat shaken by the storm that had stranded them, Chase started to walk. They hadn't gone very far, however, when Aloriah stopped and lifted one foot, feeling something stabbing her through her sneaker. It was then that she realized she had on her rattiest pair of sneakers, the pair that the sole was starting to separate from the canvas upper. Much to Chase's amusement, she hooked her fingernail at the front if the sole, providing a comical voice to demonstrate what her problem was.

"Mmmm." said the sneaker, "This road has really tasty rocks."

Dropping to one knee on the side of the road to give her a place to sit so that she could pull the offending rocks out from between her foot and the damaged sole, Chase gave a dramatic sigh.

"You know, it's really sad when you feel the need to wear the pair of sneakers you use for picking up loose change when you work for my dad. Anyone would think that he doesn't pay you enough to put up with me."

Pausing for a moment, Aloriah turned and looked at him with a serious expression.

"Well, you know, he really doesn't pay very well considering what a rotten companion you are. I mean, seriously. Here you were in a nice dark place with a willing partner and you only kissed her?"

Acting like he was going to dump her onto her backside, Chase grinned at the way she wrapped her arms around his neck to keep her seat.

"Well, if you had hugged me like that, I might have had better ideas."

Both laughed as Aloriah finished cleaning the rocks out of her shoe, and then they started walking again. To prevent her sneaker from filling right back up, Aloriah started doing a strange little shake step, stepping firmly on her left foot, then shaking the right foot to dislodge any rocks as she brought it forward. Seeing her odd step, Chase started doing a similar step as if he were her mirror image, making her giggle.

"What are you doing?" she asked, and he did his best to look innocent.

"Shouldn't we both be part of the Ministry of Silly Walks?" he joked with only the slightest hint of a smile, referring to one of the most popular Monty Python skits. "Otherwise, people will think I'm walking with someone who's mentally challenged."

Aloriah lightly thumped him on the upper arm and he pretended she'd really hit hard enough to hurt.

"I'll show you mentally challenged." she muttered, but Chase just grinned at her. Both jumped when a pickup honked at them, and then pulled over beside them.

"You two ok?" yelled the elderly man behind the wheel, and Chase stepped closer to the pickup while Aloriah bit her lip to hold back a giggle, thinking there was more than one way that question could be answered.

"We're fine, but the rig we were in isn't. I don't have a cell signal, so we're walking into town to see if there's a pay phone that still works."

The man looked them over carefully as if looking for weapons, then indicated the back of his truck with a jerk of his head.

"Hop up in the back. Its 20 miles or so to the next town, and you don't have much daylight left."

"Thank you!" they said in unison, and Chase helped Aloriah to climb over the tailgate before doing so himself. They had both barely seated themselves when the truck started moving, so as they bounced over the road, Chase worked his way to where he was close enough to put his arm over Aloriah's shoulders, putting his mouth close to her ear so she could hear him over the wind.

"Good thing I'm wearing a loose fitting shirt. He may not have given us a ride if he'd seen my nipple ring."

Shaking her head, Aloriah leaned close so he could hear her reply.

"Your dad really does need to pay me more to put up with you."

Chase's response was a grin and a kiss on her ear that made her sigh, wishing they were anywhere other than in the back of a stranger's pickup.

In fairly short order, they reached the town, and hopping out of the back of the truck, Chase went to thank the kind man and offer him some money for his trouble. Smiling at the young man, the older gentleman turned him down.

"It's real nice to see young folks still know how to be polite, though." The old man said with a wink. "You two be good, now."

Making their way into the hotel where the old man had dropped them off, Chase explained the situation to the clerk and was shown where there was a pay phone. He made the call while Aloriah filled out the paperwork so that they could get a room for the night. Calling collect, Chase almost laughed at the tone in Jack's voice when he accepted the charges.

"Calling collect, Chase? What happened to the cell phone?"

"Well, there's a slight problem with cell phones when a late season tornado takes out the cell towers."

There was a moment of dead silence as those words sunk in, and then Jack's voice was full of concern.

"Are you two all right?"

Feeling strangely touched that he and Aloriah mattered more than the truck, he confirmed that they were fine, then added, "But the truck's on its side and the trailer has seen better days."

Jack breathed an audible sigh of relief, and then asked how he could get in touch with them. Aloriah, coming to get his credit card to pay for the room, had thought to bring a business card for the hotel, so Chase gave the information as she went back to the clerk. Within a few minutes, Jack had promised to inform the customer of the delay, and wished them a good evening. By the time Chase reached the clerk, the only thing left for him to do was sign the charge slip and collect the key.

As they went down the hall to their room, Chase pulled Aloriah tight to his side, never so thankful for her presence in his life, and pressed a kiss to the side of her head.

"Thank you for letting me know you were sensing trouble, sweet. That could have been much worse if we had been in the truck."

Tears coming to her eyes as she silently thanked all the powers that be for the man at her side, one who not only accepted her strange gift, but had just thanked her for using it, Aloriah whispered "You're welcome."

Chapter 16

Settling into a room with nothing but the clothes on their back didn't take long. After they had each taken a shower to wash what Chase was calling "the tornado grime" off, they went for a walk to a nearby restaurant for supper. On the way back, Chase insisted that Aloriah enjoy the warm evening while he paused at a drugstore for a moment for "entertaining supplies", coming out with a small box in a paper bag and not allowing Aloriah to peek. She didn't inform him that she was getting more and more proficient at reading him, so she was aware that he had purchased condoms. Chase's planned surprise when he got them back to the room was delayed, however, by a message for him to call his uncle.

"Hey kiddo!" Was the cheerful greeting after Jack accepted the second collect call of the day. "Guess you'll be doing your three day rest stop there. Is it a totally abysmal place?"

Looking at Aloriah, Chase grinned, thinking of lots of fun things they could do with three days.

"No, not abysmal at all."

Hearing something in the boy's voice that reminding him of his father, Jack, sitting in his office in Greenville, closed his eyes and pretended he didn't hear what he thought he did, but it still took him a moment to collect himself and continue with what he'd wanted to say. He cleared his throat.

"Okay, so by the time you get up in the morning, your truck should be at..." he looked at the name of the garage, "a place there in town called Shiney's. There wasn't much damage to the truck itself once they got it stood back up, but what's left of the load needs another trailer to be brought the rest of the way. It'll take Jason a day or two to get to you with the new trailer, and then the two of you can swap the load over. You've already been cleared to collect whatever supplies you need out of the sleeper tomorrow."

"Thanks, Uncle Jack."

Jack smiled, but then couldn't resist his comment.

"Make sure Aloriah can still walk well enough to get herself into the truck, okay?"

Not waiting for an answer, he hung up, leaving Chase at the other end of the line staring at the phone in some shock. His uncle had never made such comments to him before, and it wasn't until he had finished relating the conversation to Aloriah that he saw the amusement in it.

After a night of seriously *trying* to make her incapable of walking, they were laughing as they walked into the yard at the garage and saw the damage. The passenger side of the truck had bad scratches in the paint and a couple of dings, but it really wasn't as bad as it could have been. When he had introduced himself and produced both his i.d. and the key to the door, the mechanic, a fellow of about Chase's age who introduced himself as Buddy, promised to have as much of the paint work repaired as he could before they got the load swapped over.

While the men talked, Aloriah gathered some clothes for both herself and Chase into one duffle, pulled the bag Chase called the shower bag out of its storage bin under the bed, and climbed back down. When she hit solid ground again, she yanked at the top of her jeans, muttering about the way they were stretching out of shape. Buddy looked over and eyed her, then asked Chase candidly "She got any sisters like her back home?"

Hearing the man, Aloriah looked at him in total disbelief, and instead of feeling upset that the man was ogling his girlfriend, Chase was amused by her reaction.

"Nope, she's an only child."

"Damn." Buddy muttered. "That's one hot lady you got there."

Thinking the man might be a couple of knights short of a Crusade, Aloriah picked up the bags and brought them over to Chase, who took the biggest one before sliding his arm around his lady's waist. Thanking Buddy for the compliment, she and Chase started for the door, but she felt the man's eyes checking out what Chase cheerfully called her *rear view* until they were out of the door and walking down the street.

"You think he might have had brain damage?" she asked as soon as they were out of Buddy's sight and hearing range. Chase laughed and agreed that might be possible, but he had started to notice that, between the healthy food and practicing self-defense whenever they could, she was starting to turn fat into muscle. Since they hadn't been near a scale since leaving his house, he wouldn't have been able to get her to check it, but her softness was definitely starting to feel a bit firmer when they made love, and her clothes weren't as skin tight.

Arriving back at the hotel, Chase asked if they had a work out space, and at the affirmative answer, waggled his brows at Aloriah. She didn't even have to ask any more what he meant by that. He was suggesting that they do some stretches and practice her self-defense moves.

In matching sweat suits and sneakers, they soon drew the attention of several of the employees, who had never seen Tai Chi practiced up close and personal. When they moved on to practicing Aloriah's self-defense, the employees mostly flinched and moved on the first time Chase was thrown to the floor, even though his response was to laugh and compliment her. The moves became more and more intense as they continued, and when Chase looked at the door to realize they were totally alone, he wrapped his arms around Aloriah from behind to kiss her ear.

"Way to go, sweet. When no one can stand to watch you throw me, you've definitely learned the moves correctly."

Aloriah laughed softly, knowing that it was his ability to take the painful looking falls without getting seriously hurt that was really what sent the watchers packing wherever they went.

"We just make a good team."

Chapter 17

By the time the replacement trailer arrived and they walked back to the garage to switch the load over to get back on their way, the employees of the hotel had spread rumors around town that the young lady riding with the good looking trucker should *not* be messed with. Buddy seemed afraid to even look her way, but Aloriah simply did the duties that Chase had assigned her and didn't even crack a smile, at least, not until they were several miles down the road. Then she started laughing about the rumors about her in town. Chase didn't help, because every time she paused for breath, he would make a wise crack, making her laugh again until tears were running down her face.

"You one *bad* mamma-jamma." he told her the first time she started getting control of her laughter.

"Beware the she-hulk." he said in his best Arnold Schwarzenegger imitation the next time.

"Don't make that lady come after me, momma. I'll be good!" he teased in a little child voice.

Soon, she was begging him not to set her off any more.

"Seriously, I can barely breathe."

Chase bit his lips together to prevent further comments, but if she could have seen behind the sunglasses, his eyes were still dancing with mischief while he plotted to spread the rumors about her even further.

After delivering the load to the customer, they checked into a hotel for their ten hour rest break, and, while she enjoyed a nice, hot shower, Chase went down under the guise of getting them something to munch while they watched television. Instead, he invited all the truckers he passed in the hall to come and watch their self-defense demonstration before they headed back out on the road the next morning.

Before breakfast, they were doing their Tai Chi stretching when Aloriah noticed the crowd at the door, but it wasn't the normal group of female employees trying to get a look at Chase. This time, the crowd was mostly men, and she could feel their eyes primarily on her, making her very uncomfortable. When they started to practice the self-defense moves, she found herself having to concentrate harder to ignore the gasps and groans from their audience. She and Chase were both breathing hard and sweating like crazy when they finished, and there were hoots and applause from their audience as Chase smiled from ear to ear.

When they started walking out of the hotel fitness room to return to their room to shower and finish packing, the other truckers thanked Chase for inviting them to see the "demonstration", and for just a moment, she wondered why he would do such a thing. That was when she noticed that all the truckers, big, small or in between, stepped back and treated her with the same kind of respect they treated him with. Once they were out of everyone's sight, he wrapped his arm around her shoulders.

"There." he stated. "That should get the rumor mill going *big* time. Before you know it, every trucker you meet will know not to mess with you."

With a skeptical look, she snorted. "And you're sure of this why?"

Chase kissed her on the nose.

"Because my dad did a demonstration like that with me my freshman year of high school, and did the same again when I first started driving. Having the whole school see what I was capable of just two weeks after I'd fought off six bullies, giving two of them concussions, made it so I didn't get picked on for the rest of my time at school. Letting a select group of truckers see the same makes it so that I get respect and no one tries to mess with my loads."

Making like she was going to tweak the nipple with the ring in it, grinning when he protected it by covering it, she just had to ask.

"So why the lip ring and the nipple ring if everyone already knew you were scary?"

The mischievous gleam she had come to love came back into his eyes.

"Because Dad wouldn't hear of me getting my ears pierced."

When she rolled her eyes, he laughed softly.

"Actually, mom let me have the lip ring done because I thought it would look really tough when I turned 16. The nipple ring was something I had done when I turned 18, because I had decided that I was going to drive for the family business, and both Dad and Uncle Jack thought that the owner's son should be a good example for the other employees. No one else is allowed face piercings, so I shouldn't have one, either."

As they reached their door and Chase fumbled for the door card, Aloriah thought back to when he had put the lip ring back in while in New Orleans. Brushing her finger across the mark on his lip, she grinned when he looked at her.

"I think it looks tough, too," she said softly, "but I prefer kissing you without it."

To prove her words, she stood on tiptoes to kiss him, and he moaned softly, pulling her close. It was getting really hard to think about getting into the truck to drive to their next destination when she kissed him like that, but with a sigh, he pushed the door card into the lock mechanism and opened the door so they could hop through fast showers before getting back on the road.

He would just make sure that *his* shower was very cold.

Chapter 18

Another two weeks on the road delivering a few things along the west coast, and then the truck was traveling east again with a load for Lansing, Michigan. Chase was in good spirits, as he had been told that a replacement for Brian had been found, so he was going to get the week furlough he had been promised in August. That was in addition to the normal time he got off from his birthday until New Year's Eve, so he and Aloriah would have plenty of time to get Christmas presents purchased and wrapped, visit with family and friends, and just enjoy lazing around the house before they went back out on the road again.

Shortly after passing Kalamazoo on I-94, Chase's phone rang, and he pulled it out of his pocket thinking it was Jack with information about where they were going after dropping their load, as it was not quite noon. He was more than a little surprised when he heard his father's voice at the other end of the line.

"How long will it be before you get to your drop point?"

The matter-of-fact tone set off Chase's internal alarms, and Aloriah reacted to the emotions she was feeling by looking over at Chase with wide eyes.

"An hour, maybe a little over. Why?"

Kyle ignored the question.

"Good. Jack will call the customer and inform them that you're just going to pull the trailer into their loading bay, unhook it, and leave. Jason will be by tomorrow morning to take the trailer off their hands, *and* take the rest of your scheduled deliveries. You need to get Aloriah to Eastern Maine Medical Center as soon as you can."

"Dad, what's going on?"

Never having heard him speak to his father in that tone, Aloriah put her hand over onto his leg, but her attempt to comfort him only made her feel his distress at his father's odd behavior even more. As if realizing that he was alarming his son and his son's girlfriend, Kyle let out a deep sigh and tried to break the news as gently as he could.

"I just got off the phone with Kelly Starbird. Aloriah's dad crashed his car late last night, and he's in intensive care." There was a pause, as if Kyle was trying to decide whether to go into further detail, and when he continued, his voice was gentle. "It doesn't look good, and I think her mother will really need her if things go south."

Despite knowing how things had been left between them, Chase was quite sure that Aloriah would want to be able to say goodbye if it came to that. It was easy to promise that he would get her home with all possible speed.

"Call me when you hit the Gardiner toll booth, and I'll meet you at the hospital with your car so you don't have to try to fit the truck into the parking garage, ok?" Kyle continued, and Chase could almost hear the smirk in the tone.

When Chase brought the Mustang home, Kyle had pretended he was wiping drool off his face, and had joked more than once that Chase would arrive home one day to find that the car had been "stolen". What better excuse for him to be able to drive the Mustang than to trade it for the truck, and save his son from a trip all the way to Greenville when he should be by his girlfriend's side?

"Just be careful, Dad. I don't want to be repairing either you *or* my baby."

Kyle laughed softly, then his voice was serious again when he said "I love you, kiddo."

Hearing the wealth of emotion in that simple statement, Chase responded with, "I love you, too, Dad."

Hanging up the phone and putting it back in his pocket, he put his hand over the hand Aloriah still had on his leg, and broke the news to her as gently as possible.

"Your Dad was in an accident. He's in ICU."

When she didn't seem to respond short of gripping his leg a little tighter, he took a glance over to find her staring straight ahead while tears flooded down her cheeks. The only sound that came out of her was when she drew a shaky breath and gave a slight cough as she tried to regain control of herself.

Lifting her hand to his lips to place a kiss on her fingers, he asked gently "Do you want me to pull over?"

Another deep breath, less shaky than the last, and she was seemingly back in control.

"No. We need to get this load delivered, and then I take it you've been ordered to bring me home."

There was no question in her tone, and it was Chase's turn to take a deep breath.

"Dad thinks your mom is going to need you."

The tears were drying up, and a slight smile touched her lips.

"Your dad is a very smart man." One more deep, sighing breath, and she started to reach for the I Pad. "Shall I plot our course, Captain?"

Smiling at the question that had become something of an inside joke, he responded with the expected answer. "Plot our course, Navigator."

Aloriah gave one final sigh as she typed "Lansing, Michigan" in as the start point and guessed where the ICU might be. "Is he at Eastern Maine or St. Joe's?"

If not for the fact that he was driving, Chase would have face palmed.

"Sorry. He's at Eastern Maine."

Secretly knowing that he had given himself a mental face palm, Aloriah wanted to smile as she typed in "Eastern Maine Medical Center, Bangor, Maine" in the destination, then clicked the button to get directions. Looking at the route with the least amount of hours to travel, she grimaced.

"Do you have a passport?"

The word "passport" made Chase groan. The quickest route from Lansing to Bangor was to go into Canada, through London and Hamilton, and cross back into the US by Niagara Falls. He had done that before, but this time, he hadn't planned on going into Canada, so his passport was in his fire safe in the house in Greenville. He didn't even have to actually say the word "no" because it was written all over his face. Aloriah shrugged.

"That's okay. Neither do I, and I really didn't want you trying to smuggle me into Canada and back out."

A tap on the screen.

"Says here that going around through Toledo and Cleveland is about sixteen and a half hours."

She reached for the log book, checking how much time he'd been on the road and how far they were from arriving in Lansing.

"Since we got a late start this morning that gives you about seven hours to drive before we have to take the stop."

Chase chewed his lip. Since they hadn't started the drive until 9 that morning, they would have to be off the road at 8 p.m. if they took the next 7 hour shot as one long drive, 9 p.m. if they stopped for an hour long dinner. He'd have 12 hours of rest on the page for the day. If he started back out at 5 a.m. on the next sheet, stopped for a breakfast, and drove straight through, he'd still be okay on that log page, unless Uncle Jack or a weigh station between here and there checked to realize that 5 plus 3 only equaled 8 hours of rest for the overnight, not the technically required 10 hours...

Might they understand that he wasn't technically "on duty" and let the timing slide, especially as the next day's sheet would have a maximum of ten and a half hours driving? As they pulled into the warehouse where the load was being delivered and saw a man waving his arms madly to direct them to the proper space for them to park the trailer, Chase made his decision.

"I can have you in Bangor between 4:30 and 5 tomorrow afternoon if you're willing to take the blame with me should we get caught." He outlined his plan to take half hour meals, push until 9 that night and get up again at 5 the next morning, which wouldn't really tax his system, and take just half hour meals until they arrived in Bangor. The differential between the two times only depended on how many times they had to stop to refill the tank on the truck. "We'll technically be serious outlaws according to the law, because my rest break overnight will be two hours short."

Aloriah looked at him over her sunglasses.

"Getting me there isn't worth losing your license, or even worth taking a fine. We'll leave at 7 a.m. and get there when we get there."

Chase, trying to bring back a little levity, muttered "Brown-noser."

Aloriah pretended to be upset, but was actually quite delighted that he would make such an offer for her. The longer she traveled with him and the more she got to know all the little idiosyncrasies that were Chase, the more she was certain she loved him with all her heart, and to offer to risk a blotch on his perfect driving record meant he felt the same way about her. No matter how many times he had said it, he had just proved his love to her by offering a simple act of kindness.

Chapter 19

Although Aloriah had convinced Chase to not mess up his driving record by shortening his rest period, she did let him talk her into shortening their normal hour long meal breaks to a half an hour, getting them into the hotel at just before 8:30 p.m., and out the door the next morning at 6:30 a.m. after eating breakfast, but skipping the stretch and self-defense practice. They had 9.5 hours left to drive according to the map program, and since they only stopped for lunch and to fill the truck, they pulled into the hospital just before 5 p.m.

Kyle had touched base with them about mid-day after getting an update on the patient, and had been given the ETA, so he was standing in the lobby talking with Kelly when they drove up to the door. Chase briefly shut off the engine to walk Aloriah in, and Kyle, after giving them each a hug and telling Kelly to call if there was anything he could do, swapped keys with Chase and climbed up into the cab of the truck with a smile, giving them a wave.

"You have a really nice dad there." Kelly told Chase as she hugged him. "And thank you for getting my daughter here so fast, even if she does look like you've been starving her."

Chase winked at Aloriah over the top of Kelly's head.

"I would have had her here sooner, but she wouldn't let me break the rules. And the weight loss is her own fault. She barricades her plate so I can't sneak on extra food."

Hearing the playfully whiney tone to his voice when he spoke of the barricades, Kelly smiled.

"I'd rather you didn't break the rules, and my daughter looks very happy about getting thinner, which is all that matters." Then she took a deep breath for what she had to tell her daughter. "Just about the time that Kyle arrived at the front desk, I was coming out to see if you were here yet."

Aloriah took her mother's hand as tears began to form in the older woman's eyes, and Chase watched curiously as Aloriah's eyes widened. The words *brain dead* had whispered through her head, but Kelly still said the words aloud for Chase's sake.

"They've confirmed he's brain dead and are only keeping him on life support until they harvest his organs. I asked them to hold off the harvesting until you arrived." Kelly sniffed, and the tears began in earnest. "I wanted your confirmation that their machines are right."

Chase wrapped his arms around her while Aloriah went and got some tissues from the receptionist. When Kelly had regained control, she got permission for all three of them to go in to say goodbye before Bruce's final gift to the world was taken and the machines unplugged. Letting go of

Chase's hand, Aloriah approached the battered, bandage wrapped person in the bed and touched the one hand that was scratched from all the flying glass, but left unbandaged because the cuts weren't deep.

She closed her eyes for a moment, taking a couple of deep, cleansing breaths, and Chase witnessed something he had never seen before. The lights in the room dimmed slightly, the air seemed somehow heavier, and for just a moment when Aloriah opened her eyes, they appeared to be dead, with not a flicker within the golden depths. Then she dropped the hand she was holding, backed up a couple of steps, and her eyes returned to normal.

"They're right. He's no longer in there. It's just an empty shell." Looking more drained than Chase had ever seen her, she took her mother's hand for just a moment, and then headed for the door. "I need to step outdoors for a moment."

Concerned, Chase started to follow her, but Kelly put a gentle hand on his arm.

"She needs to be alone. She won't be long."

"Can you explain what that was? It might help me to understand her better."

Kelly could sense that he was seriously asking so that he could help her daughter, and the fact that he cared that much gave her very warm feelings toward the young man.

"How much has she told you about her heritage?"

Chase thought for a moment about the almost three months they had been on the road, and the things that Aloriah had told him about her family to pass the time as they were driving or resting. Weeding out the painful things about the way her father had always treated her, he pulled out the things that Kelly most likely needed to know that he was aware of.

"She told me your family is from Nova Scotia, a mix of French and Mi'kmaq. Her father is..." he corrected himself, "*was* Penobscot. She also told me and showed me many times that she's empathic. I suspect that little hidden talent was what kept us from being hurt in a late season tornado in Oklahoma last month and from getting shot at a truck stop in August."

Kelly looked at Chase with new respect. Whatever it was that Aloriah had sensed about him in New Orleans, she had trusted him with things she had never shared with anyone outside of her direct family before. Clearing her throat, she decided it was time to trust him with her own family secret, suspecting that he would be the one to help Aloriah claim her heritage.

"Have you ever heard of the shamans that the natives believed in?" At his nod, she looked him straight in the eye. "Aloriah is the last shaman of my family tree. Her grandmother has been trying for years to get her to stop burying her ability and let it come out, but it's hard to live in this world when there are so many people around, always overwhelming you with their emotions. She put up internal barricades when she was a child to protect her sanity, and I think she's afraid to let them down now."

Understanding hit Chase, thinking back on

some of the things he had observed while they traveled. When tired, she would often rub her temples, particularly when they were around other people. When it was just the two of them, she seemed much more relaxed, but always seemed to know what he was thinking and feeling, sometimes before he knew it himself. Looking at Kelly, who was watching him closely, he asked "Are you able to do what she can?"

Kelly frowned.

"I have the empathic ability, but nothing like what she has. I wouldn't have been able to touch Bruce's hand to confirm what the doctors were telling me. Her ancestors were able to look into their people and, when necessary, cast out demons and do spiritual healings. They could remove pain and allow the women who were good stitchers to close horrific wounds. There were even some that were able to predict the future and keep the tribe from harm."

Chase's hand automatically went toward the scar on his shoulder and he remembered something he had seen in Aloriah's eyes the first day she saw that. She had seemed to know it was a scar from a knife wound before he had explained. Then he thought about the bruise and small puncture she had been tending at the point that she had spotted the scar. While she had her hands on him, the injury had seemed to hurt a lot less than it did even several days later, when it was nearly healed.

Aloriah came around the corner just then, and Kelly smiled at him, the look in her eyes telling him that she had trusted him with their family secrets for a reason. Smiling back at her, he stepped forward to offer Aloriah a hug, which she accepted, placing her head against him and closing her eyes, wrapping herself in the comfort he still seemed to wear like a cloak.

"So," Chase said softly, "are you ladies hungry? Supper's on me."

Aloriah's stomach growled in response, making both Chase and her mother laugh softly, and then Kelly excused herself to tell the doctors that they could proceed with the harvesting of the organs. She had already discussed his wish to be cremated with the tribal undertaker, so she would contact the man in the morning to have the body prepared for the funeral.

Pulling the key to his car out of his pocket, Chase led the way into the parking garage. The first time he pushed the button for the security system he'd had installed, the distant beep made him wrinkle his nose, making both ladies giggle as he led the way up to the second level. A second push told him they were on the right level, but he didn't see the car. Craning his neck and putting a hand over his eyes like a visor made the ladies giggle some more.

"You know, you could have just used the free valet service to avoid having to hunt." Kelly told him dryly, and Chase looked at her in exaggerated shock.

"And let someone other than me drive my baby? Sacrilege!"

"Didn't your dad drive it here?"

Aloriah bit her lip to avoid giggling at the

look of comic distaste on Chase's face.

"Yes." he growled. "But only because it was necessary. He'll never be allowed to drive her again unless it's another emergency like this."

When they came into sight of the car, Kelly's jaw dropped open and she fully understood how the young man could be so possessive of it. She had only seen a '67 Mustang at a car show, and the fact that this one had been modified with a turbo supercharger was obvious. Going over to sigh dramatically, Chase patted the hood.

"Hi baby! Did you miss me?"

Hearing a noise from Aloriah, Kelly turned to see her trying very hard not to laugh at the dramatics, and she turned back to Chase in time to see him grin from ear to ear and wink. When he opened the passenger door to allow the ladies in, Aloriah insisted that Kelly take the front seat, flipping the seat forward to climb into the back. The roar that echoed through the garage when he started the vehicle before asking Kelly to choose the restaurant made her want to choose one that would involve a long drive, but she opted for something closer for the sake of her daughter's growling stomach.

"How about the Olive Garden by the Mall."

Chase smiled and drove them over, assisting Aloriah out of the car before dropping his arm around her shoulders as they walked in. He showed Kelly what kind of treatment her daughter had been getting when he insisted on holding chairs for each of them before seating himself. As when they were in New Orleans, he kept playfully trying to sneak extra food onto Aloriah's plate whenever he thought she wasn't looking, and Kelly found herself truly enjoying his antics.

Despite the fact that her ability to sense emotions was miniscule compared to her daughter's talent, she found that she didn't even need her empathy to sense the way he felt about Aloriah. Every touch, every smile, and even his playful antics were full of love and respect. Looking at her daughter's smiling face and happy eyes filled her heart with joy.

When Bruce had kicked Aloriah out onto the street in August, Kelly had been angry at her husband and terrified that her daughter was going to be hurt or killed. Even the call from Teresanna Benton when they had found Aloriah's cell phone at Chase's house and accessed her contact list so that they could inform her mother that she was safe hadn't done much to alleviate her fears, as she was worried that Chase would use her daughter for a while and put her back onto the streets. But seeing the two of them together like this, she could finally go home with forgiveness in her heart for her husband. It may not have been his intention, but Bruce had driven their daughter into the arms of a man who saw beyond the outer shell, and truly cared about the woman inside.

As they left the restaurant some time later, all of them playfully groaning about having eaten too much, Chase had a sudden brainstorm, but as he had learned to do with Aloriah, he approached the subject carefully.

"So Kelly, did you want me to just drop you

off at the hospital so you can get your car and go home alone, or would you prefer to have me follow you so you can get some clothes and come spend the night with us in Greenville? I really don't think you should be alone at a time like this."

Momentarily stunned by the offer, Kelly stopped and simply stared at Chase. Had he really just asked that?

"Wouldn't your family be a little put out to have me just show up at your house unannounced?"

Confused by her response, Chase tilted his head.

"Why would they be upset that I brought you into my house?"

Sensing that they weren't on the same page, Aloriah gave her mother a gentle smile.

"Chase lives by himself in a farmhouse with a spare bedroom. His folks live about a mile further up on a private road, but if you think you'd rather spend the night in a guest suite, we can probably arrange for you to stay with them."

Chase added a bit more detail.

"Staying at Casa de Kyle is almost like being in a fancy hotel. It has a swimming pool, fitness center, and two story library. The guest room is two rooms and a bath with soundproofed walls, so you won't even hear the family moving around if you don't want to."

Kelly wanted to laugh at herself. She had forgotten all about who Kyle was, as the man had come off as so relaxed, so normal, so unlike a lot of the rich people she had come in contact with over the years in her job as a hotel housekeeper. While the thought of being treated like she was the rich person appealed to her on one level, she decided she might take that offer at another time. For the moment, though, the thought of all the things she needed to accomplish over the next few days hit her like a wreaking ball, and she sighed.

"Either sounds like fun, but I really have so much to do. There's making arrangements with the undertaker, and getting some black clothes, and..."

Chase stopped her.

"Unless you want your daughter wearing jeans and a black t-shirt, she'll need to come back to town to go shopping herself. You can come and stay at my house tonight, and I'll drive you back in the morning so the two of you can shop together, if you'd like that. We can help you with the other arrangements, too, as we really have nothing else planned."

Aloriah reached out to touch her mother, and Kelly found that she had missed the effortless melding of their minds. Aloriah's voice whispered in her mind, *Let him do this for you, mom.*

With a deep sigh, she made her decision.

"Okay. Drive me back to the hospital to pick up my car and follow me out to the island. If you're willing to let me take the back seat on the drive to Greenville so I can maybe take a little nap, I'll come stay in your spare bedroom."

Kelly's car was a small, nondescript vehicle that Kyle had always called "death-boxes", a vague green color with large patches of rust, but when she turned the key, it started right away. The motor didn't run smooth, however, so it didn't take long for

Chase to realize why Kelly had been hesitant about following them to Greenville. The little car might not have made it!

When they reached the house Aloriah had grown up in, Chase was in shock. The small single story house was covered in unpainted wood siding, which had a kind of grayish look about it. The front stairs were broken, the handrail missing, and the rail holding up the porch roof on one corner so rotted that it was bent, making that side of the roof sag. When Kelly turned the key in the lock, she had to pull the knob hard and wiggle it before the lock actually disengaged.

"I thought he said he was going to fix that." Aloriah said quietly.

Kelly just shrugged.

"He was always going to get to it when he had time, but he just never found the time to get to it."

The inside wasn't in any better repair than the outside. The kitchen sink had no cabinet doors, just a curtain hung around it to hide the pipes underneath. There was a constant grinding noise coming from the refrigerator. The kitchen table had one leg shorter than the others that had been propped up on two books. Going down the hallway with Aloriah, which reminded him of the hallway of a trailer one of his friends had lived in when he was younger, Chase peeked in at the bathroom to find that the floor was plain plywood that was starting to rot out around the shower and toilet.

Aloriah stepped into her room, having to stand sideways because the room was barely big enough to fit the twin bed that was jammed in it, and pushed aside the curtain that served as her closet door. Apart from the clothes she had brought in her suitcase when he picked her up in August, there was a single black dress hanging there that was very obviously for a much younger girl. All of the rest of the clothing she had left behind, mostly because it was too small for her to wear, had been either sold or brought to thrift stores.

"I wore this for the funeral of both Grampy Starbird and Grammy Starbird when I was in seventh grade." she told him as she pulled it out and held it in front of her. There was no way it was going to fit around her, and the edge of the skirt fell about mid-hip. "I think I grew a little since I last needed it."

Chase smiled as she put it on the bed to bring out to drop into the donation box her mother kept, and then she opened her drawers to pull out everything left in them. The only items were a pair of socks that had holes in both toes and a belt. Smiling at him, she wrapped the belt around her waist and hooked it.

"Hey, it fits again!"

Looking around her room, she grabbed the books that were crammed under the edge of the bed and handed them to him. "The Hobbit" and "The Lord of the Rings" trilogy, very ratty looking copies that she told him with a smile she had read to death. With a shrug, she made her way back out to him and followed him back down the hallway.

Like her daughter when he'd picked her up, Kelly had a single battered suitcase in hand that felt like it was almost empty when he took it from her to put into the back of the car with Aloriah's books. He turned to see the two women on the porch, Kelly doing the pull and wiggle technique to relock the door, and was almost tempted to tell her to leave the door unlocked. Apart from the television set in the living room that looked like it had seen better days, there was really nothing of value in the house.

As they drove back out to the main road off the island, Kelly suddenly asked him to stop, as she'd seen the lights on in the undertaker's house.

"I might be able to save us a trip out to the island." she told Chase as she got out with the paper bag she'd brought into the back seat with her, which she said held the clothes she wanted to have put on her husband for the wake.

While her mother was out of the car, Chase looked at Aloriah, who was trying hard not to fidget. His voice soft, he said "So that's how you grew up?"

She sighed.

"Dad liked to drink and he liked to gamble. He didn't like to spend money on what he didn't consider absolute necessities."

A frown crossed Chase's face.

"So how did you and your mom afford the trip to New Orleans?"

Aloriah smiled.

"When I was really small, Mom started putting money away in a savings account that had my name and hers on it. She kept the account book in her locker at work so he could never find it, putting money in it every week from her tips from the hotel. It wasn't that much, so he never missed it when she handed him what was left from paying the bills, but enough for two round trip tickets to New Orleans, a cheap hotel for a week, and a couple of things like ghost walk tickets as a special graduation present for me when I finished high school."

Putting his hand over hers, Chase gave her a smile.

"You need to help me convince your mom that I'm giving her an early Christmas present by buying you each a nice black outfit for the funeral, okay? This isn't the time for her to have to worry about money issues, nor to be as stubborn as her daughter about having me buy her some clothes."

Knowing how stubborn he was about buying things for those he cared about, despite all objections, she kissed him on the cheek.

"Just turn those sexy green eyes on her and she'll melt, like I always do."

Remembering too many times that she had resisted that melting, Chase gave her a dubious look.

"Yeah, right."

Kelly rejoined them at that moment, smiling through a few tears that had slipped out while she was making arrangements with the undertaker.

"Okay, let's go see this house of yours in Greenville." she said cheerfully, although both of the young people knew she was faking the cheerfulness. They also pretended they didn't notice the soft sounds of crying coming from the back seat as they wove through the small towns and farmlands along the way.

Chapter 20

Kelly was still asleep in Gram's old bedroom when Chase and Aloriah crept carefully down over the stairs to start breakfast. Aloriah started coffee while Chase pulled out the griddle and pulled bacon out of the freezer to toss into hot water. Almost cursing aloud as he suddenly realized they hadn't stopped for fresh eggs, he pulled open the refrigerator door to find that his mother had been one step ahead of him. The refrigerator was stocked with fresh fruits and vegetables, a carton of eggs, milk and coffee creamer. The post-it note on the eggs said simply "Welcome home".

Peeking over his shoulder to see what he was grinning at, Aloriah smiled along with him. Pulling out strawberries, she started slicing them for a nice batch of waffles and strawberries to go with the bacon. By the time Kelly came down into the kitchen, rubbing her eyes, breakfast was almost ready for the table, and Aloriah greeted her cheerfully while filling a coffee cup for her.

"Who are you and what have you done with

my daughter?" she asked, making both Chase and Aloriah laugh at her reference to the way Aloriah had been grumpy until almost noon before she had started riding in the truck with Chase.

They had just finished breakfast when the land line rang. Chase answered it, and, closing her eyes for a moment, Aloriah identified the caller as his mother. She smiled as she put the dishes into the sink for washing and yelled "Tell Mama T. good morning for me."

Chase laughed and called back "She says 'Right back atcha'."

As he related what had happened the night before, Kelly and Aloriah washed and put the breakfast dishes away. Kelly looked around the kitchen and, like her daughter, noted the very feminine feel of things. Aloriah was just finishing explaining about Gram Godfried, Chase's older cousins all wanting to move out of Greenville, and was getting ready to tell about the barn house when Chase interrupted the discussion by coming back into the kitchen.

"We've been invited to trade the Mustang for the minivan, as it's a more comfortable ride to get in and out of, and there's just Angela to pick up if she happens to miss the bus. I can introduce you to my mom and show you where I grew up before we head back into the city." He wrinkled his nose and joked, "I *guess* I can trust them not to hurt my baby."

"Where's Lynn?" Aloriah asked, and Chase smiled.

"She's at UMO, studying hard." And he told Kelly about his younger sister who was Aloriah's age.

Dressing warmly against the cold breeze, they loaded into the car, Aloriah climbing back into the back seat so that she could watch her mother's reaction at seeing the Benton house. Despite the slightly cloudy sky, the house was still impressive, and Aloriah almost laughed at her mother's exclamation of "Oh, my!"

When they entered the house, she repeated that exclamation. Kyle, recognizing her from the day before, came across the room to greet her with "Thank you, Kelly! It's nice to know that all my hard work can still inspire such awe!"

Looking at Aloriah and Chase with a gleam in his eye as they removed their coats, Kyle said "Jeans and t-shirts?"

Teresanna came in from the kitchen in time to hear him.

"No dunkings until they get back from shopping." she warned, and then walked directly to Kelly while Kyle pretended to pout. "Welcome to our home. May I take your coat and take you for a tour?"

As soon as Kelly was out of earshot, Chase looked at his father and said "Can we talk in your office?"

As the door closed behind them, Chase told him what he'd seen of the house where Kelly would have to spend her first winter alone. Aloriah explained why the house was in such sad shape. Kyle sat down at his desk and drummed his fingers on the top as both his own child and the young lady who he was coming to think of as one of his own spoke of their fears. Fear that Kelly would be too stubborn to accept if Chase were to offer her a place to live rent free, living in a house that her daughter would be returning to from time to time. Aloriah's fear that the neglected house would fall down around her mother's ears or that the poor woman would freeze to death, and that she would have to plan a second funeral in the spring.

Kyle thought, long and hard, about the problem. Then he suddenly smiled. Glimpsing his thought, Aloriah looked at him in shock, unable to stop herself from speaking aloud.

"Code violation?" she asked, and Kyle looked at her a moment in surprise, and then laughed as he looked at Chase, remembering some conversations they'd had when Aloriah wasn't in the room with Chase.

"You know, it is a little disturbing when she does that to you." Looking back at Aloriah, he smiled. "Yes, code violation. I could call in an anonymous tip to have the local code officer check the house to see if it's fit for habitation."

Her eyes lit up as she caught the rest of the thought. There was no way that the house would be considered fit to live in, meaning her mother would be given an edict, move or get arrested. Smiling back at Kyle, she thanked him with a tear in her eye, pleased that the argument over her mother moving would never happen, and therefore leave no hard feelings between mother and daughter.

"You are the most brilliant person I've ever met." Chase harrumphed and she smiled at him. "And you're getting there. But your father's idea is perfect. The code officer will condemn the place. She'll have to move."

Kyle added another thought.

"I know every business owner in this town. What do you think she'd like to do so I can start bragging her up to those who might offer her a job?"

Aloriah smiled even wider, having missed that part of the plan. "She's been a housekeeper at local hotels for as long as I can remember."

"Then I'll start spreading the word that I'm looking for a job for a housekeeper."

Then he winked, making Aloriah feel much better about the coming winter and her stubborn mother.

Chapter 21

Getting into the van, Kelly was again insistent that Aloriah should sit in the front, saying she would be more comfortable in the back. Chase, seeing a sad look on her face, sought to lighten the mood by telling stories as he had when he brought Aloriah to Greenville the first time, but when Aloriah looked back and saw the tears running silently down her mother's face, she unbuckled her belt and slid to the back, giving Chase a kiss on the cheek along the way.

"Thank you for trying." she told him, and sat on the bench style seat, hooking into the other seatbelt, before wrapping her arms around her mother to let her cry out her grief.

Looking at them in the rear view mirror while stopped behind a school bus, Chase found himself wondering if Aloriah's talent could be passed on to him. It was almost as if he could see their emotional states, and had the strangest feeling that Aloriah was the older of the pair and Kelly the one who was just 19. Shaking his head to rid himself of that image, he continued driving them into the Bangor Mall so they could look for black clothing for the funeral at several stores.

After he had parked the van and helped the two women out, Kelly gave him a watery smile as she dug in her purse for a tissue.

"Sorry about that. I think I'm under control, and suddenly I'm not."

Chase smiled back at her.

"Fully understood. That's why I didn't think it was a good idea to leave you alone at your house last night."

Kelly tilted her head and looked at him as she wiped the last traces of her grief off her face, thinking how much more mature he seemed than most boys his age. Teresanna had invited her to his 21st birthday party the following week, but he seemed like he was 20 going on 40. Looking at her daughter, Kelly wanted to laugh, because she often thought the same about Aloriah, who had always seemed like such an old soul in such a young body. Might that be why fate had intervened in New Orleans, putting these two old souls together, simply because it was meant to be so?

Chase offered her his arm, waiting while she took it, and then offered his other arm to Aloriah, making them laugh when they were able to see their reflections in the glass of the door by commenting that he felt like a Chase sandwich. Graciously opening the door to let the two ladies precede him, he told them that they could shop wherever they wished, as the clothes were being purchased as an early Christmas present. Kelly started to object, but Aloriah shook her head.

"You might as well save your breath. No matter how stubborn you think you might be, he'll out-stubborn you every time."

"You talk like you've tried to out-stubborn him before."

Aloriah made a comic face of disgust as she nodded, and Chase looked proud of himself as he pointed at the clothes she was wearing.

"That was her last attempt when her jeans were getting so loose that she couldn't climb in and out of the truck safely. I can out-stubborn the best of them."

Kelly laughed at the exchange and decided that she would do as suggested, leading the way into the first store to start looking for black things. Expecting the kind of shopping trip her husband had always forced on her, where she was expected to buy the first thing that fit correctly and had the lowest price tag, she was a little startled when Chase left her and Aloriah at the clearance racks, having forced her to admit to what size she was wearing. He returned a short time later with dresses that he thought might look nice on them that he had pulled off the full price racks, and led them over to the fitting rooms so he could get an idea of whether they liked his choices.

Seeing her come out in the first dress, he wrinkled his nose, stating that the ruched look just didn't work for her. Since she agreed, she was quite pleased with his opinion. Kelly passed Aloriah on her way back to the fitting room, as her daughter came out in a lovely flowing dress that looked beautiful on her, but was definitely a size too big.

She heard Chase laugh and promise that he would be back with the proper size. Not only did he return with that dress in a proper size, but he also had a lovely coppery colored long gown that Aloriah looked at longingly, but objected to by gently stating, "Chase, sweetie, we're buying for a funeral, not a prom."

Kelly saw his eyes narrow and felt the slight increase in his annoyance level, but his voice was calm when he insisted "Just humor me and try it."

She was on her way back out of the fitting room with the first dress that looked good on her when Aloriah stepped out of her own fitting room, asking that her mother help her to zip up the long gown. Stepping back to take a good look, she was stunned with the way the coppery fabric made her daughter's eyes pop, taking all the attention away from the slowly disappearing weight issue and putting it on the beautiful golden eyes that came from Kelly's side of the family. When Aloriah gave her a smile and went to show the gown to Chase, his triumphant grin warmed Kelly's heart, and his exclamation was loud enough to be heard all over the store.

"Wow, baby! You look like an actress on the red carpet! I have to find somewhere to take you so you can wear that!"

Aloriah laughed and thanked him for the compliment, and her happy smile when she stopped to allow her mother to undo the zipper did Kelly's heart good.

After finding several nice dresses they all could agree on in the first store, Chase insisted that they put them on hold and move on to the next store. He worked his magic there, too, finding several more possibilities to put on hold before moving on to the next store, and the next. By the time they had finished their rounds, it was time for them to stop for lunch, and while they ate, Chase directed the talk to which dresses they liked best, which ones they had reconsidered, and whether they wanted to continue shopping or make a purchase and return to Greenville.

When they both wanted to buy and go back to relax for a while with a swim in the Benton pool, but Kelly couldn't decide which of two dresses she liked best, Chase surprised her by insisting that she get them both just in case she decided she wanted to wear one for the wake and the other for the funeral. She started to open her mouth to object and found herself getting that narrowed eye look that he had used on Aloriah. She wisely backed down and let him just do what he wanted, reasoning that she could sell the dresses later on the internet if she found herself short on money over the winter, and it saved her from the lecture she was sure he was quite capable of giving her.

For her part, Aloriah had to back down on the idea of leaving the long gown in the store. Chase kept insisting that she looked so beautiful in it, he would find somewhere to take her so she could wear it. Kelly had to bite back a laugh when Aloriah, who would have argued until she was blue in the face not too many months ago, just rolled her eyes and gave up the fight.

Chapter 22

The following day, after Angela went off to school, the Bentons and the Starbirds loaded into the van to go to Bruce Starbird's wake. Kelly found herself put into the middle of the van, with Kyle and Teresanna sitting in front, and Chase and Aloriah sitting behind her. All four seemed very determined to keep her from sinking into her grief, and as they pulled into the hall where the ceremony was happening, she appreciated their efforts, as she was able to enter with a quiet dignity and greet the undertaker calmly.

Taking her arm, the older man escorted her to the casket to ask her opinion on whether she wanted it left open or closed before the first mourners arrived. Chase followed them with Aloriah on his arm while Kyle and Teresanna took up stations at the door, allowing the family a moment alone with the deceased should anyone arrive early.

Holding her mother's hand as they observed the damage from the accident that the undertaker couldn't conceal, Aloriah again made the lights dim as she eased her mother's grief, allowing her to remain dignified as she made the choice to close the casket. Kyle, watching from the door, raised an eyebrow at Chase, who mouthed "Later".

The strong arm on Aloriah's shoulder allowed her to remain dignified herself as the two of them made their way back out to the van. While Kelly settled herself for the ordeal of the wake, Chase helped Aloriah to get the memory boards she and her mother had stayed up late the night before making from a handful of old photographs, lamenting that Bruce had sold the camera so that there were no recent photos.

The undertaker, with a smile, helped Aloriah set them up, praising her for thinking of a way for the mourners to see Bruce Starbird without having the last memory being that of the damaged shell in the casket. By the time the first of the mourners arrived, Kelly and Aloriah were seated at the front of the hall, where the undertaker had placed them, to accept condolences after the mourners had passed the casket. Teresanna was greeting people at the front door and asking them to please sign the guestbook, and Chase and Kyle, in matching black suits, were standing at the doors leading from the entrance into the hall proper, ready to assist if anything got out of hand. Aloriah found she couldn't look at the two men, as the fact that they looked like they were secret service men made her want to laugh.

Expecting most of the mourners to be friends of her father, Aloriah was a little surprised when several of her former classmates came through. That was, she was surprised until she shook their hands to accept their condolences and discovered that the main reason they came was in the morbid hope of seeing the dead man's body. They luckily didn't stay for long with the lone exception of the boy who had taken her virginity the night she had stupidly been drunk at a party. His eyes lit up when he saw her slimmer body in the flattering dress, and he leaned in close to her after grabbing her wrist so she couldn't back away.

"If you had looked like this in high school, I might have asked you out a few times after that party." he whispered, and Aloriah gave him a glare.

"If I'd looked like this in high school, I might not have been depressed enough to get drunk at that party." she whispered back, and as if he had heard their whispered conversation, Chase was suddenly at her side.

Despite the smile on his face, Chase had a very menacing air about him that made the boy drop her wrist and back away a step as Chase murmured "Is everything okay, darling?"

Wanting to laugh at the look on the boy's face, she told Chase that all was fine, then introduced them.

"Chase Benton, this is..." she seemed to fumble for his name, as if she didn't really remember him, "Patrick, was it?"

"Patrick Mitchell." he provided, and Aloriah forced a smile she didn't really feel.

"Patrick Mitchell, this is my boyfriend, Chase Benton."

Chase also gave a false smile as he took the offered hand and squeezed hard enough to make

Patrick's eyes widen in pain. As soon as he got his hand back, Patrick left the building while Chase turned concerned eyes on Aloriah, suspecting he knew what that was about, but needing to confirm she was okay before he took up his station again.

"Are you alright?" he whispered softly, and Aloriah leaned forward to give him a quick kiss.

"I'm fine, and thank you for coming to my rescue...again."

"Is Patrick the one I think he is?"

She looked into his eyes, and Chase saw the answer to that without her having to say a word. He gave her a hug and whispered, "His loss."

As Chase made his way back to the door, Aloriah cleared her throat and found her mother looking at her with a gleam in her eye. Although Bruce had never been told about the party and Patrick's role, Kelly had known right along. She was sincerely hoping that Patrick had taken a good look at the kind of man who deserved to touch her daughter and felt jealous. As Aloriah sat back down beside her, Kelly glanced back at Chase to give him a smile and mouthed "Thank you."

Chase smiled back and mouthed "Any time."

Chapter 23

On the morning of the funeral, they loaded back into the minivan, and because it was a Saturday, Angela was along for the ride, having been promised that they were going to go out to dinner at her favorite Indian restaurant after the funeral. She and Kelly were having a lively discussion as to whether Lamb Curry or Keema Mutter was the better lamb dish for a first timer when Kelly's phone rang.

Excusing herself with a smile, Kelly picked up the call to find the undertaker on the other end of the line. After a couple of minutes, everyone in the van was alerted that something was wrong when Kelly said loudly, "What do you mean, 'they've misplaced him'?"

A couple of minutes more, and she sighed and said "That should be fine. We're on our way from Greenville and should be there shortly."

She hung up, dropped the phone into her purse, and gave a heavy sigh.

"The crematorium sent the wrong persons

ashes back. They're pretty sure that Bruce's ashes are on their way to the other person's undertaker in Portland, but they won't be able to check until the ashes arrive there on Monday. In the meantime, we have an empty urn to say prayers over."

Trying hard not to laugh, Aloriah leaned forward to place her hand on her mother's shoulder and looked at her solemnly.

"Um, Mom? What did you always tell him when we were trying to get ready to go somewhere and he was procrastinating?"

Kelly bit her lip for a second, her eyes dancing, and then she shared the thought with the other occupants of the van.

"I always told him he was going to be late for his own funeral."

There was a snort from the front seat as Kyle tried not to laugh outright, Teresanna covered her mouth and found something very interesting to look at out the window, and both Aloriah and Chase were biting their lips. It was Angela, with tears rolling down her cheeks as she tried to fight it, who let out the first giggle, and soon everyone in the van was sharing in the laugh. When they regained composure, Kelly asked Kyle if he could pull over at the next place that had a restroom so she could repair her smudged makeup.

The small general store where they stopped turned into a stretch break for everyone, and Kyle bought everyone containers of fruit juice. Seeing him at the cash register, Kelly decided on the spur of the moment to play the lottery, joking that her luck surely couldn't get any worse, and then they got back on their way. As they finished their ride, Kelly was prone to an occasional snort of laughter whenever she turned her head to look at Aloriah, so when they got to the funeral, she insisted that Kyle and Teresanna sit next to her while Aloriah, Chase and Angela sat behind her.

"After all," she joked, "it wouldn't do for me to suddenly start laughing in the middle of the funeral service."

The following morning, while Chase and Aloriah were making breakfast in the kitchen, Kelly was enjoying her coffee and watching the news. The lottery numbers were put up on the screen as the reporter announced that there had been a single winner of the $150 million jackpot that had been drawn the night before. When they announced the location of the store where the winning ticket was purchased, Kelly walked out to the kitchen to ask where the store was that they had stopped at the day before.

Chase told her, and she said, "Well, someone who bought a ticket there is a multi-millionaire."

Aloriah and Chase exchanged a shocked look, and Kelly suddenly remembered her offhand urge to buy a lottery ticket. Racing up over the stairs to her purse, she pulled out the ticket, and when the news story repeated in the next half hour, she was shaking as one number after another matched. Then she screamed for someone to please come and confirm that she wasn't dreaming.

Pulling up the lottery site on his laptop, first Chase confirmed it, and then Aloriah did before all three started screaming in unison and hugging each other. Kyle's plan to get her out of the broken down house didn't have to be put into action. Kelly had won the lottery!

Arriving at the Benton house a short time later for Chase's birthday party, which had been moved up a few days to allow Lynn to be home, Kelly had both Kyle and Teresanna confirm the numbers as well before she would truly believe it had happened. Kyle, always the practical one, insisted that they call Jack to accompany Kelly to the store to fill out the claim form for her winnings, as he would welcome the chance of being the financial advisor for her, and when asked what the first thing she wanted to do was, she smiled.

"Knock down that piece of crap house I've been living in and put up a nice, energy efficient bungalow."

"Well, you can live here in Greenville while that's happening." Chase told her as he hugged her.

When it came time to blow out the candles on his cake, Chase joked that it was just an exercise in futility because his wish for Kelly had already come true. Beaming at him, she thanked him for that thought with a kiss on the cheek. Then she teased him that his birthday present from her was her daughter.

Chapter 24

Within a couple of days of signing the paperwork for her win, Kelly had Chase and Aloriah help her clean out the house in preparation for its demolition. Most of the things in it were hauled to the local dump, where everything that still worked or could be easily repaired got set aside for the thrift shop, whose profits went to the local food pantry. Everything that Kelly wanted to keep, which was, as she put it, a very depressingly small stack, was hauled to Chase's house in Greenville, where he had donated a corner of his garage next to the Guzzi for her to use until the bungalow was built.

When repeatedly offered the opportunity to house sit while Chase and Aloriah were away, she agreed to stay only until her house was ready. Despite the drive to visit each other, Kelly remained adamant that the kids didn't need her underfoot, but she welcomed the idea of making sure that nothing happened to the old farmhouse during the coldest part of the winter while they were traveling.

Instead of quitting her job at the hotel, she took a voluntary leave of absence, allowing the hotel to keep on some of the other housekeepers that it was thinking of laying off during the slow spring season. She told Aloriah that, once the bungalow was built, she didn't want to just sit around all the time, and would need something to occupy her mind, so she would work, but not as hard as before.

   With all the distractions involving her mother, it seemed to Aloriah that Christmas was upon them before she was ready, but Chase had been purchasing presents without her, and brought out everything he'd been storing in the attic. When Chase went to help his parents put up decorations for the big Christmas gathering of his extended family just two days before Christmas Eve, she and Kelly turned the kitchen into a production line to get all the presents wrapped in time. By the time he returned for a late supper, they were finished, but very punchy, making each other giggle at the stupidest things. Kelly kept apologizing, but Chase thought them very amusing. They reminded him of the way they'd been behaving in New Orleans when he first noticed them, giggling together at the back of the tour group.

   By the time Christmas morning dawned, Kelly was very nervous. The largest family gathering she'd ever attended had been her own wedding, where Bruce's parents, his one brother, and her parents at been the only ones in attendance apart from the minister. Her two sisters, who had been feuding at the time, had both refused to come, and like her daughter, she had never really had close friends at school.

   With Chase having prepared them by

explaining about Uncle Jack, Aunt Kathleen, and their four children, all of whom were married and had children, Kelly was all for burying her head under the pillow and hiding until Aloriah and Chase left. Rolling her eyes, Aloriah finally convinced her mother to get on the nice outfit they had purchased for the occasion and get into the car.

They arrived right after Jack and Kathleen pulled in, so Chase introduced them as he helped pull Christmas presents out of their car. Aloriah hurried over to open the door, and let everyone else precede her, almost knocking Kelly off her feet when she stepped through the door to find her mother standing there, just staring at the biggest decorated tree she'd ever seen. Coming past for a second load with his Uncle Jack, Chase teased Kelly by saying "Did I mention Dad likes to have the biggest Christmas tree in town?"

Kelly responded by punching him on the arm.

"No, and you could have prepared me!"

Jack laughed.

"I think I like you, Kelly! You might beat some sense into this boy."

Chase stuck his tongue out at his uncle as they playfully tried to get through the door at the same time.

Angela came by to collect coats and put them into Kyle's study, suggesting that Kelly go join Teresanna and Kathleen in the kitchen for a hot toddy. Aloriah went over to the tree to help Kyle put presents under it, finding it was an almost never-ending task when the others followed Chase and Jack in, beginning with the twins, Chris and Danny, who each had a wife and two children in tow.

Jack Junior, who still went by the nickname "J.J.", and his wife came in next. Their single child, who was Angela's age, had accepted an invitation to his girlfriend's Christmas gathering, and they kept joking about feeling like they were on their honeymoon. Kitty and her fiancé were the last to arrive, with her young son from her first marriage already conked out for a nap.

When all the presents were finally put under the tree and all the adults who were old enough to drink had hot toddies in hand, Aloriah realized why her mother had been hesitant about being in a crowd this large. Having taken down most of her internal barricades during her time in the truck alone with Chase, Aloriah was having a hard time blocking all the emotions. When no one was looking, she slipped up into the room at the top of the spiral staircase to put back up her mental blocks, trying to prevent the full-blown migraine that was trying to gain a foothold. She was just coming back down when Chase, looking a little anxious, found her and made sure she was going to be alright before they rejoined the crowd.

Kelly, having numbed her empathy with a couple of hot toddies, was actually enjoying the crowd. The younger children, in particular, seemed to find her fascinating, as she had accepted a children's book from Angela and was reading to them in the living room as she had when Aloriah was young, making up different voices for each character. Unable to offer a toddy to his lady, Chase settled for keeping his arm around her as they went from room to room, visiting with just a couple of people at a time and doing whatever he could to help keep the migraine at bay.

The traditional pot-luck brunch was served up in the kitchen, but because the crowd was so large, a couple of card tables and several TV trays were brought into play so that everyone was able to find a seat with a place to set their plate. With the exception of Kitty's toddler, the children seemed quite happy to go off into the living room to eat, so the adults were given the run of the large dining room table.

It was while they were at the table that Kyle saw Aloriah rubbing at her temples and the concern on Chase's face. As soon as the meal was over, he pulled Chase aside to discover what the problem was and, before Aloriah knew what was happening, she was being handed a hot toddy by Kyle.

"It seems to have helped your mom." he told her, and despite her protests about her age, he stood firm that she shouldn't go home with a migraine because of his large family, even arguing that she was old enough to drink with her parents approval in bars in New Orleans. Kelly, wandering past to hear the conversation, gave express permission, insisting that there was no need in getting a headache on Christmas. There was a look that passed between Kelly and Kyle that made Chase clear his throat, but Aloriah's head was just painful enough that she didn't comprehend what it was about.

Drinking the toddy did seem to help somewhat, blocking out some of the overwhelming qualities of the emotions, and when Kyle suddenly disappeared and a very muscular Santa Claus made an appearance, she was glad that she had let him talk her into it. It would certainly have been a shame to have had to sequester herself because of a headache. She would have missed the photo opportunity afforded by the big man.

Santa Claus had never been quite so much fun when she was growing up.

When all the other presents had been distributed, Santa gave up his seat to Chase, who came over to take her by the hand. Much to her bemusement, she was brought over and settled into the big, warm chair, and then Santa, with a grin that was visible even under the fake beard, handed his son a small box. When he dropped to a knee in front of her, Aloriah was in shock.

"Last June," he began, "I had the good fortune to be the knight in shining armor for a damsel in distress. In our time together since then, I have found her to be not only the princess I rescued, but my soul mate. Aloriah Starbird, I don't ever want to lose you. Will you marry me?"

It took a moment for the words to sink in, and when she couldn't get her voice to work, she nodded. The room erupted as he pulled out the beautiful diamond and peridot ring, and she was touched beyond belief that he had included her birthstone. His hands were shaking as he put it onto her finger, and when he smiled up at her, still on his knees, she leaned forward to share a sweet kiss and seal the deal.

Chapter 25
January 2018

After the very intense time in Greenville, Aloriah was actually looking forward to the quiet of riding next to Chase in the truck, so when they started out the second week of January to pick up a load from a furniture manufacturer in Guilford, Maine, she breathed a sigh of relief. Looking over at her with a soft chuckle, Chase couldn't resist teasing.

"Is my family really that bad?"

With her head leaned back against the seat and her eyes closed, Aloriah just smiled.

"Not really just your family, love. That was just way too much going on to be called a relaxing trip home."

With his own sigh of relief, Chase had to agree.

"Hopefully the next trip home will be quieter." Then, considering that they were going to have to eventually think about planning a wedding, he couldn't help grinning. "And if it isn't, we may have to do like my folks did and get married in Las Vegas, then just come home to tell them we're already married and they missed it."

That comment made Aloriah's eyes pop open, and she looked at him with a confused frown.

"Your folks got married in Las Vegas?"

Grinning over the fact that he'd managed to get her to sit up and take notice, Chase shrugged.

"Well, you know how it is. Small town. Little mistake involving birth control pills and antibiotics. What better way to have a full term baby without people counting back to figure out you had a big wedding in April and the baby was born in November than to just not have the wedding in town?"

Her jaw dropping over the fact that there was no lie in any of what he'd just said, she could imagine Kyle's ribbing if his son ended up in the same shoes.

"Hmm. Maybe we'd better just plan on that big wedding in town so we don't have the excuse for your dad to tease us forever about whether or not I was pregnant at the service."

Tipping her a wink, Chase asked her to pull out the I Pad.

"We need to get from Guilford, Maine to New Orleans."

"New Orleans?" she squealed, and Chase laughed.

"Poor Cody. He doesn't have sound-proofed walls."

Aloriah blushed even as she laughed. Chase had been pretty amorous before their trip home, when they were just using condoms for protection. Even with her mother just down the hall, he had become even more so since she'd made an appointment with a doctor in Greenville and got herself on the pill. Kelly had laughed when the subject of the strange sounds in the house at night came up one morning in the hallway, and told her daughter that was what normal young people did, but Aloriah really didn't want to have to think about meeting Cody in the hallway on the way to the bathroom and know that he'd heard them.

If he hadn't been driving, she might have punched Chase in the arm for saying such a thing and getting her all embarrassed.

They pulled in to find that another driver had been by to drop off the trailer for the manufacturer to load, so the new chairs and tables to be delivered to a bar in New Orleans were almost all loaded on. Leaving Aloriah to mark the beginning of the off road, but on duty time in the log book, Chase climbed out of the cab to find out how much longer it was going to take to finish loading. Then he looked at the manifest to see exactly where he was going. He laughed out loud when he saw the address. Not only were they going to New Orleans, it was a delivery for Cody's bar.

Climbing into the truck to back it into place and hook up the trailer, he looked over at Aloriah, who was waiting for the exact address in New Orleans before she told him how long a drive it was going to be.

"You can just leave it as New Orleans in general. I'm pretty sure we're going to take a minimum of three days, and when we get to the city, it's an address I can get us to pretty easily."

"You've delivered there before?"

Chase just nodded, sure she wouldn't sense any dishonesty. He had delivered there just once, when Uncle Jack had forgotten Chase wasn't of age and shouldn't have been hauling liquor...

Thinking about the delivery, Chase decided that he could arrive at mid-afternoon on the third afternoon, which would give very little time for the crew to get the furniture set up before the crowd filled in, or they could take their time and arrive early on the fourth day. At their first stop, he called Uncle Jack and asked him to tell "the customer" to expect them early morning on the fourth day. Jack, catching on that Chase was trying not to let Aloriah know who they were delivering to, laughed and said he would.

Chase was very cheerful this time out, whistling and singing under his breath for the entire trip. Thinking it was just because they were going to get to surprise Cody with a visit right after they'd become engaged, Aloriah thought nothing of it. She just watched the time, carefully making sure the log was correct, and assuming Chase was just taking longer rest breaks so they could spend more time practicing self-defense, stretching, and being together in their room without her mother right down the hall. It also amused her that, whenever he bumped into truckers he knew, Chase took great pleasure in lifting the hand with the ring he'd given her on it and announcing that she was his *fiancé*.

It wasn't until they pulled onto the familiar

street in New Orleans, and pulled up in front of a very familiar bar that Aloriah realized that they weren't just stopping to visit with Cody. Looking at Chase, who had a very triumphant grin on his face, she realized that she had been thinking that she could always read his mind. Between the engagement ring and this, he was getting good at sometimes masking his true emotions in order to surprise her with something, and she had to smile. It was nice to know she could be like a normal human sometimes.

Chase got out of the truck to unlock the door on the trailer, roll it up out of the way, roll down the ramp, and take off the straps that had held the load secure. Aloriah pulled a baseball cap on over her dark hair, covering her eyes and most of her face, and glanced down at the body that was still overweight, but a good 50 pounds lighter than when Cody last saw her. Grabbing the manifest to do her part of the job, she stepped into the bar and paused for a moment while her eyes adjusted.

The inside of the bar was almost bare, the few remaining tables and chairs held together with duct tape. Two men were replacing one of the windows that had also been duct taped, and there was a new mirror behind the bar.

She bit back a gasp and looked down at the clipboard in her hand, announcing loudly in her best imitation of a Boston drawl "I got a load of chairs and tables for..." she paused as if struggling to pronounce the name, "Cody Boud-rocks."

Snorting, Cody came out of the back room and started toward her, wondering who this could be when he had requested Chase, growling, "That be pronounce 'Boo-droo'!"

She lifted her head, looking at him with a broad smile. He stopped, shocked, and suddenly broke into his own broad smile as he hollered loud enough to shake the rafters.

"Cherie! Is you! Comment faites-vous?"

Aloriah laughed when he grabbed her to give her a rib-crunching hug, then backed off again and looked her over from head to toe.

"Look at y'all! Has dat Chase been starvin' you? You about half de size you was las' time!"

Knowing he was exaggerating, she nonetheless smiled at the compliment.

"Good food, good company, and lots of martial arts. Does wonders for a body."

Cody grinned.

"So you learnin' self-defense while you wid him?"

Aloriah looked at him and joked "Duh!"

As they made their way back out to the truck with the other bar employees in tow to start the unloading, he asked her question after question about what she was doing traveling with Chase, how many places she'd seen, whether they'd had good holidays. Aloriah laughed as he didn't give her time to answer one question before asking the next one until Chase's voice came from inside the truck.

"Hey, Gator Boy, why don't you give her time to breathe between questions?"

Cody gave Aloriah a wink and jumped up inside the truck to hug his friend.

"I figure we gonna have some time to visit so

I get de questions out now and she can answer den."

While they were hauling the new furniture in and setting it up, Cody kept up a constant stream of chatter, eventually getting the story out of them as to what had happened when Chase went back to Maine that had resulted in Aloriah traveling with him. When he asked about Kelly, Aloriah told about the accident and her lottery win, and Cody teased "Maybe I come to Maine and get me a rich widow."

In fairly short order, they had the entire load off the truck and into the bar, and then Chase rolled the ramp back up, rolled the door down, and promised Cody they would come back out on the motorcycle for supper. Just before he reached over to hug her, Cody pretended to throw a punch at Aloriah. With the speed she and Chase had been practicing, Aloriah blocked him, caught his wrist, and spun him around with his hand behind his back.

"Trés bien, chere!" Cody congratulated her. "Keep practicin' and you be fast like the rattlesnake, like your man is."

After another bone crunching hug for both her and Chase, Cody sent them off, telling them to treat his house like their own. Looking at the clock, Chase grinned.

"You know, we have about 3 hours until suppertime."

Aloriah smiled, pretending she didn't know what he was talking about.

"Ah. Plenty of time for a nice hot soak in a bathtub."

She laughed at the big puppy dog eyes he gave her, then watched the road as they went deeper and deeper into the bayou, finally reaching Cody's house. When Chase backed the truck into his customary spot, then honked the horn, she expected someone to come out of the door. He laughed and explained about the spiders and snakes, and she made a face that made him laugh. Warning her not to stir up any ant nests on the way to the porch, he showed her where Cody hid the key, let them in, and then showed her to his room.

A couple of hours later, they emerged from the room to shower, change and get ready to go into town. Aloriah was playfully walking bow-legged down the hallway, and Chase laughed at her antics before throwing her over his shoulder to carry her into the bathroom while she squealed. The shower also took an unusually long amount of time, and, just to make sure they got into town, Chase left Aloriah in the bathroom to comb and braid her hair while he went to get dressed.

When they passed in the hall to swap rooms, his shirt was open, and she pretended she was going to tweak his nipple ring, which made him decide to press her towel wrapped body against the wall to steal another kiss. They were both laughing and breathing heavily when he released her, but they had promised Cody they were coming for supper, so they finished getting ready.

As they walked out to the garage after carefully locking back up and putting the key back in its hiding place, Chase identified the noises for her, laughing when a gator bellowed from somewhere behind the house, making Aloriah grab onto him for protection. He opened the front door to the garage and turned on the light, thumping on the trash can lid and watching a snake slither out while Aloriah watched it go, wide eyed. As they got onto the motorcycle and each put on a helmet, Aloriah was shaking her head, finding it hard to believe that someone would voluntarily live in such a place.

After parking next to Cody's motorcycle in the same lot where they always parked, and taking the helmets off so they could talk while they walked, Chase dropped his free arm over Aloriah's shoulder, escorting her back to the bar. They didn't notice as they walked the always damp streets that a scrawny young man did a double take, then pulled out a cell phone and talked excitedly into it.

The bar was filling up rapidly when they walked in, but Cody had saved them space next to the waitress station by hiding two bar stools behind the bar. Chase was greeted by name by many of the patrons, and soon had introduced his fiancé to all the patrons and employees that he knew. One big guy in particular stood out from the crowd, and Aloriah greeted him as she walked by.

"Hi, aren't you Bear?"

Turning to see who had said his name, the big trucker grinned.

"Well, I'll be darned! We meet again, and back here in New Orleans, of all places! How you doing, kids?"

With the jokes that went back and forth between Bear and Chase about his arm, it soon came out that Bear had forgotten who he was dealing with, and grabbed Chase from behind about a year after Chase started driving. Reacting on instinct,

Chase had the arm broken before he knew who it was, and had graciously paid for the hospital. When Kyle got wind of it, he had tracked Bear down to remind him not to surprise Chase again.

It wasn't long before Cody set bowls of gumbo and tall glasses of sweet tea in front of them, and they talked with patrons and laughed with Cody while they ate. Chase noticed that Aloriah would occasionally stop, rub her temples, and take a deep, sighing breath before the smile would return to her face.

After about two hours of watching her suffer, Chase made their excuses, told Cody they would see him at the house, and picked up the two helmets. Bellowed goodbyes rang throughout the room as they made their way out, and they promised to come back to visit again before they left New Orleans. As they stepped out the door, Aloriah took her helmet from Chase so that he had a free arm to drape around her shoulders, but her head was seriously starting to pound from all the conflicting emotions of the crowd. There were so many emotions hitting her all at once that she missed the feelings coming from three men who approached them, one from behind and two from the front.

Before they knew the danger they were in, Chase was grabbed by the shoulder and yanked away from Aloriah, and he gasped as a knife blade was driven through the leather jacket he had on and plunged into his side just below his rib cage. Reacting instinctively, with the famous speed Cody was so fond of bragging about, he struck behind him, disarming his assailant and knocking him back, but leaving the knife sticking out of his side. A few more quick moves, and Chase managed to slam his opponent against the wall, rendering him unconscious, but every movement was hampered by the knife in his side. As he spun to see what was going on with Aloriah, his foot slipped on the damp street and he fell to one knee, but was unable to regain his feet. Reaching back, his brain fogged with pain yet knowing that the police would want to confirm fingerprints on the weapon, he removed the blade without touching the handle, and pressed his hand to the blood that now flowed free.

When Chase was ripped away from her side, Aloriah saw the two men, saw the gleam of blades in their hands, and her brain went instinctively to the moves they had been practicing. Despite the pain in her head, disarm and neutralize was all that mattered. The first man lunged and she dodged his strike, grabbing his knife arm and slamming it, harder than she'd ever practiced, against the knee that she was bringing up, hearing a satisfying crunch as his elbow bent backwards and broke. He went to his knees with a scream of agony, clutching his broken arm.

The knife he'd dropped was still near him on the ground, but her eyes were already on the second assailant. Having seen what happened to his companion, he did a slashing motion instead of a stabbing motion. She very briefly felt the sensation of the knife going across her bicep as she dodged backward, but ignored it as she stepped in before he could swing his arm back for a second slash. Catching him by the knife arm with both hands and driving her own shoulder up under his while she yanked downward, she heard his shrill scream as if from a distance as she popped the arm out of its socket. His knife also clattered to the ground, and then she was using his dislocated shoulder as leverage to throw him onto the hard ground with every ounce of adrenaline in her system helping to make it a solid throw.

As he gasped in pain, she went back after the first man, who was trying to ignore his broken elbow to grab his knife with his other hand. Stomping his fingers, she grabbed the back of his head and drove his head, hard, against her knee. He crumpled to the ground, unconscious, and then she was back after the one with the dislocated shoulder, who was just getting back up and looking for his knife. He had regained his feet when she hit him in the stomach, and as he inadvertently bent forward from that hit, she grabbed his head and did the same as she had done to his buddy. As she let go of the back of his head after slamming his head into her knee, he crumpled to the ground and lay still.

She looked around, seeing three assailants down and out, and then her eyes focused on Chase, down on one knee with his hand pressed to his side, blood gushing from between his fingers. His name burst out of her in a scream as she rushed to his side.

"Chase!"

He was absolutely white, breathing as if he was fighting the urge to vomit, but his eyes were closed until she dropped to her knees beside him. When he lifted his head and looked at her, the pain he was in slammed into her, and she screamed for someone to get some rags out of the bar and call an ambulance. Stunned people were standing all around on the street, unable to believe what they had just seen in just the few minutes from the time the door opened and the couple had stepped out onto the street, but not one reached for a cell phone.

Growling, Aloriah put her hands on Chase's face and told him "I'll be right back."

Racing back into the bar, she screamed Cody's name, then barked "I need bar rags and an ambulance! Chase has been stabbed!"

Josette grabbed the phone and dialed while Cody grabbed the rags and raced for the door, which Aloriah had already disappeared back out through. Bear came out right behind Cody, and seeing the unconscious men and three knives clearly visible, he started directing other bikers and truckers who came out of the bar to "Keep these people back" and "Don't touch anything unless one of those assholes tries to get up. Then you *sit* on them until the cops get here!"

Aloriah had knelt back down next to Chase, putting her hand over his and gently lifting it so that Cody could pack a heavy wad of bar rags over the wound. Pressing her own hand over the spot, realizing that Chase was in so much pain that he barely recognized her, she took two deep, cleansing breaths and did something her Gramma Northrup had told her could be done, but she had never *knowingly* done herself. She looked deeply into Chase's eyes and drew the pain out of him and into herself, seeing his eyes widen as he realized what she was doing.

"Aloriah, no!" he croaked, but was too weak between the pain and blood loss to fight for very long. As she began to pant with the pain, he sank down so that his buttocks were between her thighs, and with his pain removed, he felt himself starting to slip into unconsciousness. He was only barely aware when the EMTs arrived and gently lifted him away from her to put him onto the stretcher.

Cody, seeing the blood on Aloriah's arm that didn't belong to Chase, pointed that out to the EMT and got Aloriah loaded into the ambulance with Chase. "I'll be right behind you, chere! Don't worry."

Two police cruisers arrived at the same time as a second ambulance, and, recognizing the three assailants as members of the same gang that had been responsible for the death of a police officer in June, the police pulled out handcuffs to lock each man to a stretcher and carefully recovered the knives as the men were put into ambulances. The assailant Chase had knocked out was already starting to come to, but the other two, who were going to need some medical help themselves, were still unconscious. As soon as the men were on their way to the hospital, members of the gathered crowd seemed to come out of their stupor, and one after another told of the attack on the couple, and the fierceness of the young lady as she took on two assailants after her man had been stabbed.

Listening to the various accounts that all amounted to Aloriah kicking butt and taking names while Chase had been grabbed and stabbed, Cody pulled out his cell while picking up the helmets the couple had been carrying. As he stepped back into the bar, he dialed Kyle's number and told him what had happened. The one question Kyle kept going back to actually had Cody laughing by the third time it was repeated.

"*Aloriah* kicked butt and *Chase* got stabbed?"

Chapter 26

Aloriah was pacing in the waiting room, the gash in her arm sutured, by the time Cody arrived with clean clothes for her. Even he, who had seen her outside the bar, was a little taken aback by how much blood was on her, most of it belonging to Chase.

"Have you heard anything?"

Aloriah was shaking, her head throbbing, and she couldn't feel Chase through the other emotions in the hospital. She shook her head, tears rolling down her face as she tried to speak, her voice already hoarse from her tears.

"The last time I saw him was when we were in the ambulance. They were giving him fluids and getting blood lined up for the emergency room, but no one has come out to tell me anything."

Handing her the clothes, Cody encouraged her to change while he went to check on things. The nurse outside the emergency room was a distant relative through his granny, so she told him, on hearing that the girl in the bloody shirt was the fiancé, that the young man had been brought into surgery.

"It was a long blade. They have to go deep to fix all the damage."

Cody went back out to Aloriah and sat down, telling her they were still working on him. She sighed and looked out the window, rubbing her temples. Cody remembered seeing her doing that at the bar and sat down beside her.

"Dat headache you got. Migraine?"

Not willing to open up to him about her *gift* yet, she just muttered "Sort of."

Cody sat staring at her, and then sighed. A couple of his relatives claimed that magic was real, people had *gifts* that those sensitive to magic could feel, and one of those relatives who claimed to be able to see what other people's *gifts* were had been at the barbecue. She had claimed that both the women Chase sat with were so *gifted*, the daughter more so than the mother, but he couldn't remember what she'd called it.

"Cherie? You special? You feel emotions?" Then he grimaced and admitted the full truth. "That what my great-aunt Emmaline say."

Aloriah gave a short snort of a laugh. His great-aunt. Her grammy. People who had been brought up thousands of miles apart, but still believing in the *gift* of empathy and the miracles the shaman had performed. Sighing and deciding he would find out eventually, she confirmed what he had just asked in his own special way.

"My ancestors were shaman. They could feel emotion, remove pain, and pray people better."

Cody looked on her with new respect.

"Well, how 'bout dat?"

He put his hand on her arm, patting gently.

"I don't need any shaman power to know you gotta nasty headache and need sleep. I wake you if somethin' happens," his voice lowered to a whisper, "but I see what you do for Chase befo' the ambulance come. You need sleep after that."

Cody pulled off his jacket and put it over her shoulders, tucking her in as best as he could. The jacket smelled of Old Spice instead of Axe, but it was warm and comforting nonetheless. Fighting to stay awake, Aloriah simply got to the point she couldn't fight any more.

Cody watched television for a bit. He watched other people come in, and he watched the other people leave. Finally, a doctor came out and recognized Cody, as the good doctor D'Entremont was a regular at the bar on his nights off.

"You with the stabbed kid?" the doctor asked, and Cody nodded.

"It was a tricky one, but he's stitched up. He's sleeping off the anesthesia and getting blood transfusions, but a lot will depend on the kid himself." Looking at the records, the doctor pointed at Aloriah.

"That the fiancé?"

Cody nodded again.

"Let her sleep. I'll come back out when he's awake and you can wake her up then." The doctor smiled. "He wouldn't go under. He kept calling for her. If not for the blood loss, he would have been a real bear to hold down."

Cody smiled at that, thinking that definitely sounded like the Chase he knew. If he had that much spirit before getting closed up, he would be just fine.

He turned to find Aloriah's eyes open, seeming to focus on him, but there was no emotion in them. In a voice that didn't sound anything like her normal voice, she spoke, and Cody recognized the French he'd grown up with.

"Merci." she said.

"Il vivra." she said.

"Nous marier." she said.

Then her eyes closed and she slept as if she had never opened her eyes to speak. Cody looked at her, thinking *shaman*, remembering what she'd said in French to tell his great-aunt Emmaline later.

"Thank you."

"He'll live."

"We marry."

He sat down and flipped channels, feeling better about Chase's chances, but praying anyway. Beside him, Aloriah slept and said nothing more.

A little over an hour later, there was a bellow from down the hall. Cody, who had fallen asleep, came awake at the same time Aloriah did. The bellow was repeated moments later, and was just two words.

"No!" short and sharp followed by the long, drawn out howl. "Reeeee!"

Coming to her feet, Aloriah whispered "Chase."

Cody was about to stop her from following the call when the doctor stepped out and sighed, signaling her forward.

"The king has spoken." the doctor told Cody with a smile, letting Cody come along as a witness.

Chase, barely able to sit upright, was nonetheless trying, his hand blocking the port in the I.V. line where the nurse was trying to insert a syringe filled with morphine to put him back to sleep so he could mend. He grimaced fiercely each time he tugged at the sutures in his side, but he refused to lie back until he saw that his fiancé was okay.

The moment she stepped in, their eyes met and he smiled, letting the nurse and her assistant push him back onto the bed. Aloriah held the hand that the I.V. was taped into the back of, and he let go of the port with the other hand to place it on top of hers. The morphine was administered with no further fuss, and as he relaxed, he gave her a sad smile.

"I was supposed to take care of you."

She smiled and corrected him gently.

"But it was my turn."

His eyes closed, but when Aloriah tried to remove her hand, his fingers clutched hers and his eyes started to open. The nurse who'd been holding the syringe smiled, shaking her head at the boy's tenacity, and got Aloriah a chair so she could hold Chase's hands, thereby allowing him to sleep, but be somewhat comfortable.

Sometime later, Aloriah opened her eyes. Her neck was horribly stiff from sleeping sitting up against the side of Chase's bed, but what had awakened her was a hand gently playing with the long braid she had made of her hair before going to the bar. As she looked up, she saw Chase with the most serious face she had ever seen. He was looking at her, and it was his hand that was playing with her braid.

Standing, she leaned carefully over him to give him a kiss, and as she backed away, she finally saw the slightest hint of his normal smile. Then he sighed deeply and looked into her eyes, running his tongue around the inside of his mouth to get a little moisture in there before speaking.

"I know what you did last night." he said, his voice soft and very gruff, nothing like his normal tone. Pain touched his eyes. "I don't ever want to see that kind of pain in your eyes again because of me."

Unable to stop herself, Aloriah gave him a wry smile.

"Then you'd better not come into the birthing room when we have children."

Something closer to his normal smile touched his face, and although it didn't actually come out, he mouthed "Smart ass."

It was Aloriah's turn to look pained as she had to admit to the limits of her gift.

"I couldn't stop the bleeding, so I did what I could do."

Realizing that he would have done the same if their positions were switched, Chase gave a gentle tug on her braid to bring her down for another kiss. She was just starting to straighten again when a deep voice from the door made them both smile.

"Eww! You could at least put a sock on the

doorknob if you're going to do that!"

Aloriah smiled at Kyle as she turned.

"Hey there, Daddy K! What are you doing so far from home?"

Kyle grinned as he came into the room.

"Cody called me last night to say Chase got grabbed and stabbed while you kicked butt and took names. I *had* to come see if it was true!"

Aloriah made a face and said "Oh shoot! I knew I was forgetting something. I forgot to take names!"

Chase brought his hand up to his face as he closed his eyes and shook his head. Kyle's grin just got bigger.

"I like this girl! She's even more annoying than you!"

Coming around the bed, he gave Aloriah a tight hug before holding her back so he could assess the damages she had sustained. Seeing only the bandage that peeped out from under her t-shirt sleeve, he smiled and nodded.

"Very good, grasshopper. You learned well in your time with Chase."

Stepping closer to his son, he smiled as he patted Chase's hand.

"I've also heard from Cody that you were their first target. They meant to prevent you from protecting Ree so they could kill her for her part in putting their other gang members away for life."

Chase sighed, looking disgusted.

"And they would have succeeded if Ree wasn't such a good student."

Another voice came from the door.

"Lucky for you, the one who stabbed you had no idea where the internal organs are. He managed to miss everything of any importance."

The doctor came in and smiled, holding out his hand to introduce himself.

"Dr. Michael D'Entremont."

Kyle took care of introducing himself and Aloriah, then the doctor gave them the run through of his concerns should they follow through with transferring Chase to Maine, which was what Kyle had already been discussing with the Chief Physician. Concerned that he was going to be treated like an invalid, Chase sat frowning until the doctor had finished.

"So I have to spend months at home before I can go back on the road?"

"You're going to need some physical therapy as your muscles knit back together, so yes, I would recommend that you not go right back to driving."

Kyle looked at both Chase and Aloriah sternly.

"And I hope you've had enough of visiting New Orleans, because this is your last trip here. I'm not taking the chance that other gang members are going to try to get back their bad ass reputation by killing you next time. If Cody wants to visit with you, he'll have to freeze his Cajun tail feathers to come to Maine."

"Yes, sir." Aloriah said with a sassy salute, and Kyle tried not to smile at her.

"I need to teach you how to do a proper salute." He grumbled instead.

Chase was still frowning, not liking the idea

of what might happen when he got back to Maine and his mother got the full story. He could easily see himself banned from ever driving again. Her migraine easing, Aloriah closed her eyes for a moment to see what the frown was about, and then smiled at him.

"Don't worry, sweetie. We'll find something to occupy our time if your mom bans us from driving."

Thinking about how they'd spent the afternoon at Cody's before heading into the bar, Chase found his spirits starting to rise, and his devilish smile returned to his face. Maybe being kept at home wouldn't be so bad with Aloriah living with him.

After a while, Kyle headed out with Cody to bring Chase's motorcycle back to the swamp, arrange for Cody to find it a good home, and drive the truck back to Maine. Chase, after a token protest, was resigned to getting onto an airplane with Aloriah and flying back to Maine so that she could oversee his recovery in Greenville.

Chapter 27
June 2018

It was officially one year to the day since he had met Aloriah in New Orleans, and Chase was more nervous than he'd ever been in his life. For the umpteenth time, he adjusted his tie, ran a comb through his hair, and looked at himself in the full length mirror, checking one more time to make sure that nothing marred his appearance. There was a knock at the door, and Wade, his best friend throughout school, poked his head in.

"The minister says it's time. You ready for this, bub?"

Chase let out a deep sigh, thinking that, since planning for this day and physical therapy had been all he'd been allowed to do since January that was a rather stupid question to ask.

"As ready as I'll ever be." he muttered.

As he and Wade made their way to the minister's side, Chase clenched his hands into fists to prevent himself from fidgeting. The organist smiled and started playing the introduction to the bridal march, which cued Chris's daughter, Rachel, to start down the aisle, dropping rose petals of a deep blood red as she walked. Angela came next, smiling, having been chosen to be the maid of honor since Aloriah had no close girlfriends from her past. Then, as the small group of mostly family members rose to their feet, the doors to the back of the small church were pushed open to reveal Kyle and Aloriah.

She had been working out with Teresanna since January, and was a full 100 pounds lighter than she had been when they first met, but still very well rounded in all the right places. The gown she and her mother had chosen accentuated her curves, and Chase felt nothing but pride as his father escorted her down the aisle. The white gown also accentuated her naturally dark skin, and her long, black hair had been French braided with little white flowers worked in. The simple veil over it all had small sequins worked into the design, and she had never looked more radiantly beautiful.

Arriving at her groom's side, she accepted the kiss on the cheek from her father-in-law, so very glad that he had volunteered to stand in for her deceased father, and then looked into Chase's sparkling eyes as the minister began the ceremony.

When the time came to say their vows, Chase found that his nervousness had disappeared, and he spoke the vows with his entire heart, meaning every word. Aloriah did the same, and when the minister gave the final blessing, she smiled at him with so much love in her beautiful golden eyes, he thought for sure that he was going to simply fly out of the church.

The kiss to seal the vows was a true melding of their souls, and when he stepped back, a little breathless, and heard the minister ask them to face the gathered witnesses, he couldn't resist giving his new wife a little wink.

"Now you're stuck with me forever." he whispered, unable to stop grinning.

"Stuck like glue." she confirmed in her own whisper, turning to face their family and friends with the biggest smile she had ever worn.

"Ladies and gentleman, I give you Mr. and Mrs. Chase Benton."

The End

Author Debi Emmons was born and raised in a small Maine town. She still lives in Maine with her husband, Bill. Her works have appeared in local newspapers as well as Playgirl magazine, and Ms. Emmons has three books in The Tiger Series Romances available.

Of herself, Ms. Emmons says "I'm tall and have brown eyes. All else is subject to change without warning."